Counting the Ways

'How do I love thee? Let me count the ways.'

Quietly Edie laid down the book, and for a little while they sat in silence, shoulder to shoulder, on the pink settee in the front room of 11 Cherry Villas.

'I love the way you read,' Lewis told her.

'What, me with my funny Geordie voice?' She laughed . . .

'When I go home,' he said, 'I'll never think of the Brownings without remembering you.'

She froze. 'You're going home?'

'Not yet. Another month, perhaps. But it's getting nearer by the day . . .' Gently he put his hand up to her cheek. 'I knew it. You're crying. Don't, Edie. Don't cry for me.'

About the author

Brought up in a Sunderland mining village, Jennifer Curry has been a full-time mother, teacher, freelance writer and broadcaster. She is best known as a poet and anthologist for children, and has also written novels for children and plays for both the theatre and Radio 4. Her anthology *The Last Rabbit* won the Earthworm Award in 1992, and she is currently chair of the judges' panel for the Roald Dahl Foundation Poetry Competition. The mother of two grown-up sons, she now lives with her second husband in a historic water mill in Norfolk.

Counting the Ways

Jennifer Curry

CORONET BOOKS
Hodder and Stoughton

First published in Great Britain in 1997 by Hodder and Stoughton
A division of Hodder Headline PLC
First published in paperback in 1997 by Hodder and Stoughton
A Coronet Paperback

10 9 8 7 6 5 4 3 2 1

British Library Cataloguing in Publication Data

Curry, Jennifer
Counting the ways
1. English fiction – 20th century
I. Title
823.9´14 [F]

ISBN 0 340 68019 9

Printed and bound in Great Britain by
Mackays of Chatham PLC, Chatham, Kent

Hodder and Stoughton
A division of Hodder Headline PLC
338 Euston Road
London NW1 3BH

This book is dedicated to the
bright memory of my cousin
Kathie Edwick

ACKNOWLEDGEMENTS ∫

I should like to thank the following people for their help with this book:

* my son, Graeme, who gently bullied me into writing it instead of just talking about it;
* my husband, Tym, who kept me going and listened and bravely commented, even when he knew it hurt;
* my agent, Pat, who stuck with me and was patient and long-suffering;
* my editor, Carolyn, who saw, and rooted out of me, things I didn't even know were there; and
* Pamela Oldfield, who didn't know me, but had confidence in me when I most needed it.

Part One

May 1960

Ancient Blossom Tradition to be Restored

At yesterday's meeting of Donchurch Chamber of Commerce it was decided to reinstate the ancient Maytime Blossom Procession, last held in the area in 1913. The President of the Chamber, Mr T. Tompkinson, said it was hoped that the event would attract visitors to the area, as well as giving pleasure to those who live and work here. He was confident that landowners, fruit farmers, Parish Councils and other Local Bodies would participate willingly in order to make this a thoroughly worthwhile occasion.

Maps of the procession route and complete details of all other planned activities will be widely distributed from 21 February.

Cutting from the *Donchurch and Tillerton Gazette*,
6 January 1960.

1

'Lewis! It's all right! The police have found her.' Maureen Harrison put the phone down and stood for a moment staring out of the window across the wet lawn, towards the neat rows of apple trees dripping in the green spring dusk.

Lewis shivered. He took off his glasses and rubbed his hands across his face as if wiping away a nightmare. 'Where is she?'

'At the police station. Donchurch High Street. I said we'd pick her up straight away.'

As they drove towards the market town, speeding along lanes nestled deep beneath the apple blossom, Lewis turned and looked at his wife's profile. Her expression was serious and preoccupied, as it always was when she was at the wheel. But he could see something else there. A tightness about her mouth. A narrowing of the grey eyes. 'I'm sorry, darling,' he apologised. 'I know it's a bind, all this, but she—'

'Not now, Lewis,' Maureen interrupted him. 'Let me concentrate on the road, please. This rain has turned it into a skid-pan.'

They found Helen sitting quietly in a small, drab interview room. She was wearing clothes Lewis did not recognise, all much too big for her, with a shapeless grey cardigan pulled around her shoulders. They made her slim figure look pitifully thin, almost shrunken. A policewoman was bending over her, smiling with professional kindness, watching her sip strong tea from a thick mug. 'Drink it all up, dear,' he heard her say. 'Two sugars. Do you good.'

Lewis looked steadily at his mother, trying to submerge his

alarm. Her hair was immaculate as usual, her lipstick perfect, her rouge subtly blended over her beautiful high cheekbones as it always was. It was one of her absolute rules of life, to 'put a brave face on things', in every sense. Despite that, he could see the fear behind her deep-set eyes. Briskly he strode across the room, dropped a kiss on the top of her head.

'Lewis!' she exclaimed, reaching up for his hand, holding it tightly. 'I'm so sorry about all this. I begged them not to bother you.'

'We've been worried sick, Mother. Where've you been?'

She shrugged, delicately. 'I just went out, that's all. I got bored. You know how it is. I . . . stayed away longer than I meant to.'

'But you've been away all day.'

Helen's face changed. She straightened her back. He could see that she was determined to bluff it out. 'There's no law against that, is there? I'm surely not expected to . . . clock in and out?'

'Of course you're not.' He laughed, put his arm round her and gave her a little hug. 'But in the pouring rain! And you hadn't locked up or anything. Fortunately, Mrs Sammes saw your door standing open and—'

'There you are, then,' Helen said brightly, as if she had won a small victory. 'With a neighbour like Mrs Sammes, you and Maureen have no need to worry about me. Have you?'

Maureen, who had been standing listening just inside the doorway, gave a sudden click of irritation. She crossed the room and fell on her knees in front of the woman, forcing her to meet her level gaze. 'You'd put an egg on to boil, Helen. Don't you remember? The cottage could have gone up in flames. That's *worrying*!'

Helen blinked rapidly, stared down at the tea in her hands, then placed it, hardly touched, on the table. 'I suppose I'd better go home, then,' she said. 'And eat my hard-boiled egg for supper.'

Lewis stretched out his hand to help her to her feet, but she ignored it pointedly. 'You're coming home with us tonight,' he told her. 'To Greenways.'

'No!' she protested. 'I don't want that.'

'Please. Just for a few days. Sara's set her heart on it, and Jane and Robert are coming over for the weekend.'

Maureen nodded briskly. 'A real family get-together. It's all arranged.'

'Well, then, what can I say?' Helen gave a bleak smile. 'Just like Christmas. Thank you.'

There was a light knock on the bedroom door. Helen padded across in her bare feet to open it, belting Maureen's dressing gown around her waist, and found her granddaughter hopping up and down on the landing, her arms full of clothes.

'Hi, Gran!' Sara exclaimed, and kissed her. 'Isn't this *great*?'

Helen grimaced. 'Not really. I'm in disgrace, sweetheart.'

'No, you're not!' Sara said. 'Not with me, anyway. Look, your clothes are still wet so Mum said I had to bring you this.' She held up a chestnut brown woollen dress, neatly cut and elegant. Helen gazed at it without enthusiasm. 'Mm! That's what I thought too.' Sara giggled. 'So I brought you these instead.' She handed her a pair of blue corduroy trousers and a baggy pink pullover.

'I can't wear *your* things,' Helen remonstrated. 'An old lady like me.'

'Course you can!' Sara sat on the bed and watched as Helen wriggled into her clothes, and then gave a yell of delight. 'You look great! Not a day over twenty-five.'

Helen grimaced. 'Twenty-five! Oh, God, I wish I were, Sara.'

The girl's face softened. 'Don't look so worried, Gran. It's all over now.'

'I'm afraid not. It's all just beginning, really.'

'What do you mean?'

'This happy little . . . family reunion. They've decided the time has come when I need looking after. They're trying to work out what to do with me. Where to put me. As if I were a corner cupboard or something.'

Sara stared. 'It's not that at all. This weekend's just a jolly. Because of Blossom Sunday.'

'So how is it that nobody invited me before?'

'They imagined you'd think it was all a bit twee, I suppose.

It's just a tourist attraction, really. But now – they've decided you need "taking out of yourself".' She grinned. 'At least it stops them agitating themselves about what I'm getting up to.'

'What *are* you getting up to?' Helen asked sharply. 'How's Davey these days?'

'Gran! Don't you start. You're supposed to be on *my* side.'

'Sorry!' Helen laughed, but almost immediately her face clouded. 'Oh, darling, do make the most of being fifteen, won't you? It's a dreadful business, growing old.'

'Please, Gran. Don't be sad. Please.'

Helen sniffed and blew her nose abruptly. 'No. I mustn't. I never *was*, you know. I was only thirty-seven when Bertie – when your grandfather died. Lewis had just turned seven. So, Jane was ten, I suppose. And I just . . . got on with it. Never even thought about sitting around moping. But now . . .' She shook her head and gave a rueful smile. 'I *am* old, sweetheart. I've had my three score years and ten. I – I get frightened. Sometimes I think I'm beginning to . . . run down.'

Sara looked at her seriously. 'What were you doing, Gran? Walking about in the rain all day?'

Helen closed her eyes. 'Don't tell the others. Please. I'd gone out to see . . . to see Jimmy Trotter. There was something terribly important I had to tell him before he began work in the bottom orchard.'

'Jimmy Trotter?' Sara looked puzzled. 'Who's . . . ?'

'My farm manager, sweetheart. During the war. But, of course, *now* I remember he's been dead for years.'

Next morning Maureen and Sara drove over to Tillerton to pick up the things Helen needed for the weekend. Penny Cottage seemed to shine in the sunlight, its old grey thatch still glistening from the overnight rain. It sat, snugly attached to its neighbour, Primrose Cottage, at the corner of a quiet little square, facing on to the Church of St Michael and All Angels. The pair of them looked as neat and demure as two spinsters of the parish, tidily dressed for the Sunday service.

Maureen parked the car and they pushed open the little wooden gate and walked up the brick path between rows of nodding campanula that scattered raindrops on their shoes as they passed. The scent of Virginia stocks lay heavy in the air, and hidden among the drenched blossoms of the white lilac, a thrush repeated its song like a peal of bells.

Sara smiled as her mother unlocked the blue-painted front door and went inside. 'No wonder Gran loves it.'

Maureen nodded. 'It is pretty, isn't it?' She glanced into the sitting room. There was a full bottle of milk standing in the hearth. As she went over to retrieve it she noticed that the old patchwork cushion that always sat in the corner of the sofa had been laid on top of the writing desk. That wasn't like Helen at all. Usually she was absolutely meticulous, a stickler for order in absolutely everything. She plumped up the cushion and put it back in its right place, then tried to push the niggle of worry out of her mind. No point in making mountains. 'There,' she said, 'that's better. I'll nip up to her bedroom now and pack a few clothes. You could check the house plants for me, would you, darling?'

Sara wandered dreamily around the cottage, watering the geraniums from a copper jug, carefully turning their pots so that they would catch the sun. It seemed as if, all her life, these same scarlet geraniums had stood there on the broad windowsill, tidy and homely in their neat clay pots. And all her life, it seemed, her grandmother had been there too, nodding her elegant head, smiling encouragement as she listened to her latest news. Sara didn't want anything to change. Gran in Penny Cottage ... her mother and father at Greenways ... the gardens, the orchards ... they made up her whole world. She just wanted it all to go *on*, the same as always.

As she moved across the room to water the primula in the brown lustre bowl on the dresser, she glanced casually at the dozens of photographs that filled up every spare inch of surface. Then she put down her jug and began to examine them in greater detail. Suddenly she picked up a silver frame, carried it to the window and stared at the young, carefree face of her father. His head thrown back, he was laughing in the sunshine, a basket of apples held in his arms. She was still gazing at it when Maureen came running downstairs, carrying a small overnight bag.

'There! I think I've got everything,' her mother told her. 'Are we finished, do you think?'

'Look at Dad.' Sara smiled. 'Better than any film star, wasn't he?'

Quietly, Maureen took the photograph. 'This was always Helen's favourite picture,' she said. 'She took it herself, just before he joined the Air Force. He must have been . . . twenty-two, I suppose.'

'I hadn't realised he was so handsome.'

'Oh, he was. Before the war. Huge brown eyes. Shining.'

'Poor Dad!'

'No! Lucky Dad!' Maureen corrected her. 'He might have been quite helpless, darling. For weeks we didn't know. And then it seemed like a miracle. He could have a proper life, after all.'

'But what if—' Sara began, but her question was drowned by a heavy knock as Mrs Sammes thrust her pale, jowly face around the door.

Sara's heart sank. Mrs Sammes always managed to depress her. She was the sort of woman who just had to *say* the thing you were trying your hardest not even to *think*. She supposed that it was because the poor thing was so much alone in the world that she was such an old moaner. According to Gran, *Mr* Sammes had died just about a year after he'd married his Emmeline, before they'd even managed to start a family, so she probably did feel a bit sad sometimes. And – Sara tried to be charitable – she was very kind-hearted. She really did want to be helpful. It was just that Gran never really wanted to be helped.

Mrs Sammes nodded at them lugubriously. 'Here you are!' she said. 'Just popped in to see if there was anything I could do. How *is* poor Mrs Harrison?'

Maureen gave her a bright smile. 'She's fine, thank you, Mrs Sammes. But she'll be staying with us until Tuesday.'

'Just till Tuesday!' The woman shook her head in concern. 'But is she fit to be left on her own?'

Maureen's face changed. 'I know she's becoming a little forgetful . . .'

'Oh, it's more than that, my dear.'

'You're worried about her wandering away, you mean? It's just happened twice . . .'

'Three times at least, to my knowledge.' Mrs Sammes sighed deeply, her brow ridged with anxiety. 'I found her at the other end of the village last week. Said she had some shopping to do at Broxdale's, would you believe?'

'Broxdale's!' Try as she might, Maureen could not conceal her dismay.

'Yes! There you are! They closed down in nineteen forty-four if I remember rightly. When their son was killed. A tragedy, that. Mr Broxdale said there just didn't seem any point any—'

'Gran's all right!' Sara interrupted her impatiently. 'Lots of old people get absent-minded. It's quite normal.'

But Mrs Sammes shook her head doggedly. 'I don't want to be a Job's comforter,' she insisted. 'You know me, always try to look on the bright side. But her mind's going, poor dear. There's no getting away from it.'

'I really don't think things are as bad as that,' Maureen protested.

'You don't know, though. It's me that sees her every day, isn't it? How long have we been neighbours, Mrs H. and me?'

Maureen shrugged. 'She moved here when Lewis and I got married.'

'That's right. Must be sixteen years, not a day less. And it's always been 'Mrs Sammes this' and 'Mrs Sammes that'. Even though I asked and asked her to call me Emmy, that seeming more friendly, you know. But now . . .' Her large podgy face took on the look of a bewildered baby. '"Mrs Tolly", Maureen. Why should she suddenly call me "Mrs Tolly"? I just can't understand it.'

The plan was that the Blossom Procession should start in the big clearing behind Gates Farm, then wind its way through five miles of orchards, passing by Greenways and Tillerton Rise, until it converged on the playing fields behind Donchurch. The event had been organised to bring visitors into the county in the quiet month of May and to coax them away from the beaten track. But it was not a new invention. In the tranquil, sunlit years before the Great War, every village had held its own rural ride and picnic when the blossom was at its best. It had been a way for the landowners and fruit farmers to celebrate with their workers the promise of a bumper crop to come. In those days everyone had driven along the orchard ways in open farm carts, or travelled on horseback. All the animals and vehicles were decorated with flowers and with blossoming branches, all the countryfolk dressed up in their finest clothes, as if they were going to a wedding feast. And feast they did, at the end of the day, when the cider barrels were rolled out, and the band played on the green, and young and old danced together until the first stars were in the sky.

But now, as they got ready to join the lumbering cavalcade of tractors and cars when it arrived at their own farm gate, not all the Harrisons were convinced that it had been a good idea to try to revive the old custom. Helen, sitting waiting in a low cane chair beside the door, winced at the sound of her daughter's petulant voice.

'I do think it's a shame, really,' Jane was saying, 'turning that lovely old rural tradition into a tourist thing.'

Her husband, Robert, puffed out his cheeks solemnly and nodded. 'I think you're right,' he assured her.

Helen frowned. 'But what do you two know about it? You weren't even born when we held the last one!'

'Of course we weren't,' Jane conceded. 'But I do know it used to be . . . spontaneous. A natural expression of the way ordinary people *felt*. Like Harvest Festival, and all those other lovely things. Now – well, it's just a sort of gimmick, isn't it?'

'Sad!' Robert said. 'I do think it's rather sad.'

Maureen glared at her sister-in-law. 'We invited you because we thought you'd enjoy it,' she said. 'You didn't have to come. Lewis thought a family outing would be fun.'

'Of *course* I had to come.' Jane laughed, lifting her arm and shaking the charm bracelet on her dimpled wrist. 'Good heavens, Greenways was my home for twenty-one years. The orchards were my whole life, weren't they? Of course I had to be here.'

'Well then—' Maureen began, but at once Lewis interrupted her.

'The orchards are part of *all* our lives.' He smiled. 'And today, look, the sun has come out, the blossom has never been more beautiful, and we're all here together to celebrate that. So – who cares if it's just a tourist gimmick?'

Helen breathed a sigh of relief. Her lovely Lewis. Always the peacemaker. The gentle one. How could she ever have borne it if he hadn't come back from the war? She gave an involuntary shudder. She knew in her heart that she shouldn't love him so much, care so much more passionately about his well-being than about Jane's. But she couldn't help it. Jane had always been her father's daughter. She had his blunt, square-cut features, his stocky, broad-shouldered build, already beginning to run to fat. And she had Bertie's practical, business-like approach to life too, always more interested in budgets and balance sheets than in poetry or music. No doubt that's what had first attracted her to young Robert Prescott, all those years ago, when he was still a humble teller in the Market Bank at Donchurch, not the important branch manager he was now. Helen hoped that Jane had also inherited Bertie's kindness, his capacity for devotion. But, watching her as she pouted at her reflection in the hall mirror, tugged at her sandy hair, tweaked the silk scarf at her throat, she felt dubious. Bertie had always been a happy man. Jane never seemed satisfied with anything. 'And the worst thing is,' Helen told herself wearily, 'it's probably all my fault.'

Just as depression was beginning to wrap itself around her like a grey blanket, Sara arrived in the porch, glowing with delight. 'They're coming,' she called. 'They look wonderful! The horses are all plaited up with flowers and ribbons. You lot go on without me – I'm coming on my bike with the others.'

And then she was off again, flashing down the drive in her sapphire summer dress, her black hair sleek and shining in the sun. Kingfisher on a bicycle, thought Helen, smiling quietly to herself.

'Kids!' Jane grumbled, as Sara rang a clarion call on her bell. 'We weren't like that when we were young.'

'No,' her mother agreed sadly. 'I'm afraid you weren't, my dear.'

*   *   *

Well, I have to admit I rather enjoyed it, after all.' As they sat around the huge refectory table, eating a late supper, Jane shone in the candlelight, which made the glass and silver glitter and sent their shadows stretching and shivering across the pale walls of the beautiful old room. 'It wasn't half as bad as I expected.'

'Auntie Jane!' crowed Sara. 'It was marvellous, you know it was.'

'You certainly seemed to be having a good time, Jane,' Lewis agreed. 'I thought you were going to pull out your handkerchiefs, and join in the Morris dancing.'

She laughed. 'They were rather fun, weren't they? I haven't seen Morris dancers for ages.'

'Oh – that reminds me.' Lewis's face lit up. 'Talk about ages. You'll never guess who I bumped into, Maureen. Haven't seen the man for twenty years or more.'

'Which man?' Maureen smiled. 'What *are* you talking about?'

'Jonny! You remember him, darling? Jonny Crozier, of all people.'

Maureen stared. 'Jonny Crozier? Here?'

'Yes. I bumped into him in the tea tent. Came back specially for the do, apparently. He's staying with the Bowmans. Of course, Phylly's his cousin, isn't she? I'd forgotten that.'

'I remember him,' Jane joined in, with a sharp glance in Maureen's direction. 'The young vet, in Donchurch. You used to be very thick didn't you? Ages ago. The three of you, I mean.'

Maureen picked up her half-finished supper and carried it out of the room. 'Excuse me,' she called over her shoulder. 'I just need to check things in the kitchen.'

Her feet tapping on the old tiles, she crossed to the Aga and pulled the heavy kettle on to the hot plate. Then she turned to the dresser and lifted down her blue and white china cups, one by one, from the middle shelf. Very slowly, very carefully, taking her time, breathing deeply, she wiped the inside of each cup with a snowy cloth, and laid it in its saucer. Then, methodically, she took her box of silver apostle spoons from the drawer. Her hands were shaking so much that the spoons made a chinking noise as she laid one in each saucer. She got cream from the fridge and poured it into a little jug, filled a bowl with cube sugar and placed the silver tongs on top. And then, try as she might, she could think of nothing else she could do to keep her in the kitchen any longer. She took another deep breath and turned her face to the dining room.

When she returned to her place the talk had moved on. Robert was showing off the carved applewood pipe he'd bought. Applewood, he explained, was a fine wood for carving, so the man had told him. That was something he'd always been interested in. He was thinking of taking it up himself, as a hobby. Relaxation after a busy day at the bank.

Lewis gave Maureen a worried look as she slipped into her seat and lifted her wine-glass to her lips. 'You OK, darling?' he asked her. 'You look washed out.'

'I'm fine. Just a bit tired.'

He nodded sympathetically. 'Poor love! You've been on the go all day.'

Helen was watching her. 'You've done very well, Maureen,' she said. 'Taken care of us splendidly. You always do.'

'Thank you.' Their eyes met, and held.

'But now,' Helen continued, 'if you'll all excuse me, I think I'll go to my room.'

'Mother!' Jane complained. 'Aren't you going to stay for my lemon torte? I made it specially – my little contribution.'

'No, dear. It was very kind of you. But I do need to rest now. I have a tiny niggle of a headache.'

She got slowly to her feet and at once Sara was beside her, finding her bag, her book, her spectacles. 'I'll come up with you, Gran. Tuck you in.'

When their pudding plates had been cleared, Maureen led the way into the drawing room. Jane followed her and gave a murmur of pleasure as she looked around. She stooped to smell the huge sprays of lilac that stood in a stone pitcher on the hearth, then wandered over to the french windows and gazed out at the garden, now drenched in dusk.

'It's getting dark.' She sighed, blotting out the evening with the heavy, rose-patterned curtains, running her hand luxuriously across the smooth folds of the material. She turned, smiling about her, taking it all in – the flowers, the sunny water-colours that hung against the ivory-painted walls, the dark shine of old furniture gleaming in the lamplight. 'Such a lovely room!' she said. 'You are lucky, you two.'

As Maureen poured them coffee, Robert dropped into an armchair, lit up his applewood pipe, and filled the room with plumes of fragrant blue smoke. Jane bit into a chocolate mint and ran the tip of her tongue over her lips with sensual relish. Then, suddenly, her mood changed. Her face became earnest. She laid a plump white hand on Lewis's sleeve. 'Mother seems to be getting very frail,' she told him. 'Robert and I are rather worried about her, aren't we, Robert?'

At once Lewis felt the happiness of the afternoon drain away from him, leaving him desolate and empty. He didn't want to talk about his mother with Jane. Not with anyone, not even Maureen. Because talking about her would somehow make it official – that there was something wrong, some problem that had to be solved. He would rather go on pretending that everything was always as it had been, that his mother was still as strong, and wise, and capable as she had been all his life.

His father was a shadowy figure. A bluff, hearty, half-remembered giant, laughing as he hoisted him high among the apple boughs to pick the finest fruit. And there was an old photograph Lewis had that showed him as a little boy sitting on Bertie's shoulders and wearing his tweed trilby, ludicrously over-large so that it had slipped down over his face and turned his ears into pan-handles. But that was all faraway childhood-time.

It was Helen who had been the fixed figure in his life, always *there*, somehow able to do everything, to make everything right. When Bertie had died, a young man still, and vigorous, killed in a stupid fall from a ten-foot ladder that should have left him with a twisted ankle at the worst, Helen had simply stepped into his shoes. She was the one who'd run the orchard, found new and expanding markets for their fruit, fought off competition by adding to the varieties they grew, persuaded her labour force to work with an energy and devotion they'd never displayed while her husband was in charge. And she'd still had time, all the time in the world it seemed, for him and Jane.

For years she'd been in sole charge of Greenways Farm until, on his eighteen birthday, she'd made Lewis her partner. And then, when the war came, she'd taken over the reins once more while he was in the Air Force, and held them firmly, and safely, until he was out of hospital and sufficiently recovered to be useful again.

Even when he married and she'd moved out of Greenways, she'd gone on working by Lewis's side. She'd always been the one he turned to when the workers had needed an expert supervisor for the first pruning of the young trees. That was the picture he carried of her in his mind's eye, her hands quick and light among the branches, her face incandescent as she explained exactly how, and where, and why to make the vital cut.

His mother had lived her life like a clear light, he thought, more intensely, more positively, than anyone he had ever known. He took off his glasses and rubbed his eyes wearily. But now, after all these years, it seemed that she was beginning to shine less steadily.

'We're a bit worried about Mother too,' he admitted to Jane, blinking in the soft lamplight. 'There have been one or two little . . . incidents recently.'

'What sort of incidents? Why didn't you tell me?'

'Nothing to get too fussed about. But she's . . . wandered off. Twice, in fact.'

'Wandered off? Mother?' Jane was appalled.

'Three times,' Maureen corrected him. 'And she's turned very forgetful suddenly. Can't remember names.'

'What do you mean?' Jane demanded. 'She remembers all of ours. She asked most particularly about Mike and Peter. And she definitely remembered Jonny Crozier, didn't she, Robert? I saw her face change when his name was mentioned.'

'Yes . . . well . . .'

'What are you trying to say, Maureen?' Lewis urged her gently.

'Mrs Sammes of all people. Sometimes she calls her "Mrs Tolly". I don't know . . .'

'Mrs Tolly!' exclaimed Jane. 'Mother's mixing up Mrs Sammes with Mrs Tolly?'

'But who *is* Mrs Tolly?' Maureen asked. 'I don't remember . . .'

'No. Before your time. She used to come and clean for Mother when I was tiny. About three, I suppose. My God, that's nearly forty years . . .' Her voice trailed off miserably. 'But this is terrible. I mean, I had no idea. Whatever does the doctor say?'

'She won't go to the doctor,' said Lewis.

'But that's ridiculous! We must make her.'

'You know Mother. She's as stubborn as a mule. She absolutely refuses, even to talk—'

'I did ring Dr Redwood,' interrupted Maureen.

'Well, thank heavens *somebody*'s got a bit of sense round here.' Jane flounced back in her chair, glaring at Lewis. 'And?'

'He says without examining her he cannot make an accurate diagnosis.'

'Of course not!' Robert nodded sagely.

'But,' Maureen continued, 'he says this sort of thing is very common among the elderly. Mild confusion. Forgetfulness. There's no cure.'

'But we must do *something*.' Jane stared in disbelief, demanding actions, solutions.

'What *can* you do about old age?' Maureen challenged her. 'One just has to put up with it until . . . until the problem sorts itself out, I suppose.'

'No!' said Jane. 'We have to *do* something. Look after her.'

'She doesn't *want* to be "looked after",' Maureen snapped. 'She didn't even want to come here this weekend. She wants her independence. Wouldn't you?'

Lewis shook his head slowly. 'I had thought about a companion. Live in, you know. But it wouldn't do in Penny Cottage. Much too small. She'd hate having a stranger about the place all the time.'

Suddenly Robert's face brightened. He blew a triumphant smoke ring. 'Sheltered housing, that's the thing. Independence *and* supervision. There's a splendid little development the other side of Donchurch. Customers of the bank, in fact. I might be able to pull a few strings.'

'She couldn't bear that,' declared Lewis. 'She might be getting old herself, but she doesn't want to be surrounded by old people all the time. She needs young ones, like Sara. To take her mind off old age.'

'Well,' said Robert, 'she could come to us. We've plenty of room. And Jane's got time on her hands.'

Jane's face went rigid. 'Don't be a fool, Robert,' she cried. 'Mother doesn't want to be with me. I irritate her to death, don't I? It's Lewis that she loves. For God's sake don't inflict *me* on my poor mother in her declining years. That would be a very poor joke.'

They were all chilled, paralysed, by the undisguised pain in Jane's voice. They knew she was right, but couldn't bring themselves either to accept or deny her statement. It lay among them like a block of ice.

At last Lewis said, 'The sensible answer, of course, is for her to come back here.'

'I agree.' Jane was brisk. 'It is her home, after all. Daddy brought her here when they were married.'

'It is *our* home,' Maureen contradicted her. 'A family house, held in trust, through the generations—'

'We could make her a garden flat,' Lewis interrupted, his mood lifting. 'She'd like that. Turn the utility room into a—'

'Please, Lewis.' Maureen's voice was barely audible.

'But why not, darling? It's the obvious answer.'

'*No!*' she hissed.

'Maureen!'

'No!' she repeated. 'It's my turn to have a life now.'

'What do you mean?' He couldn't understand what she was saying.

'Sara's nearly grown up. She'll be gone soon. So now I want to do something for *me*, not look after your mother. Some sort of further education perhaps . . . I don't know. Just something for *me*.'

Jane looked at Robert, her expression outraged. 'Well, I really think that's a little bit selfish,' she began, 'when you have all this.' She spread her arms expansively. 'Surely the very *least* you can do is—'

Lewis put up his hand to silence her. 'You could still do

that,' he told Maureen. 'I think it's a marvellous idea. Mother's certainly not an invalid. She can look after herself.'

'She can now. Now she's fine. Most of the time. But don't you see? She's going to get worse, Lewis. Senile dementia doesn't go away.'

'We don't know if it's that.'

'Of course we do. What else? And this is just the beginning. She's going to get more and more confused. And then, incapable. Incontinent, perhaps. You must face up to it.'

Lewis stared at her, his face like a death-mask. 'If that's true, Maureen, and pray God it's not . . . but if it *is*, surely we owe her—'

'*No!*' Maureen was shouting now. 'We do not!' Suddenly her anger drained away. She turned to leave the room, and saw Sara standing in the doorway, white as chalk.

'Please stop!' Sara begged them. 'All of you. You're not to treat Gran like . . . like a corner cupboard. Arguing about where you're going to put her. As if she had no feelings. No mind of her own. It's horrible.'

Lewis walked across and took her gently in his arms. Her thin young body was trembling. 'Sorry, baby,' he said. 'We shouldn't have got worked up like that. It's just all so difficult.'

'It's not difficult at all,' she retorted. 'All Gran wants to do is stay in her own cottage. Peace and privacy and a bit of dignity, that's what she wants. And Mrs Sammes is right next door, isn't she? Just through the wall. She sees everything and hears everything. She *likes* being a busybody.'

'So?' Lewis prompted her.

'So why don't the four of you club together and pay Mrs Sammes a little wage, just to help Gran a bit and keep an eye on her properly? That way you needn't feel worried all the time, and you needn't feel guilty either. Mrs Sammes would have something to do, and stop feeling so lonely. She might even stop being such an old moaner! And Gran wouldn't have to put up with all this stupid performance from you lot every time she had a little – a little timeslip!'

'Sara,' Maureen began, 'I'm sorry I went on like that. It's not that I don't love her . . .'

Sara managed a little smile. 'It's all right, Mum. I mean, it's great. I think you'll make a super student. I just wish you'd *enjoy* life a bit more, that's all. I don't see the point of being miserable.'

2

'There's no point in being miserable, dear!'

Maureen got used to her mother's daily advice during the last depressing months of 1939, when Lewis had gone off and joined the Air Force.

'I know there's a war on, but we must all be brave and make the best of things, mustn't we? Poor Daddy never complains.'

And then Nancy would put some more logs on the fire, plump up the pillows behind her husband's back, wipe the saliva from his chin, and forget about Maureen altogether.

Nancy Bolt had been almost forty-five when Maureen was born, the one, surprising, child of a late marriage. And though she was not exactly unwelcome – once Nancy had come to terms with the fact that what she had imagined was the change of life was, in reality, a baby – her arrival in her parents' lives was more of a disruption than a delight. Her father, Henry, had been sixty when she'd erupted noisily into the world, on the eve of his first wedding anniversary. He'd long ago been written off by his friends and family as a crusty old bachelor, married only to his farm and his considerable wealth.

And then he had met Nancy at his nephew's June wedding, seen her smiling up at him from under her tiny veiled hat, as fragile and delicate as a china doll, and come to the astonishing conclusion that he would like a bride of his own. He had proposed before the month was out, and by Christmas he was a married man and well satisfied with his new status.

A wife was one thing, however. A daughter was something else. And though, of course, he adored this beautiful, elfin child, he had always treated her more like a granddaughter, really. Fun to play with for an hour or two when he had the time and energy, but then packed off to her mother, or more often to Edna, their maid, because Nancy was having one of her 'little upsets'.

'Sorry, darling, I'm just a little bit off colour today,' she'd tell Maureen, as the child stood hopefully by her side. 'I'm afraid I'll have to hand you over to Edna. Do try not to be a nuisance.'

Then Maureen, bored with watching Edna huffing over her cooking and cleaning, would slip away and climb over the orchard wall, knowing full well that nobody would miss her for hours.

Over-the-wall was her favourite place in the whole world. Over-the-wall was where the wonderful family next door lived. Jane and Lewis and Helen, their mother, who seemed to Maureen to be everything her own mother was not. Vital, energetic, busy – but always *there* somehow, whirling around the orchard, swooping down upon their games in a burst of gaiety and laughter, gathering Maureen on to her lap while she told them all some mysterious, fantastical story. And then, just as they were longing, *begging*, for more, she was up and off again, dashing away to give her next instructions to her workers. Guiltily, in the secret places of her mind, Maureen used to imagine sometimes that there'd been a terrible mix-up when she was born, that she'd been left with Nancy and Henry by mistake and that the Harrisons were her real family.

Although she'd always adored Lewis she'd never been in love with him, even when her schoolfriends were falling in love all over the place with reckless abandon. There'd never been a schoolgirl crush or anything like that. Lewis had simply been the brother she'd never had. Part of her life. So like Helen, the way his brown eyes would shine with excitement, his face light up with sudden laughter. And his personality was split too, just like Helen's. One minute he was all movement, charging about the farm, racing his ancient bicycle, pestering Jimmy Trotter to let him help with the trees, please, *please*, to show him what to do. The next, he was in another world, sitting rapt, in the shade of the barn, with a book in his hands.

'Silly old books!' Jane used to pout. 'That's all they care about, Lewis and Mother, their silly old stories.'

And she'd take Maureen off to her room to show her her

newest doll, the one that cried, until the little girl wandered home again and sat quietly in the corner until Nancy felt strong enough to leave her darkened bedroom.

Maureen was lucky, she knew, to have had a happy childhood. If it hadn't been for the Harrisons, and especially Helen, who'd engineered it all, it would have been a different story. The Harrisons *were* her childhood. And her growing-up years.

But then, without her even realising what was happening, life began to change. A new vet, Jonny Crozier, arrived to join the Donchurch practice a year before the war began. Jonny was the most handsome man Maureen had ever seen outside a cinema. He was almost Scandinavian in appearance, with a fine athletic body, tall and loose-limbed. His dark blond hair was streaked gold by the sun, his tanned skin gleamed with health and there was a fine net of laughter lines around his eyes.

It was Robert who had first introduced him to the Harrisons and started the whole thing off. Jonny had come into the bank to open an account and Robert had been taken at once by his friendly, easy manner. 'How are you settling in?' he asked.

'Fine!' smiled Jonny. 'But it's early days, you know. I'm still a bit of an outsider here – apart from my cousin, Phylly Crozier. It was because of her—'

'An outsider!' Robert was horrified. 'We can't have that! Look, my wife and I are doing a brunch party this Sunday. Why don't you join us? Jane's a darned good cook, I can promise you that.'

For a moment Jonny looked doubtful, but Robert insisted. 'Really! Bring Phyl, of course. She's an old chum of ours. And Richard Bowman too. They've just got engaged, haven't they? Lewis Harrison will be there – my brother-in-law. And Maureen Bolt. You must join the gang.'

And then he'd laughed out loud, making the other tellers pause, their fingers busy in their cash drawers, and turn and stare at young Mr Prescott. Robert was short, and round and already his hair was going a bit thin on top. The sort of man who had begun to look middle-aged by the time he was just eight years old. It was a preposterous notion that he should have a 'gang', but he was rather taken with the idea. He determined to develop it.

When Maureen thought back to those long tranquil months of the summer of '38, they seemed to her a time of pure delight. She was sure it had never rained. Somehow the apples must have plumped up and ripened on the trees without any care or attention and every animal in Kent stayed miraculously well, and all the workaday chores just . . . got done, because she and Lewis and Jonny, and all the rest of the 'Harrison set', as they came to be known, spent their entire lives, or so her memory told her, enjoying themselves. She had never been so happy. When the weather was cool enough, they played tennis on the old overgrown courts behind the kitchen garden at Greenways. When it was hot they swam in the river. Jane organised picnic parties. Jonny had the idea of a bicycle treasure hunt. She and Lewis planned a dawn-to-dusk paper trail, hares and hounds, right across the Downs. It was the best of times. They tried to tell themselves it would last for ever. That somehow Hitler would be appeased. That universal goodwill would prevail.

But then the goodwill ran out and war was declared. Lewis enlisted for the Air Force, looking handsome and slightly scared in his smart blue uniform. A little while later Robert was called up for the Army.

'They'll *never* manage at the bank!' he protested. 'I'm sure I'd be more use to the country staying here than marching about with a gun.'

'You would!' Jane agreed, feeding Mike and Peter with coddled eggs and Marmite soldiers. 'You don't think I'll be expected to take evacuees, do you? They say there are more on the way but, really, I'm going to have quite enough on my hands with these two. And apparently the children are *awful*, you know. Head lice! And *filthy* habits.'

By the time they welcomed in the New Year, the only man left of the Harrison set was Jonny Crozier.

'Why hasn't that young vet been called up like everybody else?' Helen wanted to know.

Jane was vague. 'I think it must be something to do with his job,' she said. 'It's nice to have somebody decent left at home, anyway. The place is like a desert.'

Helen looked dubious. 'If you want my opinion, a little of Jonny Crozier goes a long way.'

'Oh, Mother! I think he's really sweet. He drops in to see me sometimes if he has a home visit in the area.' Her lips curved in a creamy smile. 'Quite often, actually. He really does want to help. So many of us poor women are having to struggle along on our own these days.'

Towards the middle of January the orchards were lashed by a mighty gale that drove inland straight down from the north-east and the huge icy land mass beyond. Maureen stared down from her bedroom, watching the apple trees bend and creak under the onslaught. Now that most of the men were away she was trying to look after the farm with only an elderly labourer and a couple of village women to help her. Her father's stroke, two years ago, had put him completely out of action, and her mother had declared she was far too delicate to get involved. Before the war, Lewis had always been at hand, and after he'd gone Helen had promised that she would lend Maureen her manager, Jimmy Trotter, whenever she needed him. But from her window, Maureen couldn't really work out what she needed. She could see that bits of branches were being snapped off the trees and whirled around high above them, but Mr Trotter could hardly help with that problem. She would just have to sit out the storm, she decided, and inspect the damage as soon as the wind had spent its force. Then she clapped her hand to her head as she suddenly remembered the new trees. Out of sight, at the exposed side of the house, a hundred maidens had been planted in the old paddock just last November. They must be taking the direct force of the gale.

Running downstairs she grabbed her coat and belted it tightly around her, shoved her feet into a pair of old boots, and let herself out of the kitchen, struggling to hold on to the heavy door so that the wind wouldn't tear it off its hinges. Clinging on to the thick ropes of ivy that grew up the walls of the house, she turned the corner and shouldered her way through the gusts towards the new trees. When she reached them she gasped in dismay. Practically all the chestnut poles that should have been holding the young trees in place had shed their ties and come loose. Some were blowing about on the ground, some had snapped off, others were bending over at crazy angles. Without them, she knew, the trees couldn't survive. Already the gale was beginning to rock their roots. Unless they were properly staked again it would tug them right out of the soft, moist soil.

Shaking and scared, Maureen battled her way back into the house and hurried to the phone. Almost at once she heard Helen's voice.

'Hello! Greenways Orchard here.'

'Helen!' Maureen tried to control the agitation in her voice.

'How lovely to hear from you, Maureen. Is everything all right?'

'Not really. Could I possibly borrow Mr Trotter for the afternoon?'

'I'm so sorry, I'm afraid you can't. He's gone down with this beastly flu. Why? What's the trouble?'

'I think I'm going to lose all the new trees in the paddock. My fault. The stakes haven't been knocked in hard enough.'

'Oh dear. Can I help?'

'No. Really! You've just got over the flu yourself. Don't worry, I'll think of something.'

Putting down the receiver, Maureen crossed to the hall cupboard and pulled from the top shelf a thick scarf, which she wound tightly round her head, and a pair of leather gloves. Then, grimly, she made for the door again.

'Darling!' she heard her mother's voice call from the next room. 'Is that you? What are you doing?'

'I've got to go out into the orchard, Mother.'

'What? In this weather? Don't you think that's rather foolish, dear?'

Shrugging wearily, Maureen let herself out into the gale that howled and screeched around her ears.

An hour later she had managed to restake and retie barely a quarter of the trees. Despite her gloves, her hands were beginning to blister from the friction of the heavy iron mallet she was using to bang in the poles. There was a tearing pain across the line of her arms and shoulders, and the skin of her face was stinging in the icy cold air. Just as she was beginning to think she could not go on for even five minutes more, she felt a strong, supporting arm about her.

'Maureen?'

She swung round. Jonny Crozier stood looking down at her in astonishment. 'What are you doing?'

'I'm trying to save my new trees, what do you think?' She had to shout to make herself heard above the wind's roar.

'I just dropped in to see you. Your mother told me you'd come out here for a little walk!'

'Oh, God!' Maureen lifted her mallet again and brought it down viciously on to the next pole. It missed its mark and knocked the pole sideways, causing one of the apple branches to break. She gave a sob of near hysteria.

At once Jonny took charge. 'Give it to me,' he insisted. 'We'll do better if we work together. Now, you hold the stake, I'll do the whacking. You check the tie. Then on to the next one. What we need is a system.'

It was just beginning to get dark when they finished the last tree, and still the wind had not abated. Maureen tried to straighten her back, grimacing with the effort. She flexed her numbed fingers, and gave Jonny a watery smile. 'Come on up to the house,' she said, 'and I'll make us some tea.'

He nodded. 'Where does this go?'

She looked vaguely at the mallet he was holding as if she hardly recognised it. 'Oh, just inside the packing shed.' She led the way towards the long wooden building that bordered the far edge of the paddock, unbolted the door, and stumbled inside. 'It stands in the corner here.'

As Jonny reached past her in the gloom, he realised that she was crying, silently, her eyes wide, her mouth open a little, and great tears rolling down her cheeks. 'Hey! Hey, what's this?' he murmured, delicately wiping away a tear with the tip of his finger. 'A heroine like you, weeping!'

His words unleashed a torrent of sobs that made her body shake uncontrollably.

'It's all right,' he said, putting his arms round her and holding on to her, patiently, until the trembling stopped. 'There!' He smiled. 'Better now?'

She sniffed and cleared her throat. 'Yes, thank you,' she replied in a small voice, like a polite child. 'I'm sorry.' And then she took a deep breath, as his mouth came down on hers.

For her, it was a new experience. She was twenty-one years

old and it was her first real kiss. Lewis had kissed her often enough, but Lewis had kissed her like a brother. Jonny's was a lover's kiss.

Maureen was in thrall. She fell in love, rapturously, recklessly, as if she were diving into a cool, blue, fathomless sea. Soon Jonny was a regular visitor to the Bolt household. Maureen could hardly believe it, the way he brought her parents back from the strange limbo of their lives.

'Nancy! How well and *pretty* you're looking today,' he'd say, dropping a kiss on her dry cheek. And Nancy would sparkle up at him, her smile transforming the dulled, lustreless face.

'I'm sure you say that to all the ladies.' She wagged her finger at him in mock reproof.

'Only when it's true!'

With her father, the response was even more miraculous. Henry's stroke had left him partially paralysed and without speech. The few visitors he had either spoke to him in loud, polite voices as if he were an imbecile, or talked over his head as if he just weren't there. Jonny behaved as if he hadn't even noticed that Henry was disabled. He'd sit by the old man's side discussing the desperate state of the war, the misery of the blackout, how on earth they were all supposed to manage on these punitive rations. And then he'd radiate optimism. 'Never mind, Henry. It might look as if old Adolf has the upper hand, but don't you believe it. We'll have him on the run before you're picking your next crop of apples, believe me.'

And Maureen noticed that her father's eyes would snap and twinkle as Jonny talked. He listened and understood and relished every word.

'Thank you for being so kind to them,' she said.

'Kind? Nonsense! I like them.'

As the spring approached, with celandines bright candles in the orchard grass and the first tiny leaves beginning to appear on the apple trees, Maureen realised that Jonny had become a vital part of her daily life. Sometimes he called to say he had a visit to make at a farm or in one of the more remote villages, and insist he carry her off with him, just for the ride. Sometimes, if he had time off and she was working, he'd come along to help, lending a cheerful hand with the watering, feeding, mulching and spraying.

'It never stops!' he complained one day, gathering up the prunings to be carted away for burning.

She laughed. 'My apple trees are just like your precious animals. Alive and kicking, thank goodness.'

The first time Jane saw them together, it was market day in Donchurch and they were having lunch in the Saddle Room of the Four Horses pub. Jonny was in the middle of a complicated and riotous story about a Large White boar that had somehow managed to trap him in the corner of its sty and had been, he was convinced, determined to devour him there and then.

'Wreaking revenge for all the bacon rashers I've devoured,' he exclaimed. 'And who can blame the poor beast?'

They were both laughing so much, heads close together, so absorbed in their own world, that neither of them even noticed Jane until she bent over their table.

'Hello, you two!' Her voice was brittle. 'Long time no see, Jonny. I've been wondering where you were hiding yourself.'

Jonny grinned, unabashed. 'Would you care to join us for coffee, Jane? We've just finished ours but . . .' He pulled up a seat for her and nodded towards the barmaid.

'Thank you.' Jane smiled frostily. 'Have you heard from Lewis?' she asked Maureen.

'Yes. About a fortnight ago.'

'Me too. You will keep the letters flowing, won't you? He's really pretty miserable. He seems to hate flying, though he was desperate to join up, wasn't he? Determined to do his bit.' She glared pointedly at Jonny.

Maureen drained her coffee cup. 'Of course I'll write, Jane. But I'm working all hours at present. We haven't finished pruning yet and here we are, into March already.'

'I'm glad you can find time to lunch with your friends anyway. And I imagine *you* are keeping pretty busy too, Jonny,' Jane purred.

'You know me,' he said airily. 'I am a slave unto my animals!' He looked at his watch. 'And, as it happens, duty calls yet again.' He stood up, pushing back his chair. 'I'll get the bill on the way out.' He smiled at Maureen. 'You two can girl-talk behind my back.' He signalled at Maureen with raised eyebrows, then patted her gently on the top of her head as he squeezed past. 'Give Nancy and Henry my love, won't you? Say I'll be round to see them soon.'

Jane watched him go, then turned a solemn face to Maureen. 'Look,' she said, 'I really don't want to interfere, and of course it's absolutely none of my business, but you do need to keep an eye on that one, you know.'

'Who? Jonny? Whatever do you mean?'

'You must have heard about the reputation he's getting. He's a terrible lady's man.'

'Oh, Jane. Please.'

'I mean it. When Robert was first called up, he was *always* round at our place. I couldn't keep him away. In the end I had to tell him. "I'm a married woman," I said, "and it's not right. Not fair on Robert."'

Maureen gave an incredulous laugh.

'You may think it's funny,' Jane ploughed on remorselessly, 'but I wasn't the only one either. He spreads his favours far and wide, believe me. Too handsome for his own good.'

Suddenly Maureen was angry. She stood up abruptly. 'I have to go now,' she said. 'I don't want to hear any more of this nonsense. As you say, it's got nothing to do with you.'

Jane was offended. 'I was just trying to give you a friendly warning,' she protested. 'Why do you think he came to Donchurch in the first place?'

'I don't know. I never asked.'

'Well, apparently Phylly told my hairdresser, and she told me – in strictest confidence – that he was on the run from a certain lady's *husband*, who was getting quite shirty.'

'Really?' said Maureen coldly. 'I'm sure you felt you had to tell me that, Jane. But I'll make up my own mind about my friends, thank you.' She picked up her basket of shopping.

'And the other thing,' Jane persisted. 'Mother can't stand him, you know.'

'Helen can't stand Jonny? Why not?'

Jane shrugged. 'I don't know. But I do know this, Maureen. Mother has always been a very shrewd judge of character. And what she wants to know is, why hasn't he been called up like all the rest of the boys? Do you know?'

'His work, I suppose.'

'I don't think so.'

Maureen looked vague. 'Some problem we don't know about then. Like flat feet or something.'

Jane's chilly laugh rang round the bar. 'Come off it. Even someone as naive as you must have noticed that Jonny Crozier is an absolutely *perfect* specimen of manhood.'

For a while Maureen was haunted by Jane's warning. Sometimes she found herself watching Jonny, imagining him with other women. Of course, he must have had lots of girlfriends. Had he kissed them in the same way as he kissed her? Smiled into their eyes as lovingly? Touched them as gently, as tenderly? But then, as the days sped by, she thrust it all away from her. Wherever the truth lay, what did it matter what had happened in the past? Jonny was with *her* now. And no matter what Helen might think of him, her own mother lit up whenever he entered the room and her father's poor, shattered face signalled his pleasure.

She wrote to Lewis.

I'm sorry you're having a bad time and not enjoying flying very much. I hope things get better soon. Nothing much seems to happen here, we haven't been bombed or anything, thank goodness. But *you* must be in the thick of things, I suppose. Fingers crossed that we'll all be together again next Christmas. Wouldn't that be marvellous? Although I thought I'd never be able to cope with the orchard on my own, and the winter was absolutely *terrible* – they say January and February were the coldest for almost fifty years – we are now having a perfect spring. Beautiful! Of course it doesn't make life any easier as far as the work is concerned. Everything is growing like billy-o and if we have a late frost . . . but I don't need to tell *you*, do I?

The good thing is, Jonny Crozier is being absolutely won-derful. He comes and helps whenever he can, and he's fun to be with and makes sure that I get out and have a bit of time off occasionally, otherwise I'd be working non-stop. He's still managing to run his car, of course, because of his work. He asked me to send you his 'best regards' and says he might even drop you a line one of these days, though knowing Jonny, I wouldn't bank on it!

Father is very frail now and Mother is terribly sad – except when Jonny is around to cheer her up. Helen and Mr Trotter seem to be managing Greenways very efficiently between them so you don't need to worry about *that*, and they're always ready to help me whenever I need it.

I bump into Jane occasionally. She never changes, does she? Still her own sweet self!

Take care, Lewis. Come home safe and well *very soon*.

Love, Maureen.

It was before breakfast, on what promised to be a lovely April day, that Jonny rang up, wildly excited. 'You must come out with me,' he urged. 'My day off, and you *must* come and see the cherry blossom. I insist!'

'Jonny, I can't. We have to do the mowing today.'

'Do the mowing another day. It can't be that important.'

'Of course it is. If we don't keep the grass short it increases the frost risk and we—'

'Maureen, sweetheart!' His voice was like honey. 'I can't bear you not to see the cherry trees and I don't know when we'll have another chance. Please, *please* come.'

She paused. Then, 'I'll see what I can organise,' she said softly. 'Just give me a couple of hours.'

'I've found this place, this perfect place,' he told her, as they drove along narrow green lanes that climbed steeply up and up, past hidden farms and hamlets that looked as if time had forgotten them. At last he parked the car at the side of the road, took her hand and led her through a little copse of hazel trees where the ground beneath shone with pale primroses and wood anemones. She stood still, trying to breathe in all the wonderful fresh scents of soil and leaf and flower, but he couldn't bear to wait. He tugged her after him, stumbling over the rough grass, until at last they emerged from the wood on to a high plateau overlooking a secret valley.

'Now! What about *that*?' he demanded.

She couldn't reply. Away below her, for almost half a mile it seemed, the wild cherry trees flowed into the distance, creamy white, swaying gently in the breeze. A sea of blossom. She had never in her life seen anything so lovely. She gazed, wide-eyed and wordless, then turned towards him with a radiant smile.

'I love you,' he said suddenly, as if taken by surprise. 'All I could think of, when I saw this, was you. Needing to share it with *you*. I love you. I love you.'

He threw himself on to the sweet, short grass and putting his hand up to her, pulled her gently down beside him. She lay quietly in the crook of his arm, feeling the steady beat of his heart, listening to the call of the cuckoos insistent overhead. And when she felt his hand on her breast, saw his face looming over hers transfigured by desire, she felt nothing but joy. The touch of his lips, the thrust of his tongue, aroused in her a level of passion she didn't begin to understand.

'Is it all right?' he murmured, peeling off her blouse, kissing her breasts, her nipples, with quick, feather-light kisses. 'I *will* take care. Tell me it's all right.'

'Of course.' She smiled, her hands caressing the nape of his neck, her body spread beneath his. 'Of course it is, Jonny.'

On the way home, through the late April afternoon that glittered gold and green, Maureen worried about seeing her mother again. Even Nancy must be bound to see it written on her face, she thought, must notice the change in her and understand what it meant.

But her anxieties were groundless. Nancy had too many other things on her mind to register the wide, shining delight in Maureen's eyes. 'The travellers are back,' she cried, running into the kitchen to meet them the moment they opened the door. 'Camped in our back lane again, a whole tribe of them. I thought they wouldn't come this year, with the war and everything.'

'Travellers?' Jonny's voice was sharp. 'Gypsies, you mean?'

Maureen shook her head. 'Travelling labourers. They come every year at about this time. I don't know why, because there's never any work for them. I think they must have just left their winter campsite, wherever that is. They seem to troop about the place, checking out the orchards and the hop gardens for when the picking begins.'

'And they camp on your private land without so much as a by-your-leave?' Jonny was appalled. 'We can't have that.'

'But, you see, Henry always said that we must treat them charitably,' Nancy explained. 'With tolerance. He thought it was necessary for them to keep their dignity.'

'That's all very well, but—'

'The other thing is,' Maureen interrupted him, 'we daren't upset them because we really need them when the picking begins. And they know that. This year more than ever.'

Jonny looked doubtful. 'Apart from trespassing, do they behave themselves?'

Maureen laughed. 'They usually take a few eggs from the coop, and pinch a few vegetables. Maybe the odd bottle of milk. But they don't look upon it as stealing or anything wrong. Because we have so much, you see, and they have practically nothing. And, in a way, I can see their point.'

'Oh dear!' sighed Nancy. 'You're your father's daughter, you really are. That's exactly what he used to say. The real trouble, Jonny, is their wretched fires. They're not content with sticks for firewood. They wrench whole branches off our trees. And they're such a wild, lawless bunch. They look so strange, you know. Perhaps I'm being silly but they terrify me.'

Jonny had heard enough. 'I really think we should call the police. Get them moved on.'

Maureen put her hand on his arm. 'They've been coming here every April since before I was born.'

'But things are different now. There's a war on. A state of emergency. I think it's probably against the law.'

'They don't mean any harm. They always got on well with Father.'

'That's the other thing!' Jonny exclaimed. 'Henry isn't able to take care of you any longer. It needs a man's authority.' Grim-faced, he marched out of the room. 'I'm going to have a word with them.'

'You must *not* do this on your own,' Maureen insisted, hurrying after him. 'You don't know how to handle them.' She looked back at Nancy's anxious face. 'Don't worry, Mother. It'll be all right. You go in to Father now.'

The travellers were encamped in the wide lane that ran round the back of the orchard, just where it widened out to form a grassy bay, protected on three sides by a thick hawthorn hedge. They had two horse-drawn carts covered with heavy tarpaulin, and a dilapidated van. A couple of starved-looking dogs were roped to the back of the vehicle and the horses had been unhitched and tethered loosely to the fence at the opposite side of the lane. A group of people was scattered around the dying embers of a large fire, a hunch-backed dwarf of a man, five women, one of whom had a baby at her breast, and a little mob of children rolling around on the ground like puppies.

As Maureen and Jonny approached, the travellers turned and stared at them fiercely.

'Good evening,' said Jonny in a firm voice.

'Evenin'.' An old woman sitting on an upturned bucket returned the greeting. She was wearing a man's tweed coat fastened round the waist with stout string, and her rough, tangled hair and pitted skin gave evidence of a lifetime's hardship. She was evidently the spokesman. All the rest were silent and sullen, except for a half-naked boy who burst into noisy sobs and rushed to the comfort of his mother's lap. Maureen noticed with a pang that the girl who picked him up and cuddled him looked hardly more than a child herself.

'Lovely evenin' it is too,' the old woman continued, laughing with a sort of desperate bravado.

'Yes, it's been a beautiful day.' Maureen smiled down at her. 'You must have seen how fine the cherry blossom—'

Jonny was scuffling about among the ashes with the toe of his shoe, examining the piles of unburnt fuel round the outer edge of the burnt circle. 'Look here,' he interrupted curtly. 'You've been breaking off branches, haven't you?' He waved his arm grandly in the direction of the hedge. 'And you've hacked great chunks out of the hawthorn bushes.'

'Have to have a fire to cook,' replied the woman. 'And we're lettin' it out now. Can't have lights after dark, not these days. We know that.'

'But you could have used dead wood, couldn't you?' Maureen pleaded. 'There's plenty of it lying about, I'm sure. You can take as much of that as you want, you know.'

'Thank you, my dear.' The woman gave her a gap-toothed

grin. 'You always were a kind little maid. I remember you comin' here with your old dad when you were knee-high.'

Maureen blushed, struggling for words. 'We're not asking you to move on tonight,' she explained, her voice gentle. 'It's late for the children. But if you *could* leave tomorrow . . .'

'Can't do that, maid. Out of petrol, you see, or we wouldn't be here now. Can't move on without petrol, can we?' And she cackled happily, smiling about her at the rest of her family, who nodded cheerfully, knowing that she had scored a point.

'When will you have some petrol?' Maureen asked.

'Don't know. It's in short supply, isn't it? There bein' a war on. One o' my lasses here will have to stir herself tomorrow, see if she can lay her hands on any. But I can't make any promises.'

'You can't stay here indefinitely,' Jonny protested.

The old woman gave him a sardonic stare. 'We're doin' no harm, sir. Not just bein' here. There's no harm in that, is there, if we promise to use the dead wood.'

'How do we know you won't go stealing eggs, or—'

'Stealin'?' She was outraged. She glared around her for support and her companions muttered angrily. 'Do you think we'd *steal*, sir?'

'Well . . . since you ask me . . . yes. I do. Sorry.'

Maureen gave a silent groan and buried her face in her hands. The old traveller raised one brown leathery hand and pointed it at Jonny as if she were delivering a curse.

'May the Lord forgive you, *sir*, for havin' so little faith in your fellow man. We are good honest labourin' folk, that's what we are. Not thieves and vagabonds. And we've been comin' here, to this young lady's place, for fifty years or more. Year in, year out. Yes, and helped her father with his fine apple crop and earned our poor penny. And never, never in all that time, has anyone in this good place accused us of stealin'.' She dropped her arm, straightened her back, coughed, and spat juicily on to the hot ashes.

Jonny listened to the hiss of the spittle, and looked helplessly at Maureen for support. Quickly she stepped forward and crouched down so that she was face to face with the affronted woman. 'Please,' she begged her, 'don't take what Mr Crozier said personally. He doesn't know you the way I do. It's just that some of the itinerant workers do – just occasionally – dig up a few potatoes or—'

'Not us!' the woman declared. 'Never us. He had no right sayin' that.' She grabbed Maureen's arm and pulled her closer. 'You're too good a maid for the likes o' him,' she muttered. 'You want to watch that one.'

'I'm sure he's very sorry for upsetting you,' Maureen assured her. 'Aren't you, Jonny?'

Jonny shrugged, knowing he'd been out-manoeuvred. 'Look,' he said, desperate to extricate himself, 'what if I come over tomorrow with a couple of cans of petrol? My gift. Would you . . . move on then?'

The old woman looked at him, her eyes shrewd. 'And give our hosses a goin'-over too?'

'I beg your pardon?'

'"Mr Crozier", the maid called you. You're the young vet from over Donchurch.'

'How did you know that?'

She grinned. 'They do say as you know about hosses. Understand them. Two gallon o' petrol and a check-up for our beasts, and then we'll be on our way.'

Reluctantly, Jonny gave in. 'All right,' he said. 'All right, it's a deal. But I must have your word upon it.'

She raised her head proudly, like a tribal queen. 'You have that.'

'Very well. I'll see you tomorrow, then.'

'Goodnight,' said Maureen humbly. 'Thank you. We will see you for the apple picking, won't we? It's going to be a heavy crop.'

The travellers' faces were inscrutable. She put her arm through Jonny's and they began to walk away together down the lane, now cobweb-grey in the twilight. Suddenly the woman's voice shrilled after them: 'Mr Crozier! Sir! Before you go.'

Jonny looked back, wondering what new demand was going to be forced upon him now. 'What is it?'

'I was just wonderin', sir. How is it you're not in the Army? As you see, all my lads have been taken. All gone off to fight for King and country.' Her voice was sly. 'Seems strange that you're still here.'

Silently Jonny turned on his heel, listening to the raucous laughter echoing at his back.

After a few minutes Maureen said, 'I've often wondered that, Jonny. Were you exempt because of your job or something?'

He smiled down at her. 'No. I was too ill.'

'Too ill. What with? You've never told me.'

'Diabetes.'

'You have diabetes?' Maureen was horrified. 'How terrible! You should have . . .'

He laughed. 'Just on the day. The day I went for my medical. Then it cleared up. A miracle!'

'What do you mean?'

'It's the easiest thing in the world to fake, darling – sugar in the water.'

'What?' Maureen could feel her heart thumping. She stopped in her tracks and looked at him furiously. 'You did *that*? You cheated, just to stay at home? When poor Lewis, and Robert, and Richard Bowman, and all our friends are over there being shot at and attacked and heaven knows what. How *could* you?' She felt betrayed, physically sick. She stalked away from him, tears stinging her eyes.

At once he had her by the shoulders, forcing her round to face him again. 'Maureen, listen to me. I *hate* war—'

'So does everybody.'

'But I think it's wrong. Evil. I've got more important things to do with my life.' She jerked her head to one side, refusing to look at him. 'My life is about caring for sick animals, not killing people. War is against my principles.'

She was silent for a moment. Then, 'You should have told them that when you were called up,' she said. 'You should have been honest. Done it properly.'

'Signed up as a "conchy", you mean?' He snorted. 'What good would that have done? Prison. Or driving ambulances. Listen. What I'm trying to tell you is – you may think it was wrong, but I did it for my animals. *They*'re the ones that matter.' He gave a brief laugh. 'Before I met you I used to think that animals were better than people. That I liked them more. They are innocent, not like us. And I am good with them, you know. That's about the only true thing that dreadful old traveller woman said. I'm a healer. That's my role in life, not to go around shooting people, dropping bombs, sinking ships. I hate all that. I'm a man of peace.' He looked at her beseechingly. Her face glimmered at him through the dusk. She stood silently before him, still and grave. He raised his hands in a helpless gesture. 'But the most important thing, Maureen – why, I'd do it again, exactly the same, no matter what anybody might say or think about me – is that through staying here, I found *you*. These few months we've had together, they've been the most marvellous time of my life. The *only* time of my life! Getting to know you, loving you, sharing things with you . . . If they dragged me off tomorrow and threw me into jail for ten years or more, I'd still think it had been worth it. Don't you see? It was meant to be, Maureen. Just you and me together, like this. I know it. But you have to trust me. I'm no cheap cheat, darling. Really.' His voice fell to a whisper. 'Please say that you believe me.'

She raised her eyes to his and saw to her astonishment that he was close to tears. She couldn't bear it, the defeated despair on his face. Swiftly she wrapped her arms around him, and held him tightly. She felt his head droop down on her shoulder, heard his harsh sob. 'Oh, Jonny, yes, I do believe you, darling. Of course, I do. I'm sorry. I'm sorry.' And as she kissed him, on his neck, on his ear, on his cheek, whispering to him, persuading him to lift his head, to smile again, she knew without doubt that whatever Jonny did, she couldn't help but love him, unconditionally, for as long as she lived.

3

Almost a week had passed since the Blossom Procession, and Maureen was feeling edgy and anxious. She stared at herself in her long mirror. Smallish. Thinnish. Grey eyes. Skin OK but getting a bit wrinkly here and there. Hair? Not bad. Glossy black, thick and wavy, good, short cut. She frowned at her reflection. Usually she thought she looked quite good for her age, but today . . . She tugged the black dress off over her head and threw it on her bed. It made her look at least fifty. Forty-one was quite old enough without adding a few years! She rattled through the rest of the hangers in the wardrobe. *Not* the garish red suit. She couldn't imagine why she'd ever bought it. And the grey shirtwaister made her look like a country mouse. She sat down at her dressing table in despair. The last thing in the world that she wanted to do was go to this wretched party, but Phylly Bowman had been adamant.

'You *must* come!' she'd insisted over the telephone. 'I'm trying to get all the old set together again. It's a sort of surprise present for Jonny.'

'We're really very busy this week. Reorganising Penny Cottage for Lewis's mother. She's not been too—'

'Never mind all that. You can look after Helen another day. Jonny has to go back on Sunday.'

'So soon?'

'Quite! And, really, you and Lewis and he were almost inseparable, weren't you, before the rotten war messed everything up? He'd be devastated if you didn't come. You just can't be "too busy", Maureen. I won't have it.'

'Have you told him we're coming?'

'You're not concentrating. A *surprise* party, I said. Can't wait to see his face, can *you*?'

'Can't wait to see his face!' Grimly, Maureen decided on the cream silk jacket and skirt she'd bought to wear at her nephew Peter's graduation ceremony. 'Unobtrusive without being dowdy,' she told herself. 'That's the best I can hope for.'

Phylly and Richard Bowman lived in a new, rosy-red villa on a little estate on the southern edge of Donchurch. After a day of unseasonable dark skies and fretful winds, the weather had settled into a miserable grey drizzle by the time the party began, so all the guests were crammed inside the house, unable to overflow into the garden. Once across the threshold, Maureen and Lewis were drawn into a mass of shoving bodies and grinning faces, trapped in a maelstrom of talk and music and loud, shouted laughter.

'One or two close friends!' Maureen protested. 'That's what Phylly said. There must be at least forty – and I don't recognise half of them.'

'Better pretend you do,' Lewis answered. 'After all this time it's the safest way.'

'Don't you think we could just slip off home—' she began. And then she saw Jonny. He was standing by the fireplace, one foot raised on the hearth, his arms folded. He seemed to be listening intently to a small man with a little bald patch and a large fat stomach. Every now and then Jonny shook his head, laughing, his eyes wide, as if he couldn't believe what he was hearing. Maureen watched him, amazed. He hadn't changed at all. The way he stood. The way he held his head. The years seemed to have left him completely untouched. While she and Lewis had gone on living their quiet lives, bringing up Sara, tending the orchards, going calmly about their daily affairs and trying not to notice week by week the stray grey hair, the extra laughter line or wrinkle, Jonny had been in some enchanted land where time stood still. His hair was as blond and thick as ever, his skin glowed with health, his body was still as taut and finely muscled as that of a racehorse.

Suddenly the fat man stopped talking and Jonny raised his eyes as if looking round the room for an escape route. As soon as he caught sight of Maureen he excused himself and began pushing his way across the crowded room.

'Lew!' he said, shaking his hand warmly. 'Great to see you again. Thanks for coming.' Then he turned to Maureen, bent and kissed her swiftly on the cheek. 'You're looking *wonderful*! Not a day – not a minute older!'

She cursed herself for blushing, and heard herself babbling like an idiot. 'What a surprise all this is. Year after year and never a word from you. And now, here we all are together again as if you'd never been away. I can hardly believe it.'

Lewis laughed. 'When I bumped into you on Sunday I thought you were a ghost. What have you been doing with yourself?'

'Oh, you know. Once a vet, always a vet. I practise in Suffolk now. Lots of affluent ladies with lovely overfed pet dogs who need my *very* expensive attention.'

'And is your wife with you?'

'I have no wife.'

'I'm sorry. I thought . . . I'm sure somebody told me . . .'

'Yes. It lasted about three years. We parted without tears. On either side.'

'I'm sorry,' Lewis said again. 'Bad luck. It must be miserable.'

'Lewis!' exclaimed Maureen.

'What's the matter, darling? What have I said?'

She shrugged. 'Nothing. *Nothing*.'

Jonny laughed. 'Not to worry. I don't mind talking about the manifold disasters of my love life, really. But it is a bit boring. And repetitive. So let's catch up with you two instead, shall we?'

Lewis smiled. 'Well, we have a daughter, almost sixteen—'

'Yes! Sarah.'

'Sara,' Lewis corrected him.

'Sorry. I saw her at the Blossom party. Phylly pointed her out. She's a little beauty. Just like her lovely mother.'

Maureen shook her head, steeling herself to meet his insistent gaze. 'More like Lewis's mother actually.'

'Ah. The redoubtable Helen. Yes, I bumped into her too, but she pretended not to know me. She never did like me much, did she?'

Lewis laughed. 'When I went away, you mean? I hope you

didn't let it bother you. It was probably just because you were here and I wasn't. Mother's like that, I'm afraid!'

'I learnt to live with it,' Jonny told him drily. 'Like most things.' Then he turned to Maureen again. 'And what about Nancy and Henry? I thought about them often after . . . when I got my new job.'

Maureen's face clouded. 'They missed you, Jonny. Terribly. My father died the year after you left.'

'I'm sorry. I didn't realise or I'd have written.'

'You know how he was. He was ready to go. The worst thing was that my mother simply couldn't live without him. I . . . until then I'd never believed that you could die of a broken heart, but . . .'

'Oh, *I* believe it,' Jonny told her seriously. 'I'm sure of it. Is that what happened to poor Nancy?'

Maureen shrugged. 'She followed him within six months. She was only sixty-seven and not half as 'delicate' as she imagined.' Her voice rose, harsh with remembered grief. 'The doctor said there was absolutely no *need* for her to die.'

'What do doctors know about it?' demanded Lewis, with sudden anger. 'They're blinded by medical science. Think there must be a remedy for every ailment. But it's not like that. We can die of other things than physical illness. A broken heart can be just as fatal as a diseased liver.'

His words were so unexpected, so edged with bitterness, that for a moment neither Jonny nor Maureen could think how to respond. Puzzled, Maureen touched his hand, and he gave her a fleeting, troubled smile.

'Well,' said Jonny, abruptly changing the mood. 'So you were just twenty-three, were you, Maureen, when you came into your inheritance? Lucky man, Lewis. Your bride brought you a fortune as well as her lovely self.'

Lewis's face was like stone. 'I never even thought of that, Jonny. After my accident, when I came home, I needed Maureen. I really did. I believe she saved my life. And I've gone on needing her ever since.'

'Sorry, old chap.' Jonny looked contrite. 'Stupid of me. It was just a – a tasteless joke. I do know Maureen's value, believe me.'

Maureen looked up desperately at the two men, her veneer of composure destroyed by the emotion that trembled in Jonny's voice. 'I'm so sorry. I'm really feeling quite faint,' she said. 'It's so hot in here. I must get some air.'

'Poor love!' Lewis's face swam in front of her, crumpled in concern. 'We'd better go home.'

'No, really.'

'*Yes*, really. You haven't been yourself for days. Perhaps you've got a bug or something.'

'I'll be all right. Just give me a minute.'

'Better to make a move, I think. I'll just go and retrieve our coats. Sorry, Jonny.'

When he'd gone, Jonny fixed his eyes on her. 'Thank you for coming to my party,' he said with a wry smile. 'But it wasn't *quite* like old times.'

When Lewis awoke and looked at his watch it was three o'clock in the morning. He lay rigid, listening, staring into the darkness. He put out his hand to touch Maureen, and realised that she was not beside him. Alarmed, he clambered out of bed and opened the door on to the landing. The sound of muffled sobbing was unmistakable. He found her in the spare bedroom, kneeling beside the bed, her arms stretched across it, her head buried in the pillows. He dropped on his knees beside her and held on to her heaving shoulders.

'Whatever is it, darling? What's the matter?'

She gulped, swallowing back her tears. 'Nothing. Really. I'm sorry I woke you.'

'Are you still feeling ill?'

'No. I just can't sleep. I'm so tired.'

'What are you worrying about?'

She shook her head.

'Is it Mother?'

'Of course not. She's going to be fine.'

'Sara, then?'

'It's *nothing*, Lewis. I'm just over-tired, I told you. Perhaps I need a holiday or something.'

'It's more than that. It's been days now, hasn't it? I did wonder—'

'What do you mean? What's been days?'

'You had a funny spell on Sunday evening during supper, do you remember? Then tonight, feeling faint at the party . . . it's not like you.'

'It was just too hot and stuffy, darling. Please! Don't make a fuss.'

'But I've been wondering . . . You don't think you could be – pregnant, do you?'

She stared at him, her face tear-stained and swollen. 'Pregnant?' And then she gave a whoop of wild laughter. 'Pregnant? After sixteen years. Oh, Lewis, I hardly think so.' The laughter died as she saw his crestfallen face. 'Would you have liked that?' she asked him, surprised.

His smile was sheepish. 'I would, rather. I've been thinking about it ever since last Sunday. Yes. I'd come to the conclusion it would be . . . lovely, really. We're still not too old. But, of course, now that you've decided to go back to college . . .'

He watched her face intently, wanting her to offer him just a glimmer of a possibility perhaps.

'Poor Lewis,' she said. She climbed to her feet, put her hand out and pulled him up with her. 'No, I'm definitely not pregnant. I'm sorry to disappoint you, but I'm afraid you're going to wait until you're a grandfather before you have another baby in your arms.'

For the next few days Lewis dragged about like a ghost. Usually he was at his happiest, working among the trees, especially when they were in blossom. But this year the satisfaction drained away. Wherever he went, whatever he did, Maureen was on his mind. She seemed so strained, so remote. It was nothing that she said or did. She looked after him and Sara with the same careful attention, supervised the work in the farm office with meticulous detail. But all the same, she didn't seem to be *there* somehow.

He frowned. They had been married for almost seventeen years and it had worked out well. He didn't think they'd ever even had a row. They'd argued, of course, but usually it was just over a technical matter about the running of the orchards, and it always ended in mutual agreement. And Sara had brought them nothing but delight. Their friends, he knew, considered them a fortunate couple with more than their share of the good things of life.

But something was eating away at Maureen and he didn't know what it was. He knew that she had never really liked Jane, and he understood that. Jane was a prickly creature, always had been. But she seemed to hold Helen at arm's length too, and that he couldn't understand. Before the war Maureen had adored Helen, had seemed to love her even more than her own mother, poor Nancy.

Lewis threw down the sharp little hook he'd been using to trim back the long grass at the base of the trees where the mowers couldn't reach. He stood up, stretching his back, and walked slowly to the lower boundary of the orchard where the apples stopped and the meadowland took over. He rested his elbows on the field gate, his eyes following the flight of the swallows as they soared and swooped in the clear air. The war had changed everything, he thought. Even though it was old history now, and his little part in it had come to a sticky end as long ago as 1940, nothing had ever been the same since then.

When he'd gone away Maureen had been a sweet-faced girl, strangely young for her age. She'd always been quiet, rather shy and serious, but that came of having parents like the Bolts, he'd imagined, far too old and self-absorbed to care for her properly. And behind her grave, grey eyes there'd been a shine, a sparkle of happiness. What set her apart from the rest of their set was that she'd always had a wonderful understanding and gentleness towards the sort of people that none of the others even seemed to notice. He remembered one day he'd stood and watched her when she had not the least idea that he was there. She was concentrating fiercely, making a daisy chain for the little girl of one of the apple-pickers. Her mother had had no choice but to bring the child to work with her, she said, even though she was obviously poorly. The woman had needed the day's pay, and could find no one to leave her with. Lewis could see that the child was very dirty. She had a runny nose and sticky eyes and smelled strongly of urine and unwashed clothes. But Maureen smiled at her as if she were a princess of the royal blood, crowned her with her coronet of daisies and was rewarded with a rare, wide-eyed smile that he'd never forgotten.

So where had it all gone, he wondered. That warmth. That quiet radiance. When he had come back to Greenways, invalided out of the Air Force and so stricken with despair that he thought he'd die of it, it had been Maureen who had willed him back to life. There was nothing she wouldn't do for him, no task too menial. But he could tell even then that she was not the same Maureen he had left behind. It was almost as if she were urged on by a sense of *duty*. As if by caring for him she was playing her own part in the war effort.

He wrinkled his brow, trying to remember it all exactly as it had happened. When her parents had died, one after the other so quickly like that, leaving her entirely alone without any family of her own, it had seemed the most natural thing in the world that she should become absorbed into the life of Greenways, with him and Helen, and that the three of them should run their orchards together. And after that, the next step had seemed natural too. They were both free agents. There was no one else in their lives, no secret lovers or persistent suitors, and they had always been – there was no other way to describe it – best friends. Their marriage had seemed almost inevitable.

Lewis pushed open the wooden gate, feeling its rough warmth beneath the palms of his hands, and strode down towards the river path. He needed to walk, he decided. The exercise might help to relax him, budge him from this morbid preoccupation. But try as he might, there was no way he could stop thinking about it. Was that all it had been then, between him and Maureen – simply a marriage of convenience? Entered into because they'd both been lonely and had needed each other for help and comfort? And had Maureen come to regret it as the years passed, to resent it more and more? Was that why she seemed so bitter sometimes? Why he found her weeping in the small hours of the night?

If so, he could not blame her. She was a kind and loyal wife, he knew that, and he had tried his very best to be a good husband, to take care of her, to *value* her. But should they not have given each other more? Where was the passion?

As he gazed at the water swirling past him, noticed a coot busy among the wild flags at the river's edge, his thoughts turned inevitably to Edie, as they had done, day after day, for twenty years. He had thought that he and Edie had loved each other as much as it was possible for two people to love. They had been the whole world to each other. And yet Edie had turned against him too, cast him aside with a few polite words, been 'too busy' even to come to the station to say goodbye. If Maureen couldn't love him, and Edie couldn't love him, perhaps . . . perhaps the truth of the matter was that he was unlovable. Savagely he hurled a pebble into the water, heard its splash and the staccato alarm call of the coot, and then he turned and stumbled along the path that led him up through the orchard and back to the house.

'Lewis?' Maureen called, as he banged the door behind him. 'Is that you? Supper won't be long.'

'Sorry,' he shouted back, trying to control the tremor in his voice. 'Just give me an hour, will you? I've got some work to do.'

Doggedly he began to search through the books on the tall shelves that lined the room from floor to ceiling, working his way mechanically along each row. Straining his eyes, standing in very close so that he could scrutinise every binding, he examined shelf by shelf. Then he began to lift volumes out and drop them on the floor so that he could push his hands through and grope around in the space behind. At last his fingers closed over a small, thin book, its cover velvety, soft to the touch. He tugged it out and carried it over to his desk. With trembling fingers he switched on his special reading light, adjusted his glasses, opened the pages and stared, once again, at the inscription on the flyleaf.

To my dear friend, Lewis, with my sincere wishes for a very happy life.

Edie. (Edith Batey. MRS)
October 1940

He groaned. 'Edith Batey. MRS'. Why bother to look at it? He knew the inscription by heart. He'd read it again and again, day after day. Sideways, upside down, back to front. Always searching for some hidden meaning, some special message. Some reflection of what they'd been to each other, he and Edie, during those long months. What had happened to her?

How could she have been so cruel? So cold? How could she possibly have imagined that he could have 'a very happy life' without her?

In a sudden burst of anger he hurled the book across the room, aiming for the wastepaper basket. It ricocheted off the edge and fell, its pages splayed open, on to the rug. He dragged out a sheaf of invoices from the desk drawer, opened it up at random, and tried to concentrate on the figures that danced before his eyes.

'Dad!' He heard Sara at the door, her voice worried. 'Are you OK? Can I come in?' She was already across the threshold, hurrying towards the desk, peering over his shoulder. 'Dad! You mustn't.' Firmly she closed the file and slipped it back into the drawer. 'You *must* leave the office stuff to Mum.'

He smiled bitterly. 'I leave too much to Mum. It's not fair. Why should she do so much for me?'

'Don't be silly. She likes helping you.' She looked at him suspiciously. 'What's the matter with you? Why have you hidden yourself away in here?' She stared at the piles of books he'd pulled out of the shelves. 'What *have* you been doing?'

'Nothing,' he said. 'Just looking for something. I've found it now. Just a reference I needed.'

Suddenly she noticed the little green book lying beside the paper basket, and snatched it up. 'What's this doing here?' She stared at him accusingly. 'You weren't going to throw it out, were you?'

'I don't want it any more.'

'But you can't throw it away, Dad. It's beautiful.' She examined the front cover. '*Sonnets from the Portuguese* by Elizabeth Barrett Browning. Oh, she writes such romantic poetry, doesn't she? Romantic life too!'

'You have it, then, if you'd like it.' He watched her open the book and read the inscription, a little frown between her eyes.

'But it was a special present,' she said. 'From a friend. You can't just get rid of it.'

He heard his own voice, loud with anger. 'I don't want it any longer, do you hear?'

He could see the hurt in her eyes, the bewilderment. 'Sorry,' she said. 'None of my business.'

She carried the book to the window seat, curled up in the

corner and began to browse through it, turning the pages slowly, pausing now and then to read a line or two, then passing on to the next poem. Lewis sat in his chair, his eyes closed.

'Dad!' Sara's puzzled voice cut across his thoughts. 'What are these numbers here, do you know?'

'What numbers?'

'A little row of them, hidden away here inside the back cover.'

With one bound Lewis was out of his chair and snatching the book from Sara's hands.

'I'll have to show you,' she said. 'They're very faint. Just pencilled in. Here. Look.'

He followed her finger while she read out, '2 2 9 1 4.'

He stared, trying to jerk his brain into gear, force it to concentrate properly. 2 2 9 1 4. Twenty-two thousand, nine hundred and fourteen? He shook his head impatiently. It didn't mean a thing. The twenty-second of the ninth of 1914, then? September the twenty-second 1914? Somebody's birthday? Edie's birthday? Of course not. The outbreak of war, then? No, that was August. Anyway, what of it? The First World War had had nothing to do with them. Something else, then. Think, man. Think.

At last he shook his head, put down the book in despair. 'Doesn't mean anything to me, I'm afraid.' He turned away, cruelly disappointed, his thoughts in turmoil. 'Wait a minute, though. Wait a minute.' He grabbed back the book again, riffled through the pages with fingers that had become impossibly clumsy, and opened it up at page 22.

Page 22. Sonnet 9. Line 14. The words shone out at him. 'Beloved, I only love thee! let it pass.'

His smile was radiant. He closed the book gently and held it between his hands like treasure.

'Well?' demanded Sara impatiently. 'What is it? Is it a code?'

'No. It's not a code, sweetheart.'

'What *is* it, then?'

'It's a love letter.'

'What? From Mum?'

'Not from Mum.'

'Dad! You wicked old thing. I thought you two were supposed

to have been sweethearts when you were just about five years old.'

'We were.'

'So what does all this mean?'

Her father's eyes gleamed at her. 'It's a secret message, darling. Just for me. From another life.'

Part Two

June 1940

Sometimes . . . even now, sometimes, she dreamed of him. Always the same dream. Though she knew there was sunshine, for she felt its warmth, saw its brilliance, he was standing in deepest shadow. For some reason, though in the dream she could never understand why, the sun was not able to reach him. And where he was – there, there was danger. An almost tangible presence. Clutched around him like a cloak. Worn . . . lovingly. Perhaps, even . . . longingly.

The shadow. The danger. The cloak of despair. She dreamed them again and again.

The dreams had begun, she thought, after he left. But even now, in the pale stretches of the night, they returned to her.

4

Edith turned sleepily in the circle of Will's arms. Through the closed curtains a finger of sunlight stretched out and fell on his face. She lay quietly, watching as it crept slowly over his cheek, illuminated the bridge of his nose and left eyebrow, then moved upwards, shining on his temple.

It was the last morning of his leave, and she couldn't bear to wake him, couldn't face the thought of their last day beginning, and then running out of time. She had no idea when they'd be like this together again, so closely entwined, so deeply relaxed into each other that she hardly knew which was his elbow, her leg. One flesh.

She was afraid too, because she knew that Will was changing. He'd only been away from her for a few months yet already there was something new about him. Before he'd joined the RAF his life had been wrapped up in the books he read and the children he taught. Now he was still studying, but to a different end. He was doing well on his training course, coming top of his unit again and again, and it had given him a sort of . . . hard edge, an independence that she didn't recognise. It frightened her. She was terrified that it would pull them apart.

She laid the tips of her fingers gently on his cheek, longing to bind him tight so that he couldn't change, outpace her, leave her behind. At once he awoke and turned to her, smiling, cupping the back of her head in the palm of his hand, softly kissing her eyelids.

'I was dreaming,' he said, his eyes alight. 'I was flying. You too. You were with me.'

She felt a stab of jealous resentment. 'You really love it, don't you?'

'Oh, yes.' He pulled away from her, propped himself on one elbow and gazed down into her face. 'It's the most wonderful feeling. I can't describe it, pet, what it's like to be up there and hurtling through the sky. It makes you feel so free, so full of . . . power, and energy. It's like . . . taking on a new body almost, being bigger . . . and more . . . more . . . more *everything*.' He laughed. 'I wish I could tell you.'

She tried to smile, share his enjoyment, but she couldn't disguise the hurt she felt.

'What's the matter?' he asked, not understanding.

'Nothing. Nothing, really.'

'Come on, hinny. Something's bothering you.' Then his brow cleared. 'Aw, you think it's too dangerous, is that it?'

'No! Well, yes, but not more than anything else I suppose. It's just . . .'

'What?'

'Everything's so horrible here now, the air-raids and everything. And worrying about the children, and you, and missing you all the time.'

'I know, pet. And you've got Dad and Marigold to look after too.'

'I don't mind that. The trouble is . . .'

'Tell me.' Will waited, puzzled.

'You – you seem to be really *happy* in the Air Force, away from us all.'

'Oh, Edie!' He lay down and took her in his arms again. 'Listen to me. I miss you every hour of every day. There's not a night goes by I don't long to be lying in this bed with you by my side, just the way we are now. Do you believe me?'

'I suppose so, but—'

'*But!*' he echoed. 'That's the point. *But* while there's a war on life's got to be different, for all of us. Flying that aeroplane – it's not my real life, I know that. But it's wonderful all the same. Please don't hold that against me.'

'I don't. Oh, I don't, love. I'm sorry.'

'Would you rather I was sick all the time? Like some of the lads, dropping vomit bombs all over Lincolnshire?'

'No!' She gave a shaky laugh. 'It's just – it sounds awful, I suppose . . . But I'd like something wonderful too. More than just being Mum, and helping out in the shop. It keeps me busy enough but . . .'

'There's lots of other things to do, you know,' he said thoughtfully. 'The women who live round the camp all seem to be plunging into the war effort one way or another. They enjoy it. They're good fun too – oh, please don't cry like that.' He rummaged under his pillow, pulled out a big hanky and began to dab vigorously at her eyes.

'I'm sorry,' she said again, taking it from him, sniffing, laughing through her tears as she pushed away his big, anxious hands. 'Your last day too! I was determined to be cheerful and now all I can do is nag and weep.' Sadly, she laid her wet face against his shoulder.

'I love you, Edie,' he murmured. 'You wouldn't know how to nag if you tried. But I must admit you're pretty advanced in the crying stakes!'

He kissed her delicately, her lips, her throat, the tender hidden places beneath her breasts, until she turned on her back, pulling his body on to hers, hugging him fiercely in her arms as if she would never let go. Gently then, and slowly, with the sure confidence of their ten years of loving, he entered her and coaxed her body into passionate response, holding back until she'd reached the very edge before he allowed himself to come to climax.

She walked back from the station alone, having stood and waved after his train until it vanished into a distant blur. Will's father had taken David off to the shop for the afternoon.

'Faith'll look after him out the back,' Joe had promised. 'It'll be a treat for her, and it'll give you and Will a bit o' time on your own.'

He'd meant it kindly, she knew that. But now she longed to have David with her, waving his pudgy hand at a passing butterfly, crowing with delight when she bent over his pushchair and tickled the back of his neck. She trailed up the hill to meet Josie and Marigold from school, and got there just as the headmistress was opening the big playground gates.

Miss Taylor smiled sympathetically when she saw her woe-begone face. 'Josie told me her daddy was going back this afternoon,' she said. 'You must be feeling a bit low.'

Edie nodded, not trusting herself to speak.

'We miss him from school too,' Miss Taylor told her. 'One of the best teachers I ever worked with. A natural.' She nodded thoughtfully. 'However, to change the subject, I did want to have a word. I was hoping to coax you on to our Care Committee. For the wounded men, you know.'

'The wounded men?' Edie was vague.

'Surely Mr Batey told you?' Miss Taylor looked surprised. 'We're expecting a whole trainload. Any day.'

Edie's brow cleared. Of course Joe had told her. Then Will had arrived home suddenly, out of the blue, and her whole life had turned joyously topsy-turvy. But she remembered now, now that Will was gone again and the bleak monochrome of her days threatened to overwhelm her.

Joe had been summoned away from the shop to take the message himself, him being head warden of the village. He'd been scared, convinced that the invasion must be starting. It was the fear that nibbled away at all their lives. The county's long, unprotected lines of coast and crumbling cliff made it a natural target for an advancing army. But the news that reached Joe that day was about something entirely different, an invasion of another sort. Hundreds of wounded servicemen were being shipped home from the Continent, he was informed, many of them severely ill. Redbrae's Emergency Hospital was to be made ready to receive them without delay, although the exact time of their arrival was not yet known. Joe had been busy ever since, making sure that the village was ready to receive the men with the respect and attention that they had earned.

But Edie, with Will in her arms, had hardly given it a second thought. Now, standing miserably at the school gates, aching for him, wondering how far he had got on his journey, she stared at Miss Taylor.

'A Care Committee?' she repeated. 'I've never been on a committee. I always leave that sort of thing to Will or Joe.'

'Ah, well. We're all having to make changes nowadays, aren't we?'

'But what would I have to do?'

'I don't know yet. We'll have to wait until the men arrive, see what they most need. I imagine there'll be hospital visiting, taking them books and magazines, just generally being friendly and welcoming.'

Edie's face brightened, her eyes shining into life again. 'Will's just been telling me I should find something to occupy my mind. If you really think I could do it.'

'We'll have a meeting as soon as they're here. Plan our strategy. I really would be glad to have your help, my dear.'

Throughout the village, they waited in a fever of anticipation. The weather seemed to be in holiday mood, hot cloudless day followed by stifling night. Redbrae, used to grey skies and cool winds from the sea, wilted in the heat. No one could remember a June like it. Foreign weather, they told each other, wanting to blame it all on Hitler. Not what you'd expect in the north-east. And as they watered the vegetables in their allotments, they began to yearn for rain. At last they got the news they'd been waiting for. The special train would arrive at approximately two p.m. the next day.

From daybreak the little railway station hummed with activity. Vic Lawrence, the station master, and poor moon-faced Teddy Laing had been toiling away for days at the strip of garden that ran the length of the platform, and had transplanted into it every clump of white alyssum, every patch of blue lobelia that they could lay their hands on. The red they needed for a truly patriotic display proved more difficult to come by. There were poppies galore, great swathes of scarlet, in the fields that ran down towards the sea, but they were too fragile to be uprooted. And it was early in the season for geraniums. Vic sent out an SOS for red roses. All morning they arrived, in their hundreds. Some came in pots and tubs that could be buried in the flower-beds. Others, cut blooms, were delivered by the pailful, to be stood around the platform and ticket office, wherever the vicar's wife, and her church army of flower arrangers, deemed fit.

By midday the welcome parties began to arrive and the WI set up their copper tea urns and trestles of sandwiches and fairy cakes. Edie, with David plump and beaming in his pushchair, looked up and down the platform in amazement. At the far end, the Local Defence Volunteers had gathered, sheepishly clutching their strange assortment of weapons in the hope of making themselves feel official. It was only weeks since the platoon had been formed and they still hadn't got used to the idea, sweating uncomfortably in their arm-bands and raggle-taggle bits of uniform. By contrast the wardens, grouped together by the station entrance, were dapper and business-like in their black berets. This was their show and they knew it was going like clockwork, thanks to Joe Batey.

A great cheer went up as the colliery band was heard approaching. The musicians were playing as they marched, all the old favourites, and as they followed their golden banner on to the platform, thumping out 'The Blaydon Races' as if their lives depended upon it, the music was drowned in a sea of applause.

'Good lads!' called Joe.

After the bandsmen had taken their places, grinning, wiping the perspiration from their faces, the schoolchildren arrived in a straggly crocodile, watched over every step of the way by Miss Taylor and their class teachers. Again, the crowd clapped their arrival. Each child waved a tiny Union Jack, and most of the girls were wearing ribbons in their hair, red, white or blue. At their sides, their gas-mask cases bobbed incongruously. Edie's eyes scanned the column, and her face broke into a smile as she caught sight of Josie and Marigold, walking hand in hand near the front of the procession. Marigold was wearing her favourite dress, pale spring-green cotton sprigged with little white daisies, and in the strong sunshine her red-gold curls flamed around her head like a halo. And Josie looked really bonny, a perfect English rose in the pale pink dress that Edie had smocked for her at the Women's Institute classes during the winter.

Edie watched the two of them together. So different, the one from the other, even though they'd been brought up almost as sisters. Marigold was all light and movement, vivid, shining. She twisted about like a leaf in the wind, unable to stand still. But Josie was quiet and serene, like Edie, with her own colouring, pale hair, fair skin, blue eyes. She could see her smiling calmly at Marigold now, putting her hand on her shoulder, trying to persuade her to be patient. People found it strange that although the two little girls were so much of an age, Marigold was, in fact, Josie's aunt and Will's little sister. Grace Batey had died giving birth to Marigold, and now Edie felt that she had almost become her own child, as dear to her, every bit, as Josie and David.

Edie's thoughts were distracted by the sound of a bell ringing, and she saw Vic Lawrence jump into the air, waving his arm high above his head. Then, with a rush, a gush of steam, and a high-pitched whistle, the great locomotive rattled into the station. Dr Gillies, the senior consultant from the hospital, moved to the edge of the platform to greet the colonel travelling with the casualties. As the officer leapt down from his compartment, doors were flung open the whole length of the train, weary faces peered out from every window, smiling with relief that the long and painful journey was at an end, and the band struck up with 'Land of Hope and Glory'. Gradually the carriages began to empty. It seemed that everyone wanted to welcome the men in their own special way, with kisses, flowers, cigarettes, cups of tea – whatever they had to give.

First the stretcher cases were lifted off and the crowds parted silently to allow them to be hurried away to the waiting ambulances. Edie found herself standing close to Miss Taylor as the last of them was carried past, a young man in stained khaki battle-dress. His eyes were closed and he looked as pale as death.

'Isn't it terrible?' she exclaimed, appalled. 'Poor lads!'

Miss Taylor looked at her closely, then looked away. 'But at least they've come back.'

With a clutch at her heart Edie remembered Will telling her, years before, that Miss Taylor had been engaged to be married, had even fixed a Christmas wedding day. And that her fiancé had been killed in action, only one week before the Armistice. She touched the woman's arm. 'Aye. I'm really sorry,' she murmured.

Miss Taylor smiled briefly. 'Life goes on.' She gestured towards her pupils, who pressed against her, their eyes wide as they watched the wounded being carried away. 'Let's just hope that we've got something better to offer this lot when they grow up.'

After the ambulances had left, the rest of the servicemen seemed in no hurry to move on. They blinked and stretched in the sunshine, some already settled into wheelchairs, and feasted on the ladies' tea and cakes as if they were browsing on nectar. For a while time stood still. The scent of red roses hung in the warm air. The band, having exhausted its patriotic repertoire, decided to move into its special competition medley of north-country songs. The music rattled along in the background while the men talked, smiling about them, clasping the many hands that were stretched out towards them. 'Ca' Hackie'. 'Adam Buckam-o'. 'Bobby Shaftoe' . . . the old familiar tunes shimmered out from their instruments.

Suddenly a clear young voice soared up above them, silencing the chatter, stilling the clink and clatter of cups and spoons.

'Blow the wind southerly, southerly, southerly . . .'

The notes fell from the clear air like coins of gold.

'Blow the wind south o'er the bonny blue sea.'

Every head turned towards the source of the singing, and Edie gave a little gasp as she realised that it was Marigold. Propped high on a milk churn, standing tall and confident, Marigold was pouring her heart out.

'But my eyes could not see it,
Wherever might be it,
The bark that was bearing
My true love to me.'

The plaintive little tune drifted away into silence. The eyes of the listening men were hooded, brooding. Then abruptly they burst into a storm of clapping and cheering. 'Bravo! Well done!' they called. 'Encore.'

With pursed lips Edie watched as Marigold dimpled and curtsied shyly. Then the band-master lifted her down and stood to one side, clapping her himself as she ran back towards Josie.

'A lovely little singer, your Marigold,' Miss Taylor commented. 'I hope she'll make something of it.'

Edie nodded, blushing with pleasure.

'Takes after her mother, doesn't she?' the teacher added. 'Poor Grace sang like an angel.'

At last the colonel decided that it really was time to move. The hospital would be waiting for them, he said, and the men must clean up and get some rest. Within minutes the coaches had pulled into position in Station Street, and the weakest of the wounded shuffled towards them and were enthusiastically helped on board.

But Dr Gillies was anxious about disturbing the men in wheelchairs yet again. 'I don't see why we shouldn't just push them up through the village, Mr Batey,' he suggested to Joe. 'I'm sure the fresh air would do them more good than being hauled on and off those buses.'

'Good idea,' Joe agreed. 'There's plenty o' strong arms just waiting for the chance to make theirselves useful. We'll have them up that hill in a jiffy.'

When they'd worked out what was going on, some of the men who could walk well enough decided that they'd like to join the foot party too, and began to pour out into the road, where the band was all ready and waiting, and the children were buzzing around Miss Taylor, begging her to let them go as well, since it was now far too late, they informed her earnestly, to think of going back to school.

Edie turned back into the railway station to see if there was anyone left behind who needed help, and noticed a young man, his head bandaged, standing alone, still and silent. He was not far from the edge of the platform, and she realised with a jolt that he couldn't see: the bandages were covering his eyes. Only another few inches, she thought, and he might fall. Leaving David beside the ticket office, she hurried across to his side.

'Can I help you?' she asked him quietly. 'I'm afraid all the coaches seem to have gone, but . . .'

He smiled then, turning towards her voice. And though she could only see the lower part of his face, Edie thought she had never in her life seen a smile as dazzling.

'I think I'm supposed to be waiting for a wheelchair,' he replied.

'Are you?' She was doubtful. 'I don't know if there are any left.'

'Oh dear! What *shall* we do?'

His voice was low, slow, with a hint of suppressed laughter. Almost as if he were teasing her. He sounded like ... an educated man, a public-school man, Edie thought, and felt vaguely ashamed of her own northern dialect.

'Stay there. Don't move,' she said hurriedly. 'I'll find somebody.'

She looked around for a volunteer. But the place was almost empty, there was no one to ask. Stepping outside she could see that people were beginning to leave the station already, wandering off in the direction of the hospital at the other end of the village. She turned back to the young man. 'There *is* a wheelchair, out the front,' she said. 'So I think I'd better take you up myself. It's not much out of my way. The only thing is, I have my little boy with me. Could you put him on your knee, do you think?'

Again his lips curved into their miraculous smile. 'I'd like that,' he said. 'Very much. But perhaps I should introduce myself before we become so ... familiar. My name is Lewis. Lewis Harrison, Flying Officer.'

'How do you do?' She laughed, shaking his hand awkwardly, relieved that at least he couldn't see her embarrassment. 'I'm Edie. Edie Batey, Mrs. I live here. In Redbrae, I mean. Not far from the hospital. But I think we should try to hurry now – there's hardly anybody left. I'll just ask one of my neighbours if she'll bring David's pushchair home for me.'

'I'm sorry to put you to all this trouble. It's really very kind of you.'

'It's no trouble,' Edie reassured him. 'It's a pleasure. And young David will be over the moon.'

Slowly the procession wound its way along Station Street, across the main road, on as far as the village green, and up Redbrae Street. Then it swung abruptly to the left, leaving the village behind, and made towards the edge of the open country where the hospital lay sprawled in the fields. The colliery banner led the way as usual, with the band blowing and bashing along behind it. Next came the wheelchair brigade, with the wardens on one side of them and the LDV on the other. The rest of the casualties followed, taking their time, deep in conversation with the villagers who moved along easily beside them. And all around them, the children, skipping and dancing, waving their flags.

Edie, pushing Lewis in front of her, with David laughing and excited, enthroned on his knee, felt a terrible pang of sadness. He looked so young. Barely twenty years old. And a flyer, like Will. Was he really going to spend the rest of his life in darkness?

At last they reached the hospital and congregated in its trim, flowering forecourt where the Reverend Eustace Lamb was waiting, with Matron by his side. The vicar raised his hand for silence and uttered a brief prayer of thanksgiving for their safe delivery. After the Amen he begged their forbearance for just a few more moments while he made a short speech.

'You are most welcome, each one of you, to our village,' he told them in his resonant voice. 'I trust you have felt for yourselves the real warmth of our north-country greeting.'

There was a murmur of agreement from the men, and a ripple of applause ran through the crowd. Edie felt Lewis tugging at her arm, lifting up his blind head towards her.

'What's he like?' he whispered. 'The clerical gentleman?'

She thought for a moment. 'Bone thin,' she told him. 'About six foot two, with knobby knees and elbows that stick out. Big nose – sharp, pointed. Like a beak. He's a bit like a great bird, I suppose, all black from head to toe.'

He chuckled softly. 'Thanks. I can see him *exactly* now.'

Edie felt absurdly pleased.

'It *is* true what they say about the people of this north coast of ours,' Mr Lamb went on. 'We may be a bit "rough and ready" perhaps, perhaps a bit outspoken sometimes, but we really do have hearts of gold.' Again he stopped, interrupted by laughter and loud cries of 'Hear, hear!' 'Now, Matron is getting anxious, I know, and time rushes on. But I do most sincerely hope that during the weeks – months, perhaps – that you spend in our parish, the people will take you into their hearts. Yes, and into their homes. That for you, and for your sacrifice, every house in this village really will be an open house. And may God bless you all!'

When he finished speaking the clapping and cheering began again, and went on until the wounded were firmly shepherded away.

'Goodbye,' said Lewis. 'And thanks again. Perhaps I'll see you . . .' His voice trailed off lamely and a brisk nurse took hold of his wheelchair and began to push it away.

Edie swung David up in her arms and stood watching until at last Lewis disappeared, swallowed up into the dimness of the long, cool, hospital corridor. David gave a little wail of disappointment and she hugged him close. 'Never mind, pet,' she murmured.

'Mrs Batey.'

She turned to see Miss Taylor hovering at her side, bright and efficient as ever.

'We'll have our first meeting next week, shall we? Work out what we can do to help. If you have any ideas, do bring them along.'

At ten o'clock next morning, Edie strapped David into his pushchair and began her daily walk to Batey's Herbal and Pharmaceutical. She had already pushed the carpet sweeper round her own house, and Joe's, washed up her own breakfast things, and Joe's, made her own bed, and the children's, and Joe's.

When she and Will had bought their brand new house in Cherry Villas, in the spring before the war broke out, it had seemed to make sense for Joe and Marigold to move out of the flat above the shop and into the house next door to them, the other half of their semi. The little estate had been built on the edge of open countryside, well away from the sight and stench of the pit, with gardens front and back. A much better place for Marigold, Joe said, than that sprawling old flat with all the smells of the chemist's below. Besides, Edie could give a hand with looking after the little girl, and it would be nice for the bairns to live so close to each other.

But then hostilities broke out. Suddenly all three of Joe's older children were involved in the war effort and it was left to Edie to cope single-handed with Marigold as well as David and Josie. And with Joe, of course. Still . . . there was a war on. It never occurred to her to complain. She knew that women all over the country were struggling along, trying to cope with extra burdens, just the way she was.

She crossed the road and decided, as she always did, to take the short-cut through the back streets. The sun shone down on the drab little terraces, bringing into sharp focus the grimed red brick of the houses. Nothing fresh and green here. Not a tree. Not a leaf. Just sooty walls and stretches of dirty grey cobbles.

The pitmen who were not on the early shift were out in the fresh air, enjoying the warmth of the morning. The men sat on their hunkers, each one beside his own back gate. Conversation was hurled back and forth across the street, caught like a ball, considered, then tossed on to another player. When they saw Edie coming towards them they stopped talking to each other and directed their comments to her instead.

'Why aye, Edie,' called Ben Howis. 'Hot enough for you, is it, pet?'

She grinned. 'I can do with plenty of this, Benny.'

'How's your Will? Killed any Jerries yet?'

'Not yet, Chalky. He's gone to Canada now. Training.'

'Canada, eh? All right for some.'

Edie walked on, laughing when David blew Chalky a juicy kiss. She felt easy and comfortable. These were men she'd known for ten years, ever since Will had first brought her to Redbrae. He'd gone to school with some of them, had taught most of their children. Sitting there, guarding their back gates, they seemed solid and constant, as much part of the village as the pit heaps and winding wheels. She could almost imagine, for a few moments, that the war was an illusion and that Will would be coming whistling home at tea-time.

When she reached the shop Edie could see at once that they were busy. She took David into the back office where Faith, Joe's new manager, was talking to a commercial traveller. The woman's smile lit up the room as she saw David, and he cooed at her, waving his chubby little arms in the air.

'Cuddles later,' Edie told him firmly. 'Into the cage now, I'm afraid.' She put him down in the playpen that always stood ready in the corner, piled up a stack of building blocks and some squeaky toys around him, and reached for her overall. 'I'll just see what I can do out the front,' she said.

Faith nodded. 'We could do with a bit of help. Joe's rushed off his feet.'

Edie slipped in behind the long wooden counter and glanced at the little group of waiting women. 'Who's next?' She smiled.

'He's just making up my bottle,' old Mrs Surtees told her. She dropped her voice. 'Trouble down below,' she hissed.

Briefly Joe turned away from his customer to speak to Edie. 'You could see if Harry's finished it, could you, lass? Should be ready now.'

In the narrow dispensary Edie found Harry Cargill wrapping up the medicine in shiny white paper and sealing it with a blob of pink wax. He handed it over with a flourish. 'All signed and sealed for the lady.'

As she reached out her hand, Harry bent down and gave her a conspiratorial look. 'Hear you've joined our Care Committee, Edie. Good to have you on board. Lilian's delighted.'

She stared at him. 'I didn't know you had anything to do with it.'

'Oh, certainly.' He beamed. 'I was in on the ground floor. Lilian and I . . . Miss Taylor . . . we decided just as soon as Joe told me about the wounded men coming. We really wanted to do something to help.'

'Lilian and I . . .' Harry spoke about Miss Taylor with an easy familiarity that surprised Edie. Harry Cargill and Miss Taylor? It seemed strange. Miss Taylor was always such a private, contained sort of person. She didn't make friends lightly. Wondering, she looked up into Harry's face, and the secret smile he gave her left her in no doubt. It was true. And he wanted her to know it. He and Miss Taylor. It should be good news. She should be pleased for them, Edie thought. Miss Taylor had had more than her fair share of sadness. But Harry Cargill, of all people. She'd never understood him. Never really trusted him, ever since he'd first arrived.

He'd just come wandering into the shop one day and told them that he was looking for a new position. He was tired of London, he said. Nothing but war-mongering and scare stories there. He had no ties, a single man as free as a bird. He just wanted to make a new life for himself as far away from the capital as possible. He was a good-looking chap, about forty-five or so, well set up, fair-skinned, blue-eyed, with a real presence to him. And he had a fistful of references and pharmaceutical qualifications that had made Joe blanch with admiration.

But it didn't make sense to Edie. 'Why should he want to work for *us*?' she'd asked Joe. 'A little shop like Batey's. We're too ordinary for a man like that.'

'I don't know, pet.' Joe had shrugged. 'He's got scared of the bombs, mebbe. Or it might be an unhappy love affair or something. He's not letting on. But he's dead set on moving into the flat and getting on with the job, I can tell you that. And I've a mind to give him a chance, Edie. I can't see anything against it.'

Within days, Harry Cargill had taken up residence above the shop, made himself at home in the dispensary, and even learned to decipher Dr Scott's handwriting. The customers took to him at once, Marigold adored her new 'uncle', and before the first week was over Joe was exclaiming daily that he couldn't imagine how he'd ever managed before Harry had come to his aid.

All the same, there was just something . . . not quite right. Edie wrinkled her forehead, considering it all.

'Why, hinny, whatever's bothering you, pet? You've got a face on you like a wet week!'

Mrs Surtees' crackly old voice broke through her thoughts. Edie gave her a rueful smile. 'Sorry! I was miles away.'

'Dinna worry, lass. It might never happen.'

'No.' Edie gazed at her thoughtfully. 'I really hope it doesn't.'

Miss Taylor had chosen her committee carefully. She had to have the vicar because he liked to be in on everything, and besides, his pulpit and parish magazine were the most effective form of spreading news. And Brian Hunter, the butcher, because everyone knew him and liked him, *and* he had all their ration books. Young Tommy Briggs, to represent the miners. Edith Batey, because she looked so desperately lost and lonely these days, poor thing. And Harry Cargill, because he was a man on his own with time and energy to spare. Besides, more and more she had come to enjoy his company, had begun to rely on him almost. So, that made six in all. A good number for a committee, she always felt. Enough to get things done. Not enough to divide into two camps and squabble among themselves.

She presided over their first meeting herself, every inch the school teacher, neat and precise in her burgundy-coloured dress, dark hair pulled back rather severely into a tight roll at the back of her neck. 'Let's begin by working out who's going to do what,' she suggested. 'First, we need a chairman.'

The vicar's face got itself ready to accept the honour, but Edie jumped in quickly. 'It should be you, Miss Taylor. You've done everything so far. I vote for you.'

'Me, too,' chimed in Tommy, and Miss Taylor was duly elected.

'But only on condition that you drop the "Miss" bit.' She smiled. 'I get enough of that at school.'

Within five minutes all the jobs had been allocated and Edie was amazed to find herself unanimously voted in as secretary.

'Thank you,' she said shyly. 'I'll try to do it well.'

'Of course you will. You'll be first rate,' Lilian assured her, and Edie blushed with pleasure. She was used to Will being the clever one. Since Josie had been born she'd got out of the way of thinking of herself as anything other than a housewife.

The next task was to draw up a list of open houses, where the wounded men could be sure of a warm welcome whenever they needed it. And some of the houses were big enough to do more than that, they agreed. If there were a good-sized dining room it could be used to put on a spread for the men sometimes. A change from hospital food.

'Mind you, I don't know where the extra rations are going to come from,' Lilian admitted, but Brian gave her a wink and told her to leave it to him. He'd just have a word with Arn Mason, the Store manager, and Lenny Dell down the baker's, he told her. He was sure they'd come up with something.

'We have heaps of room,' offered Edie suddenly, 'now that Joe's knocked the two houses into one.'

'So you could do some entertaining, you mean?' Lilian asked.

'Yes. Please.' Feeling slightly self-conscious, Edie wrote down her own name at the top of the list.

'And we should also think about the visitors,' said Lilian.
Tommy looked blank. 'Which visitors?'

'The men's families. Sweethearts. Some of them are going to
be in hospital for months so obviously their folks will want to
visit them, won't they?'

Mr Lamb nodded. 'I was talking to a young airman yesterday.
Having his eyes operated on. Nasty business apparently. They're
taking him into Newcastle Infirmary. He was telling me his
mother is absolutely set on coming up from Kent.'

Edie stared at him. 'A blinded airman? He wasn't called . . .
er . . . Lewis? Lewis . . . Harris? Or Harrison, maybe.'

'Harrison . . . Harrison? Yes, I believe that was the name. Do
you know him, Mrs Batey?'

'Yes. Well, no, not really. I just took him up to the hospital
when he arrived. He seemed nice. I was worried about him.'

Lilian gave her a brief smile then bobbed her head, determined
to press on with the business in hand. 'The airman's not our
problem if he's going to Newcastle, poor man. But what about
the others, and *their* mothers? I thought it might be a good idea
if those of us with spare rooms should be on an accommodation
list. Make up a rota so no one gets too many. And put them up
overnight, or longer, as needs be.'

'Good idea, Lilian,' said Harry. 'Just imagine travelling three
hundred miles to get to Redbrae, and then having to trail round
looking for a bed for the night. With the black-out and the
air-raids and everything.'

'And finally,' Lilian began to finish off the meeting, 'for
the men who can't get out of the hospital, and who don't
have their families with them, we really ought to provide
regular visitors. Contact with the outside world. Ordinary life.
Ordinary people. The doctors say it's vital to the patients'
morale.'

'That's it, then.' Edie ticked the list off on her fingers. 'Open
houses. Hospitality. Accommodation. Hospital visitors. That's
what we need. And I'd like to volunteer for all four.'

'You don't need to do more than your fair share, you know,'
Lilian warned her kindly.

Edie shrugged. 'All the rest of you have full-time jobs.'

Harry raised his eyebrows. 'You have three children to look

after and Joe. *And* you come and help us out in the shop most days.'

'I *want* to do as much as I can. Please. It's important to me.'

Brian looked at her set face. 'Aye, lass,' he said. 'With your Will gone you'll be needing something to fill his space. How *is* Will?'

'Fine, I think. I haven't heard from him since he went back. There hasn't really been time, I suppose.' To her embarrassment she felt tears springing to her eyes, and blinked them back furiously.

'It's a funny old world, it is that, with all the ones we love scattered to the four winds.' Brian pushed back his chair noisily, reached for his cap and crammed it hard down over his wiry black hair. 'Damn and blast this bloody war!'

The vicar raised his hand. 'Come, come, Mr Hunter. We have to trust to God's will.'

'God's will!' exclaimed Brian. His large, florid face, which usually shone with good humour, was a mask of anger. He braced his broad shoulders and his bulky frame seemed to expand with fury. 'Pulling families apart. Separating man from wife. Dropping bombs on little children. If this is God's will, Vicar, then I don't think much of it.' And he clattered out into the blacked-out evening.

5

Edie walked briskly towards the hospital. Surprised, she noticed that the rowans already had their red berries. The war seemed to be playing games with time, stretching it out, spreading it, reshaping it. She could hardly remember what her life had been like before the wounded men came. She'd almost forgotten how peace felt, how her days had trundled calmly along, filled edge to edge with Will and the children.

Now all that was left of Will were his weekly letters, loving and tender, but strangely unreal. Letters from an alien world that she couldn't begin to imagine. She waved to a group of men walking slowly towards her on the other side of the road. One was leaning heavily on a stick. Another was pushing his friend in a wheelchair. They all wore the bright blue dressing gowns that were the patients' distinctive hospital uniform whenever they were out in the village.

'Hello there, Edie,' one of them shouted, his face wreathed in smiles.

'See you on Sunday?' she called back.

'We'll be there. We're all busy getting the old tonsils tuned up.'

'Edie's Sunday Suppers' had already become something of a legend. So far, they'd been lucky. They'd escaped without a single raid to spoil the fun. But Edie often thought that even if there were one, even if the bombs began to fall, the men would stay put and ignore the danger. Their wounds seemed to have made them immune to fear. It was almost as if they believed that, as far as they were concerned, the worst had already happened.

She tried to keep the supper numbers down to twelve each week, squashing in four men at each side of her gate-legged table and two at each end.

'Even a tinned sardine has more room,' groaned Bombardier Taffy Evans – but he kept coming back for more.

Sometimes a mother or sweetheart turned up unexpectedly, then everyone would shuffle around to make space. 'Plenty of room for a little one,' they'd chorus.

She still couldn't work out how there always seemed to be more than enough to eat, no matter how many mouths there were to feed. Neighbours brought pies and cakes, whatever they'd been making for their own families.

'You can always squeeze out a bit extra,' beamed Ada Briggs, producing two fine cheese and potato pasties and a bowl of pease pudding. 'Always enough for a bit more.'

And if the pantry ever did begin to look a bit bare she just had to say one word to Brian Hunter and he performed his famous magic trick, and conjured up feast out of famine.

Edie loved her Sundays. They'd always been the special day, the family day, and now they were that all over again. It was just that the family had changed. Joe was still there, gamely ploughing his way through suds-filled sinks of washing-up. Josie's job was to wait at table and if she'd been *very* good she was allowed to scramble up on to a welcoming lap for a story before she went to bed. But it was Marigold who was the star.

At the first of the Sunday Suppers, Taffy Evans had recognised her straight away. 'Well, blow me down, if it isn't little Miss Shirley Temple herself. Come on, my bird, what you going to sing for us tonight, then?'

Then some of the other men had joined in, laughing and clapping. '"On the go-oo-od ship, Loll-i-pop . . ."' they chanted.

Marigold was mortified. She flushed to the roots of her hair, glared at them fiercely. 'I'm not Shirley Temple,' she declared. 'I'm Marigold Batey, and I'm seven.'

Taffy looked at her solemnly. 'So you are,' he apologised. 'I see that now. The little girl with the voice of pure gold.'

And before Edie could stop him, he'd wriggled himself out of the dining room and into the lounge, propped Marigold up on the end of the piano, and was strumming away like a man possessed while the little girl sang.

Now it had got to the stage where some of the men came down especially to hear Marigold, and Matron had let it be known that in her opinion it would do the bedridden cases a power of good if Edie would take her up and let her sing around the wards too.

Edie lengthened her stride, hurrying across the hospital forecourt to the big swing doors. That was one of the things she'd better talk about today, she reminded herself. She'd have to remember to drop in and see Matron before she left. She didn't expect to be on the wards for very long. Lilian had put only four or five names on the list of men who needed cheering up, so she'd soon get back to pick up David from Ada's house.

An hour later, walking along the corridor towards Knowle Ward after she'd visited her 'special cases', she caught sight of Matron's sturdy bulk bending over a bed at the end of a side ward, just beneath the window. She popped her head through the door, trying to catch her attention, and noticed a figure sitting alone in a shadowy corner. Something in its utter stillness made her pause. Her eyes still dazzled from the window, she looked closer, and saw that the man's head was bandaged.

'Hello,' Edie said, hesitating. 'Is it . . . I think it's Lewis, isn't it?'

'Yes.' He turned his head towards her. 'But I'm afraid I don't know . . .'

'It's Edie,' she told him. 'We met at the station. The day you came. I don't suppose you remember but . . .'

'Ah!' The mouth curved into a rapid smile. '*Mrs* Edith Batey. Of course I remember.'

She realised he was teasing her again. That's how she'd introduced herself, on the platform. He'd said, 'Lewis Harrison, Flying Officer,' and she'd said, 'Edie Batey, Mrs.' As soon as the words were out of her mouth she had known how stupid they sounded. And he'd remembered after all this time. She felt suddenly breathless. 'I thought . . . the vicar told me you'd gone. To Newcastle.'

'The vicar was right. I went. But I came back.' His voice was light, bantering.

She paused. 'Does that mean . . .'

'They don't know yet. I've got to keep the bandages on until it all heals up. It's going to be weeks.'

'That must be awful. The waiting.'

'I'm learning to be patient.'

She touched his hand. 'Is there anything I can do? Some of the men come down to my house on Sundays. They could bring you with them if you liked.'

'The famous Sunday Suppers.' He laughed.

'You've heard about them?'

'Oh, yes. If I'd known it was *you* . . .'

She found herself blushing, and was grateful he couldn't see her face. 'Please come then.'

'Sorry. I'm not very good in crowds just now,' he apologised.

'There must be *something* I can do?'

He bent his head, and she looked at the blunt white shape of it, drooped and defenceless. For a while he didn't speak and she just stood at his side, holding his hand as if he were a child, watching him.

Then – 'Reading,' he said. 'What I miss most is reading. Could you read to me, do you think? Once in a while?'

'I'd like that. I come to the hospital often. What book would you like—?'

A nurse banged through the door, pushing a tea trolley, rattling it noisily between the beds. 'Tea's up,' she called cheerfully.

Lewis laughed. 'You'll have to bring a megaphone,' he told her. 'This place is bedlam.'

'Come to me, then,' she said decisively. 'My house is quiet as a grave during the afternoons. David has his sleep and the girls don't get home from school till quarter past four. I'll arrange it with Matron now.'

To her consternation he raised her hand to his lips and kissed it gently. 'Edie,' he said. 'Edith Batey, *Mrs* – you are my angel of light!'

She turned away, embarrassed, trying to wriggle her hand free from his grip.

'Don't go away yet,' he begged her. 'Sit down and talk to me.'

'All right, then. Just for a little while.' She perched on the edge of his bed. 'What would you like to talk about?'

'Everything!' he exclaimed. 'This place, for instance. Redbrae. What sort of a place is it? I haven't seen it, remember.'

'No. But it's nothing special, you know. Just a pit village, really. It used to be all right, I suppose. We have a lovely beach, high cliffs, miles of sand. And there are pretty denes running down to it. Little hilly valleys, with streams and lots of trees.'

'It sounds beautiful.'

She laughed. 'Till they sank the pit here. Now it's a dirty old place. But I like it. We've got a lovely new house with views towards the sea. It's just across the fields from the hospital.'

'You've always lived here, then?'

'No. I come from Sunderland. Not far away. I used to work in a flower shop there. Will – my husband – when he was doing his teacher-training, he used to come in sometimes to buy flowers for his mam. That's how we met.' Sudden tears caught at her throat as she remembered her first sight of Will, standing tall and shy in front of her, his hands full of roses. It all seemed a world away. She swallowed. 'Will's in the Air Force, like you. Only you're a pilot, aren't you, and he's a navigator. And—'

'I *was* a pilot,' Lewis corrected her.

'I'm sorry.'

'Don't be,' he said gently. 'I'm glad it's all over. Don't stop. I didn't mean to interrupt you.'

'I was nearly finished anyway. I was just going to say that now I've swapped flowers for pharmacy. Will's family has had a chemist's shop in this village for three generations. I help out there whenever I'm needed.'

'A busy life you lead.'

'That's the way I like it. So – your turn now. What do you do? When there's not a war on, I mean. I don't even know where you come from.'

He smiled. 'I live in a place called Greenways.' His lips puckered as if he were trying to conjure it up in his head. 'It's just a typical Kentish farm, you know. We're apple-growers, my family. Mmm – how can I describe the house? Long and low, with a green front door in the middle and a big square chimney at either end. It's a sort of dullish, reddy-brown colour, built from nice old bricks. "Tile-hung" – you know what that is? And the roof is pulled down snug nearly to the top of the upstairs windows. Like a knitted tea-cosy I used to think, when I was little. Courtyard in front, and the garden at the back, with high hedges at either side, and a wall at the bottom. And this is the best bit. There's a high gate in the wall and when you open it and go through – oh, it's marvellous. The most marvellous thing in the world, because the orchards are just *there*. It's like a . . . a great *sea* of apple trees. The smell of them, the sound when the wind blows . . .' His voice trailed away and he bowed his head. He looked bereft.

Edie laid her hand gently on his shoulder. 'You really love it, don't you?'

He nodded. 'The thought of Greenways was the only thing that kept me going when I was flying. The *only* thing. I hated it, you know. Loathed it.' He patted at his bandages with shaking hands. 'Even before it did this to me.'

'Hated flying?' Edie couldn't keep the surprise out of her voice. 'Will loves it. He says it's really exciting.'

'He must be the tough-guy type.'

She laughed. 'Not really. He teaches at the village school. I wouldn't call that a tough-guy job, would you? But he loves that too.'

'Lucky man! Loves flying. Loves teaching. Loves his wife and children too, I'm sure. All's right in his world.'

'Grace – she was Will's mother – Grace used to say that Will was born under a lucky star. Things always seem to turn out right for him.'

'Well, good for Will!'

The words came out like a sneer, and Edie froze, realising too late how thoughtless, how insensitive she'd been. 'I'm sorry,' she said. 'I wasn't thinking.'

'No. *I'm* sorry,' said Lewis. 'That was very rude of me. I do try not to be bitter. The trouble is, all I've done, all my life, is grow apples. That *is* my life. And now . . .'

'I think you have every right to be angry.'

'Do you? Really?'

'Yes. Really. But I'm sorry, I *really must* go now.'

'Don't. Please.'

'I've got to. The children! But I'll fix a time for our reading session first, shall I? What sort of books do you like?'

'Anything. Everything. Poetry. Biography. Letters. Good, meaty novels. What about *War and Peace* to start with?'

She blinked. '*War and . . .*'

'Don't worry!' He laughed. 'A joke. I'll be gentle with you, promise.'

She could still hear him laughing as she made her way towards Matron's office.

'That's never Flying Officer Harrison!' Matron said, listening in amazement. 'My word, you *have* cheered him up, Mrs Batey. Most of the time we can't get a peep out of him. What makes *you* so special, I wonder?'

'If you go on like this you'll be too busy for the shop,' Joe grumbled.

'No, I *won't!*' insisted Edie.

All the same, she admitted to herself, life was beginning to get more and more complicated. Now that Lewis was coming down to Cherry Villas twice a week for their reading sessions, and she still had her hospital visiting to fit in *and* her Suppers to organise, she could hardly find time to breathe. And there'd been air-raid warnings night after night for the past month. No bombs fell. Everyone had decided Redbrae mustn't be important enough to be bombed. The German planes ignored them, searching out the great shipyards on the Tyne and Wear. But they still had to take precautions. So, while Joe put on his tin helmet and took to the streets checking for lights, and making sure that people were all right, Edie had to zip the children into their siren suits and rush them along to the big shelter at the end of the street, where sleep was out of the question. She was tired. She was worked off her feet. And she felt more alive, more . . . complete, than she had for years.

'I won't let you down at the shop, Joe,' she promised him. 'I'll be in tomorrow morning as usual.'

He nodded. 'Aye, I could use a hand. The new stock's arrived. All our Christmas lines. We'll need to clear some shelves.'

'Christmas! It's hardly autumn yet.'

'Christmas is coming, my lass. You've got to get the goods

in the windows or the customers'll go elsewhere. Saturday tomorrow. Best time to get started.'

Next morning, when Edie arrived at the shop with the three children, Joe, Harry and Faith were all hard at work. Saturday was their regular time for 'getting things sorted out', as Joe put it. It was the one day they were never overrun by customers, because most of the miners' wives went into Sunderland on the early bus to do their town shopping.

Faith was in the back shop, the heavy lever files open on the table in front of her, punching receipts and stowing them safely away. 'I'll keep an eye on my favourite boyfriend.' She grinned, as Edie lowered David into the playpen.

'Can I punch some holes for you?' Josie asked her.

'I'm sure you can be a big help, pet,' said Faith. 'Pull up a chair beside me and we'll see what you can do.'

Marigold had already vanished into the dispensary where she was standing close to Harry Cargill, watching intently as he made up a bottle of medicine, measuring out, mixing carefully, examining the results with scrupulous care.

'I'm going to be a chemist when I grow up,' she told him. It was her favourite conversation.

'I know you are,' Harry replied, as he always did. 'And then you'll look after Batey's, and be very, very rich, and your dad and I will fly to the moon and eat green cheese.'

'No, you *won't*!' Marigold gave a delighted giggle.

Edie laughed and began to pass up big boxes of cotton wool for Joe to stack high on a shelf above his head.

He wobbled on his ladder. 'I wish we could, pet,' he called down to Marigold.

Suddenly the shop door clattered open and Edie heard heavy footsteps behind them. She swung round to see Billy Robson, the village policeman, marching inside. He stood, foursquare and determined, in the middle of the floor.

'Morning, Billy,' said Joe. 'What can we do for you?'

'I'm sorry, Joe.' Sergeant Robson looked embarrassed. 'It's not you. I've come for Harry.'

'Get away!' Joe shoved his carton of wool on to the shelf and scrambled down the steps. 'What d'you want Harry for? He hasn't been robbing the till, that's for sure.'

'Worse than that, I'm afraid.' The sergeant's voice was grim.

'Whatever are you talking about? What could he have done? He's hardly ever out of the shop, man.'

'Not now, perhaps. It's not what he's doing *now*.'

'Well, then?'

'I think you should let me talk to him.'

'You'll talk to me first! He's my employee.'

'All right then.' Billy glared. 'If you insist. What do you think he came here for? In the first place? Did you ever stop to think o' that, when you made him your *employee*?'

Joe hesitated. He had to admit he'd thought of it often, and had never managed to come up with a satisfactory answer. 'I don't know,' he said defensively. 'To get away—'

'Aye. That's it exactly. To get away – when London turned too hot for him. This fine fellow here is a Blackshirt.' His face contorted. 'A Jew-baiting thug!'

'Harry? You're talking rubbish, man.' Joe gave an incredulous snort.

'I've got proof.' The policeman threw down a large leather wallet on the counter.

At once Harry emerged from the dispensary and stood facing Joe, while behind him Marigold clutched tight hold of his hand, trembling with fear, sensing that something serious was happening to her kind uncle.

'All right, Sergeant,' Harry said, not taking his eyes off Joe's face. 'No need for a scene. I'll come with you.'

'Billy, will you tell me what the hell is going on?' Joe demanded. 'I'll remind you that this is my shop, and my chemist.'

'Aye. And your fault too, for bringing this – this Fascist to Redbrae and providing him with a roof over his head.'

'I don't believe this is happening,' murmured Joe, staring from Harry to Billy. 'I just can't believe it.'

For a while they stood as if paralysed, the three men in a tight, anguished group, Edie like a statue by the counter. Then Marigold burst into sudden, noisy sobs and at once Faith emerged from the back, put her arm round the little girl and led her gently away.

'The men have some nasty old business to talk about,' she told her. 'Let's go and find Josie, shall we, pet? And I think it's about time we had the kettle on too.'

Joe stretched out his hand towards the wallet. 'What is this proof, then?' he asked.

'Want to see with your own eyes, do you?' sneered Harry. 'Have a dabble in my murky past? Let me show you, friend. I've been waiting for these little gems to catch up with me.' And grabbing up the wallet he emptied its contents and spread them out.

Edie and Joe looked down, appalled. There were cuttings from newspapers, images that were blurred and unfocused towards the edges but all of which had, at their centre, the unmistakable figure of Oswald Mosley, marching, gesturing, inspecting his troops, spewing out his racist poison. And with the cuttings were photographs, each one an enlargement and clarification of the detail that was obscured in the originals. Harry's face stared out at them. Harry gazing admiringly at Mosley as they stood side by side on a rally platform. Harry marching one step behind Mosley through an impoverished East End street. Harry off duty, for once out of uniform, with a smiling woman by his side, her arm through his, their hands linked like lovers, as they relaxed with Mosley in a summer-bright garden.

Joe stared at his chemist. 'I took you for an honest man.'

'Oswald Mosley was . . . *is* my friend and leader. His beliefs are mine. We were trying to give back to this country its greatness. Its pride.'

'And you thought this was the way?' Joe pointed to the pictures with disgust.

'We need a pure race. Only the pure are strong . . .' The relentless oratory began – and then Harry's face creased up in contempt. 'But, of course, you wouldn't understand, you half-educated little—'

'That's enough!' interrupted Billy Robson. 'I've got the van outside. I think you'd better just come along with me now.'

'Gladly,' agreed Harry, turning on his heel.

Outside in the street a small crowd had gathered, their curiosity caught by the sight of the police van. People were peering through the shop windows, trying to see what was going on. Quietly, they stepped aside to let Billy lead Harry through, then stood watching, their eyes blank, as he drove him away. Edie moved forward to shut the shop door. She thought she'd put up the CLOSED sign for a little while, give themselves time to come to terms with what had happened, work out what they had to do. Then her heart sank. Across the road she saw the spare, lonely figure of Lilian Taylor. The woman had her face turned aside, and was hurrying away, almost running, from the shop. She must have seen the whole thing, had to stand by and watch as Harry was taken into police custody.

Edie turned and looked bleakly at Joe. 'It's Miss Taylor,' she told him. 'She was outside. She looks dreadful.'

'Better go after her, lass,' Joe said at once. 'The poor woman will be in need of a friend just now.'

Within minutes Edie was on her way, but Lilian was too fast for her. She had reached her home and vanished inside before she could catch up. Uncertainly, Edie stood on the doorstep and looked up and down the road, wondering what she should do. Church Row was a quiet, tree-lined street of old grey houses that stretched between the village school and the vicarage. Built a century before the sinking of the pit, it seemed light years removed from the grubby back-to-backs that the colliery owners had erected for the miners. This morning it looked particularly beautiful, still and peaceful. Resolutely she raised the polished brass knocker on the white door, then waited, patiently, her head raised, admiring the great horse-chestnut trees in the churchyard. There was no answer to her knock. She rapped on the door again, then, feeling anxious, she raised the letter-box and called, 'Lilian. Are you there? It's Edie Batey.'

She heard a voice from inside, very low, taut and controlled. 'I'm fine, Edie. Just a headache. But I really would like to be left alone. Thank you.'

'Oh. I'm sorry. I shouldn't . . .' Edie felt embarrassed. She'd been stupid to interfere, she thought. Of course Lilian didn't want her around when she was unhappy. 'I'm sorry,' she repeated, and began to walk away.

She hadn't gone more than a step or two when she heard the door open behind her. Turning, she saw her standing there, grey-faced, unsmiling.

'I do apologise,' the woman said. 'That was unforgivably rude of me.'

Edie shook her head. 'I just wanted to make sure you were all right, that's all.'

'It was very kind of you. Do come in.'

'No. I don't want to intrude.'

'*Please*.'

Without a word Edie nodded and followed her into the house, along a dark passageway and into the big sunny kitchen that opened out on to the garden.

Lilian sat down at the table, pointing her to the chair opposite. 'I saw Sergeant Robson take Harry,' she said.

'I know,' Edie told her. 'That's why I came. I just wanted to explain . . . well, he hasn't committed a crime or anything. It's just that they've found out that he was—'

'A Fascist. Yes.'

'You *knew*?'

Slowly Lilian got to her feet. She moved painfully, like an old woman. She pulled open a little drawer in the kitchen cabinet. Then she unfolded two pieces of paper and smoothed them out on the table in front of Edie. One was a photograph of Mosley, cut from a newspaper. A circle of red ink highlighted a face in the background, a face that might be Harry's, but blurred and fuzzy beyond certain recognition. The other paper was a letter, printed in thick, black pencil on lined paper. Edie read:

Miss High and Mighty Lilian Taylor,

We know all about you and you'r NASTY NAZI FRIEND and you'r disgusting goings-on. Why doesnt' he clear off to GERMANY? and why dont' you go with him? His MASTER, HERR ADOLF HITLER would make you both very welcome, I dont' doubt. And what *we* say is GOOD RIDANCE TO BAD RUBBISH!! Redbrae can do without the likes of you.

Edie was horrified. 'But who on earth . . .' she asked, scrutinising the letter, turning it over and over in her hands.

'Oh, an angry parent, I imagine. I punished their child, perhaps. Or gave him a bad report. Who is not important.

The thing is, I refused to believe it. Blotted it out. It seemed impossible – Harry, of all people.'

'I know.'

'He was always so loving, Edie. Gentle. Adored the children, especially your Marigold.' She gave a bitter laugh. 'It's a cliché, isn't it? "The man may be a multiple murderer, m'lud, but he was always kind to children and old ladies."' She took a deep breath. 'I – I just can't imagine him, marching about in jack-boots, screaming obscenities like those – those *monsters* in Cable Street.' She began to cry then, soundlessly, not even trying to stem the tears. 'He wanted me, you know, Edie. Wanted to make love to me, I mean. Funny, isn't it? A dried-up old spinster like me, when there were so many other women he could have had. But, you see, he saw through all that – refused to take me at face value. That was what was so marvellous. And I wanted him too. Desperately. But, I said no.'

Quietly Edie stretched out and took hold of her hand and held it.

'Why did I do that, do you think?' Lilian asked her wildly. 'What harm could it possibly have done? To *anybody*? But I said no. The headmistress of the local school having an "affair". It wouldn't be appropriate, I told him. That's the word I used, Edie. Appropriate!'

Edie bit her lip. 'Maybe it was just as well.'

'No, it *wasn't* just as well.' Lilian's voice rose. 'Whatever he's done. Whatever's going to happen to him. I don't care about that. The thing is, I'm forty-seven years old. Forty-seven! And I've never ever known what it is to be loved by a man. Not in the physical sense, I mean. And now, you see, I never will.' She fumbled in her pocket, took out a handkerchief and wiped away her tears. Then she turned a desolate face towards Edie. 'Never turn your back on joy,' she said. 'It might not offer itself again.'

6

'How do I love thee? Let me count the ways.
I love thee to the depth and breadth and height
My soul can reach, when feeling out of sight . . .'

Quietly Edie laid down the book, and for a little while they sat
in silence, shoulder to shoulder, on the pink settee in the front
room of 11 Cherry Villas.

'I love the way you read,' Lewis told her.

'What, me with my funny Geordie voice?' She laughed.

'Elizabeth Barrett Browning never sounded better, believe
me.'

At first she'd felt shy, reading to Lewis. He had a voracious
appetite for words, couldn't get enough of them. Dickens,
Thomas Hardy, Jane Austen. Books Edie had heard Will talk
about but had never read herself. They'd been through them
all. And now they were consuming poetry.

'When I go home,' he said, 'I'll never think of the Brownings
without remembering you.'

She froze. 'You're going home?'

'Not yet. Another month, perhaps. But it's getting nearer by
the day.'

She tried to imagine him back in Kent, among the apple
orchards which he'd run in partnership with his mother ever
since he'd left school.

'How . . . how will you manage, Lewis, if . . . ?'

He gave a brief, mirthless laugh. 'Oh, I imagine there are
stranger things than a blind fruit farmer, don't you? I'll just
get on with the job, I suppose. I shall still be able to smell the

blossom, hear the bees, weigh the apples in my hands. Still remember what it looked like in May when the top orchard foamed all pink and perfect.' Gently he put his hand up to her cheek. 'I knew it. You're crying. Don't, Edie. Don't cry for me.'

'I'm sorry. It just seems so cruel.'

'Read to me again. But stay close to me.'

She swallowed, and turned the page, trying to stop her voice from trembling.

> 'I love thee to the level of every day's
> Most quiet need, by sun and candlelight . . .'

Then suddenly, with a harsh sob, he turned, blindly stretching out towards her. 'Help me. Please, please, Edie. I'm frightened. Help me.'

At once she gathered him into her arms, holding his head against her breasts, patting him, rocking him, murmuring as if he were a scared child. 'Hush. There. Hush now, pet.'

Gradually his shuddering subsided and he began to kiss her, gently at first, then more and more urgently, the roughness of his bandages rubbing against her cheek.

'Edie . . . Edie . . .' he moaned, fumbling with the buttons of her dress, tearing at his own clothes.

She had no power, no will, to resist him. She felt she belonged to him, claimed by his need of her. His hands clutched wildly at her thighs as he reached for her. And then, crushing her into the corner of the sofa, he was within her, devouring her . . . until at last she floated free and he sank down heavily at her side.

They lay together, stunned and speechless. Silently he moved away and began to dress himself again, clumsily dabbing at himself with a handkerchief.

'I'm sorry,' he muttered. She didn't answer. 'I was so rough. So stupid . . . I didn't know . . .'

'No.'

'I won't let it happen again. I suddenly couldn't bear it. I – I shouldn't have—'

'No.'

'Please, Edie. Please say something, even if it's just "I hate you. You disgust me."'

Edie smiled then, reached out and took his shaking hands, and pulled him down beside her again. 'I love you, Lewis,' she said.

She stood shivering outside the playground, pinched with cold. She glanced up at the darkening sky and knotted her headsquare tighter at her throat. October already. Winter would be upon them before they knew it.

Coming out to open the school gates, Lilian Taylor looked at her in alarm. 'You don't look well,' she said. 'Whatever is the matter?'

'Nothing.' Edie smiled evasively. 'I'm fine.'

But Lilian shook her head. 'You can't fool me, my dear. You're not yourself. Not yourself at all.'

Edie took the children home for tea, wheeling David's pushchair while Marigold and Josie ran on ahead, jumping over the cracks on the pavement in case the bears should bite them. Lilian was absolutely right, she thought. She was not herself. Nobody was any longer. The war had seen to that. Before she went to sleep each night, she looked at the photograph Will had sent her from his training unit, before he'd been sent on active duty with his squadron. She looked at her husband's face and saw a laughing, careless stranger, outlined against the fuselage of his Airspeed Oxford, as unfamiliar to her now as the other uniformed men lined up beside him.

How was she to recognise her husband when she couldn't even recognise herself? She'd been in love with Will for as long as she could remember. Ever since she was eighteen and he'd come into Walsh's to buy white roses.

She smiled, remembering the Flower Shop, the colour, the smell of it. She'd always loved it, from being a little girl. When she was trailing home from school, along the drab and dusty streets of Sunderland, she'd always stopped there. Flattening her nose against the window, peering inside into its damp greenness. It was like one of the aquariums in the Winter Gardens where her mam took her sometimes, only there were flowers instead of fish. In summer time, Mrs Walsh wedged the door open with a heavy old iron doorstop, and Edie stood transfixed, breathing in the smell of wet moss, and leaves, and soil, and the heavy, languorous sweetness of lilies and freesia.

'Come in, pet.' Mrs Walsh smiled whenever she saw her standing there.

But Edie always took fright and shrank away shyly, knowing she'd never have enough money even for a bunch of anemones. One day her attention had been caught by a small white card that had suddenly appeared in the window.

> WANTED – willing and pleasant schoolgirl
> to help in shop. 2 evenings per week.
> Some Saturdays.   Apply within.
>   M. Walsh, Proprietor

Like a sleepwalker Edie had pushed open the shop door and stepped inside for the first time. 'The job in the window,' she said. 'Will I do?'

Mrs Walsh beamed. 'Why, yes, pet. I was hoping it would be you. But I'd better just have a word with your mam and dad first.'

'There's only me mam,' Edie told her. 'Me dad died last year.'

'Eh, I'm really sorry to hear that.' The woman frowned. 'Well, then, if yer mam doesn't make any objections, come along on Saturday morning and we'll see how you get on. She'll likely be pleased to have an extra bit money comin' in.'

Two years later, on her fourteenth birthday, Edie left school and began working at the Flower Shop full time. She hardly considered it 'work'. Bunching sweet peas and standing them up to their necks in cold water, swathing roses in their veils of gypsophila, she thought of her friends who had gone straight from the classroom into Royle's factory round the corner, and she could hardly believe her own good fortune.

And then, one day, Will had come in. He'd been so shy and awkward he'd tripped over a bucket of lilies standing on the floor, setting all the other buckets rattling, slopping water over the bare boards.

'Clumsy fool!' he kept saying, trying to wipe up the mess with his handkerchief.

She laughed at the comical expression on his face. 'No harm done,' she told him, fetching a mop from the cupboard.

When she'd finished arranging his roses with sprays of delicate greenery, and tied them in silvery ribbon, she handed them over with a smile. 'Some lucky girl's going to have a nice surprise.'

He grinned then, suddenly relaxed. 'My mother,' he said. 'My mother's the lucky girl. They're for her birthday.'

After that he came into the shop often. Sometimes he'd carry off a little bunch of violets, sometimes anemones. Then one day he bought freesias and Edie's face lit up.

'My favourites,' she'd told him.

'That's good.' He smiled. 'They're for you.'

Three years later, on her last day in the shop, Edie had made up her own wedding bouquet, with a small spray of freesias pinned securely at the heart of it. A whole life ago, it seemed.

Thinking about that naive girl who'd proudly married her school-teacher husband, and painted their two-room flat with yellow distemper to make it look like sunshine, Edie could hardly believe that it was *her*. Now the quiet little shop assistant had become a real person in the village, organising the welfare of dozens of soldiers. Matron and the doctors actually discussed their care and rehabilitation with her. Women like Lilian Taylor seemed to value her as a friend and equal. She ran two house-holds single-handed and did it efficiently and well. And . . .

And she was having a love affair with a flying officer who was little more than a boy. The thought of Lewis made her tremble. To start with, she was scared. Suppose – that first time, when they hadn't taken any precautions – suppose she'd got pregnant. Or suppose that Joe found out what was going on. Her blood ran cold at the thought. Joe was a stickler for 'decent behaviour', for 'doing the right thing'. And it was all so very wrong, what she was doing, she knew that. 'There was a woman taken in adultery . . .' The words hammered through her head. She was letting Will down, being unfaithful to him when he was thousands of miles away, serving his country in time of war.

But the most terrible thing was – none of that really mattered. All that did matter was her consuming passion for Lewis. He only needed to touch her with one finger and her whole body flamed into such intense desire that she could hardly stop herself from shouting out. She thought of him during every waking moment. And when she slept, she dreamed only of him. She had believed she loved her husband, but if what she felt for Will should be described as love, she had no idea what name to give the terrifying intensity of her feeling for Lewis.

The girls reached the house before she did and stood hopping up and down in the porch.

'Come on, Mam, open the door,' called Josie, as Edie manoeuvred the pushchair through the gate.

'All right. All right. What's the hurry?' She tossed her the key, then turned to unstrap David.

'Auntie Edie,' Marigold called, stepping into the hall, 'there's a letter for you.'

'What do you mean? The postman came ages ago.'

'It says . . .' Marigold hesitated. 'It's got written on it, "By Hand. Personal".'

Edie leapt forward, snatched it from her, and stared at the unfamiliar writing. It must be a message from Lewis. Alarm flickered through her. It must be something important if he had entrusted one of his friends to write a letter for him. She looked down into Marigold's surprised face, then shrugged and pushed the envelope into her pocket. 'I know what it is,' she said. 'Just a note about our next committee meeting.'

She couldn't work out how to get a moment alone to read the letter, but knew she couldn't bear to wait until the children were in bed. At last, begging Josie to keep a close eye on David, she locked herself into the bathroom.

Dear Edie [she read], Taffy Evans is writing this note for me and has offered to bring it down himself. Things are happening at last. I'm leaving here and going back to Newcastle to have the bandages removed. My mother is coming up to hold my hand and organise the doctors, no doubt. It would be very kind of you to come and see me one last time before they cart me off,

All the best,

Lewis.

P S Keep taking the Barrett Browning!

Next morning, as soon as she dared, she took David to Ada Briggs, her neighbour at number 10, muttered some dreamed-up excuse about being needed on one of the wards, then practically ran up to the hospital.

'It's a really nice day,' she told Matron brightly, avoiding the question in her eyes. 'I thought I'd take Lewis out for some fresh air.'

'You know we're losing him next week?'

Edie nodded.

The woman looked at her shrewdly. 'You'll miss him,' she said. 'I think he's been one of your favourites.'

'I have enjoyed reading to him.' Edie smiled, her voice level. 'I'll certainly miss that.'

She found him sitting in his usual place, his head bowed as he listened to the sounds of the hospital flowing around him. Instantly he recognised her step and turned his face towards her, stretching out his hand.

Within minutes she had whisked him away from the scrutinising eyes of the other patients on Lilac Ward and out into the crisp autumn air. She tucked his arm into hers and led him carefully through the hospital grounds into the dene, helping him negotiate the steep path down the bank, crunching through dead leaves, until they reached the stream.

'We'll walk here a bit,' she said. 'The sound of the water might calm me down.'

'Yes.' He nodded. 'Our own special place.' He put his arm round her shoulders, touching her cold cheek with his fingers. 'What are we going to do, Edie?'

'What did we do before? We'll just have to get on with our lives, won't we? Get through each day.'

'How *can* I get through it all without you? It's impossible.'

'We have to, Lewis. There's nothing else.'

'There is, there is!' he said impetuously. 'You must come home with me. I'll probably be invalided out in a fortnight. Come *with* me.'

She took a deep breath. 'You know I cannot do that.'

'I know no such thing. I can't live without you, Edie. With or without my eyes, I need you.'

'I have children!'

'Bring the children. Greenways is huge. Masses of space. Empty bedrooms all over the place.' He sounded like an excited little boy.

'There's more to think about than the number of bedrooms!'

'But it's such a good life there, Edie. We're right out in the country. The children would love it. We could even get them a pony! They'd like that, wouldn't they?' He laughed, throwing his head back in delight. 'I can just see young David perched up in the saddle. I've been wondering what to do with that empty stable. Oh, and it's all so *beautiful*, you know. Thousands of trees. And not a pit heap in sight.'

Edie looked at him with tears in her eyes. For a moment, she thought, just for a tiny space of time, he'd forgotten that he couldn't see, might never see again. She laughed shakily. 'It all sounds wonderful. But you might as well ask me to fly to the moon!'

He stopped her, pulling her round to face him, and kissed her fiercely. 'We have this one chance to be happy, Edie. It's now or never. I'm sorry about Will – I know it's tough on him. But these things happen in wartime. You should just hear the men talking on the ward.'

'I – I don't think I can do it, Lewis.' But even as she spoke she was trying to work it all out in her head. 'It's not just David and Josie, you see. I've got to consider Marigold too. She's got no mam of her own.'

'Marigold would come with us, of course.'

She began to weaken in the face of his certainty, his pure conviction, but still she struggled to put obstacles in his path. Almost as if she were willing him to break them down for her. 'We couldn't take her away from Joe.'

'It would just be as if she'd been evacuated, don't you see? In fact, now I think of it, the children *should* have been evacuated into the country. When the war's over she can come home again. Will's sister will be back then to take over, won't she?'

'I don't know. I don't know what will happen after the war.'

Perhaps it could all work out, she thought, staring at Lewis's rapt face. Perhaps it would be the best thing for the children. And she could find a live-in housekeeper for Joe. A nice, comfortable, middle-aged woman, a widow perhaps, who'd really enjoy looking after him in return for a bit of security. Then her heart sank. But what about Will? However could she tell Will? She shook herself, pushing the idea away from her. No, it was impossible.

'When's your mother coming?' she asked.

'The day after tomorrow.'

'You will let her stay at Cherry Villas, won't you?'

'Is that a good idea?'

'Why not?'

'She can be a formidable lady. She's used to being in charge, you see, getting her own way. Since my father died she's always done everything. Given all the orders, made sure—'

'All the more reason for me to meet her, then,' said Edie. 'Whatever happens to us, Lewis, if this is the end or just the beginning—' He tried to kiss her again but she put up her hand, gently pushing his head away. 'Whatever happens to us, I'd really like to get to know your mother. I know you think the world of her.'

7

Helen gave a little cry of triumph. N-E-S-T-I-N-G! That's what it was. She pencilled in the last blocks of the crossword. 'Springtime activity – some of the most earnest in Gravesend'. That was the clue. And 'nesting' was the answer. Easy! She threw aside the paper with a satisfied smile. If she could still do the *Telegraph* crossword in less than half an hour she couldn't be completely gaga, could she? She looked around her pretty sitting room, at the plants in vigorous bloom on her window-sill, the family photographs shining in their silver frames. No one could pretend she wasn't able to look after herself properly. Yet Mrs Sammes had been on her doorstep at half past eight this morning. What an *irritating* creature that woman was! 'I've come to give you a good going-through,' she'd declared, as if she were announcing that bubonic plague had broken out in Tillerton. 'It's no trouble, Mrs H. No trouble at all.'

Well, Helen wouldn't have a 'good going-through', thank you very much. Not from Mrs Sammes. Nor from anybody else for that matter. She was perfectly able to do her own hoovering and polishing. She would *not* be fussed over, no matter what her family thought. 'What *are* we going to do about Mother?' She hated all that. She braced her shoulders, picked up the paper again to glance through the book reviews, then frowned, wrinkling her forehead. She did seem to have the beginnings of a headache, though. What a nuisance! Jane would be here soon, for one of their lunches. And she did look forward to it so, poor girl. She didn't want to let her down by feeling off colour.

Helen had to admit that she had been shaken by the events of Blossom Sunday, and she hadn't quite got back into her stride again. First, bumping into that dreadful Jonny Crozier, when she hadn't given him a thought for years. When he'd come marching out of the tea tent, tossing his head back in a laugh, looking *exactly* the same, she'd thought at first that she was just imagining him. Conjuring him up, like poor dead Jimmy Trotter. But Jonny was flesh and blood, all right, more's the pity. She'd never guessed for a moment that she would see *him* again. She'd thought that business was water under the bridge.

And then, afterwards, when they were all having supper together at Greenways and his name came up, Maureen had looked so terrible, so . . . haunted, that Helen was afraid she might collapse in a faint all over Jane's precious lemon torte. How could the wretched man have that effect on her after all these years? When she had Lewis. And Sara. Helen had thought their marriage was so happy. A real success story. It certainly looked that way from the outside. They were always so pleasant with each other. So considerate. Never raised their voices, never lost their tempers.

'I do believe that marriage was made in heaven!' Mrs Sammes had sighed one day, and Helen had felt a glow of pride. She didn't know how much heaven had had to do with it, but she had certainly lent a hand. She'd always known that Maureen would turn out to be the right one for Lewis, such a sweet, biddable child. And, of course, the fact that they were able to combine the orchards, that the Bolts' land ran side by side with their own, was extremely fortuitous. Yes, her grand plan for Lewis and Maureen had worked out extremely well, once Jonny Crozier had taken himself off. So it was worrying that the dreadful man had suddenly staged a reappearance, she couldn't deny that. Still, Maureen was too sensible to dwell on the past. It was all so long ago. And anyway, she must know – looking at Jonny and Lewis side by side – that Lewis was ten times more the man than that . . . pretty playboy could ever be.

How one did *brood* about one's children, Helen thought, even when they were perfectly old enough and able enough to look after themselves. After all, Lewis and Jane were already middle-aged, weren't they? They could be grandparents themselves, for goodness sake. And yet it seemed no time at all since they were babies. Just like yesterday. She had adored Lewis, always, from the first moment that he'd been put into her arms, still slippery and slimy from her womb. And then, after that fearful crash, when she'd thought that he was going to be blind, she had wanted to die. If she could have given him her own eyes she would have done so, joyfully, without a moment's hesitation. But the doctors had worked miracles. He had seen again. And she had managed to bring him safely home and pass him over into Maureen's gentle keeping. Yes, she *knew* she'd done the right thing by Lewis. But Jane – she felt a tremor of guilt – Jane was a different kettle of fish.

She wouldn't, of course, admit it to a living soul, but Jane always rubbed her up the wrong way. And besides that, they had absolutely nothing in common. Jane was quite extraordinary really. She hardly ever read a book. She didn't know Vivaldi from Verdi. She wasn't even interested in the orchards, apart from a constant concern that they were operating at maximum profit. The only thing that seemed to fire her imagination was food. Helen couldn't understand it, how anyone could be so fascinated by such a prosaic subject, could actually talk about cookery as if it were an art form. As far as *she* was concerned, give her a poached egg on toast, or a little dish of tomato salad, and she was perfectly satisfied.

Grimly, she got to her feet and went up to her bathroom. Opening a cupboard, she took out a bottle of her own home-made rosemary and elderflower water, shook a few drops on to a pad of cotton wool, and carefully bathed her forehead, temples and the back of her neck. Her headache was getting worse, she decided. She must 'take steps'.

No sooner had she put the stopper back on the bottle than she heard Jane's quick rat-tat at the door. 'Just a moment, darling,' she called from the top of the stairs. 'I'm coming.'

Jane sat in her car, drumming her fingers impatiently as she waited for a gap in the traffic so that she could pull out and turn right, home towards Donchurch. Suddenly, the by-pass cleared and she found herself turning left instead, in the direction of Greenways. She might just drop in and have a chat with Lewis, she thought, since her special day had collapsed in ruins. Always, on the last Friday of the month, ever since she had left Greenways to get married, she and her mother had lunch together. It was their ritual, just the two of them. Jane did the cooking and loved every minute of it.

Looking in her mirror, she slowed down and changed gear to turn off the A-road towards the farm. The Greenways sign shone out at her – a vivid green tree with a single rosy red apple. She registered it mentally, still deeply preoccupied with her mother. The trouble was, she often thought, her mother didn't really enjoy their lunches as much as she did. Today she had just picked at that delicious salmon *en croûte*. Today, admittedly, she hadn't been well.

She'd told Jane, the minute she'd got there. 'I've just got a bit of a headache,' she'd apologised, 'and it won't seem to lift.' And despite the aspirins Jane had insisted on her swallowing, the pain had persisted. In the end, Helen had given up the struggle. 'I'm so sorry, dear. Will you forgive me? I do really need to lie down.'

Jane had hardly been able to conceal her disappointment. It was barely two o'clock. They'd only had a couple of hours and it would be a whole month before she had her mother to herself again. One day, she told herself, she'd get it right. One day they'd manage to be really comfortable together. Like the mothers and daughters she saw having coffee in the Copper Kitchen, laughing and chattering together, comparing shopping, swopping photographs.

She changed gear again, and bumped uncomfortably into Greenways' paved courtyard. The place looked deserted. Maureen's new Mini Minor wasn't in its usual place. She supposed she must be out shopping or something. And it was still far too early for Sara to be home from school. Jane walked slowly round the side of the house, then crossed the lawn, opened the gate in the wall, and stepped through into the top orchard.

At once the noise of mowers reached her, hovering around her ears like angry wasps. She wandered through the trees, enjoying the green, dappled light. Lewis and his assistant, Luke Gibbs, were cutting grass at the far end of the plantation. She called and waved, carefully moving into his line of vision, and Lewis shut off his machine and came slowly towards her, pushing his straw hat to the back of his head, mopping his brow with his hand.

'Jane!' He beamed, when he got close. 'What a surprise!' He seemed really pleased to see her. 'I was just longing for a good excuse for a break. Maureen's not here, I'm afraid. She had to go into Donchurch.'

He led the way towards the barn at the edge of the orchard and she followed him inside. The slatted wooden racks stood empty, reaching up in neat tiers towards the cavernous roof. The sun, slanting through the opened door, bleached them to pale honey-gold, and a fragrance of wood, and ripe apples, and ancient dust filled the air. Jane breathed it in like incense. 'My favourite smell in the whole world,' she said.

Lewis grinned, fished in a gloomy corner and pulled out a large stone jug, covered with a cloth. 'My favourite drink in the whole world. Maureen's home-made lemonade.'

They sat down outside, side by side on the sun-blistered green bench that had been propped against the wall of the barn for as long as Jane could remember. She leaned back, feeling the bricks warm and solid through the thin cotton of her blouse, and for a while she felt completely happy. She could sit here in the sun, she thought, drinking lemonade with Lewis until the end of time.

After a while Lewis shuffled his feet. 'Well, this is all very nice,' he said. 'Is it a social call, Jane, or was there something . . . ?'

She smiled ruefully, the spell broken. 'A bit of both. It's the last Friday in May. I've been to see Mother.'

'Oh, of course. Was it fun?'

'Fun?' Jane hesitated. 'Yes, I suppose so. I always look forward to it. Do you know,' she gave a nervous laugh, 'I'm even thinking of turning it all into a cookery book. Twenty-four years of *Lunch with Mother*. Don't you think it's a good idea?'

'Goodness!' Lewis rubbed his forehead. 'Yes. Wonderful! But who would publish it?'

'One of the advantages of having a bank-manager husband. He has a client . . .'

Lewis smiled. 'Good old Robert. He knows all the right people. So what does Mother think about it?'

'I don't know. I was going to put it to her today, but, well, she had one of her headaches. I was wondering – that's partly why I came over – do you think I should give Dr Redwood a ring?'

He shook his head. 'If she needs him she'll call him herself, Jane. She keeps saying she doesn't want to be nannied.'

'I was afraid they might be migraines.'

'You worry about her too much. At the moment I'm more concerned about Maureen.'

'Why? What's wrong with Maureen?' Jane was surprised. Maureen was always well, always able to cope with absolutely everything. Just like Helen, really.

'I don't know. She nearly passed out the other evening at the Bowmans' party.'

'Oh, so that was it!' Jane shrugged. 'I did wonder. We were a bit late because Robert had one of his wretched meetings, and you'd already left by the time we got there. But Phylly didn't say anything.'

'No, we just slithered off really.'

'Something she'd eaten?'

'I don't think so. She said it was just that the room was too hot and stuffy. All those people crammed together. One minute we were standing there chatting to Jonny about the old days, the next she's white as a sheet and—'

'She'd been talking to Jonny!' Jane exclaimed. 'Well, there you are, then. It must be difficult for her, mustn't it? Meeting up with him again after all this time.'

The silence stretched out between them. Jane, looking at Lewis's shocked face, realised that she'd made an appalling blunder. 'Oh, my God! You didn't know, did you?'

He shook his head. 'So now you'd better tell me.'

She looked around her wildly, searching for some distraction, some escape, but she found none. Lewis was watching her steadfastly.

'Oh, it's nothing. Really. All finished and forgotten years ago.'

Patiently he waited for an explanation.

She blurted it out, the words stopping and stumbling. 'It's just that Maureen and Jonny had a . . . a sort of affair, I suppose. I thought she'd have told you, Lew. I mean, it was *ages* ago. While you were in the Air Force. It was before . . . you weren't engaged or anything, not then, were you? I don't even know if you and she . . . you were just friends, weren't you? Before you went away?'

He nodded slowly.

'I thought so. But it wasn't like that with Jonny. He was *mad* about her. They were together all the time. He was never away from the Bolts' place. And Nancy thought the world of him.'

'So what happened?'

'I don't know. Maureen's never confided in me. But something went wrong and then he just upped and offed. I suppose she threw him over but I don't know why. I do know that Mother was very anti the whole thing. Right from the beginning. I often wondered whether it was Mother who—'

'Mother! What business was it of Mother's, for heaven's sake, what Maureen and Jonny got up to? As you say, we were just friends then. Nothing more.'

'Oh, come on, Lewis. Maureen was always a great favourite of hers, you know she was. She was more like a member of the family than our next-door neighbour. More like another daughter, really. That's the way Mother felt, anyway.' She paused, her eyes startled. 'Yes, now I think about it, she must have wanted her for another daughter.'

Lewis gave her a long, level look. 'Just let me get this straight, Jane. Are you telling me that Maureen was in love with Jonny and Mother caused trouble between them? Is that what you're saying?' His voice was unforgiving.

Jane's podgy face collapsed as if she were going to cry. 'I don't *know*, Lew. Please don't be so cross. It was nothing to do with me. I just know that one minute they were being lovey-dovey all over the place and you never saw one without the other, love's young dream and the rest of it. And the next – well, suddenly it was all off. Maureen was looking wan and woebegone and Jonny had departed and Mother was saying thank heavens she'd have Maureen to help her look after you when you came home from hospital because she'd never be able to manage everything on her own. So it's no good going on at me about it. You should have it out with Mother. You really should.'

8 ♪

Helen Harrison sank down into the comfort of the pink settee, kicked off her high-heeled shoes, took a large gulp of tea, and smiled. 'Well, my dear,' she said, 'by this time tomorrow . . .'

'Would you like me to come with you?' Edie suggested. 'To the hospital? I could easily arrange it.'

'What do you mean? You want to be there when the bandages come off?'

Edie felt the colour rushing to her face and prayed that Helen wouldn't notice. 'I thought I'd be company for you. You might . . . need a friend.'

'Oh, no. Thank you. It's very sweet of you, Edie. But if the doctor's news is very bad I think Lewis and I will need to be on our own to take it in, don't you? Just the two of us.' Her voice brooked no argument. 'At least we'll *know*, won't we? And then I'll take my poor boy home and we'll try to pick up the pieces.'

Edie looked at her thoughtfully. She was an attractive woman, Lewis's mother. Much younger than she'd expected, and smarter too, with her fashionable perm, careful make-up and elegant tweed costume. She seemed so warm, so frank and friendly. During the few days Helen had been staying at Cherry Villas they'd got on very well together, sitting up late into the evening while they talked about everything under the sun. But most of all, of course, they had talked about Lewis.

'Lew and I are very close,' she'd explained to Edie. 'It's more than just a mother-and-son attachment – though, heaven knows, that's strong enough. But he's worked with me in the orchards ever since my husband died. It seems astonishing, doesn't it? He was just a little boy when it happened, but he still did his share of the picking and carting and weeding and mowing. All that. And since he left school – well, he's been my other half. *And* my best friend. The orchards will be his when I go, of course.' She looked at Edie with wide brown eyes. 'But I suppose he's told you that? You two seem to talk about absolutely everything.'

Edie shook her head. 'He's often told me how beautiful the orchards are. But not much else. He's talked about his father sometimes, how he remembers him from when he was little. It's something we have in common. My dad was killed in an accident too.'

'I'm sorry. I didn't know.'

'I was just ten. He used to work down the shipyard in Sunderland and they were moving a great girder. One of the chains broke . . . He wasn't the only one. Three men died. Crushed.'

'Oh, my dear.' Helen was horrified. 'Your poor mother.'

'Yes.' Edie nodded sadly. 'That girder, it killed her too, you know. She never really got over losing my dad. She'd never been very strong. She was only forty.'

'But how did you manage? Did you go to relatives?'

'I didn't have any. Nobody close. And, really, I was old enough to live on my own by then. But the lady I worked for, Mrs Walsh, she let me have a room in her house. Over the shop. It was lovely. Whenever I woke up, whenever I fell asleep, always that smell of roses and lilies and carnations. I was happy there.'

'*I* think you're putting a very brave face on it all.'

'No!' Edie laughed. 'The Flower Shop really was my favourite place. Until I met Will, of course. Then, his family became my family, and suddenly I had a mother and father again, *and* sisters. And a home of my own.'

Helen looked around the little sitting room, taking in the three-piece suite, the upright piano, the bay window with its stained glass inserts and imitation leading. She gazed up at the ornate central light, which had been cunningly contrived into the form of a stately galleon, with an electric light bulb concealed behind each of its billowing parchment sails. She smiled warmly. 'You've come a long way from the room above the shop,' she said.

Edie wondered about the things Lewis had told her about his mother. 'Formidable,' he'd said. 'Used to getting her own way.' And yet she'd found herself confiding in Helen things that she'd hardly told anyone. Even Lilian Taylor didn't know about her father, gasping out his last agonised breath beneath a weight of steel. Or about her mother either, dwindling her days away in that terrible haze of tears and bleak despair through which a sad little girl could find no way to reach her.

Yes, she'd thought that Helen had become a friend. But now, watching her face as she talked about taking Lewis home to Greenways, Edie couldn't help feeling that, suddenly, she was holding her at arm's length. What had Lewis told her about *them*, she wondered. She felt a hysterical giggle rising inside her as she tried not to stare at the corner of the pink sofa, with Helen sitting serenely on the very spot where she and Lewis, that first time, had made such tumultuous love.

'I think you're going to miss him.' Helen went on. 'He's told me how absolutely marvellous you've been, giving him so much of your time.'

'You have talked about me, then?' Edie asked her.

'Of course! He said you were the only person who made his life here remotely bearable. But at least you'll still have all the other boys to take care of.'

Edie looked at her blankly. 'Which boys?'

'Your Sunday Suppers. Your hospital visiting. Apparently it would all collapse without you.'

'I don't think so,' Edie protested. 'I'm just one of the committee. We all—'

'Don't be modest, my dear. Everyone tells me you're the absolute *pivot*!'

Edie poured them both more tea and stirred hers slowly, watching the little saccharin fizzing and circling on the surface.

Helen put her cup on the side-table and reached for her handbag. 'I thought you might like to have a photograph of Lew. So you won't forget him.'

Edie closed her eyes and conjured up the touch of Lewis's hand between her thighs, his tongue urgently exploring her mouth, her nipples. 'I won't forget him,' she said.

'Ah!' Helen's laugh tinkled round the room like breaking glass.

'We all think that at the beginning. Holiday friendships, that sort of thing. But time goes on, doesn't it?' She handed her a postcard-sized photograph of Lewis, laughing, holding out a basket of apples towards the camera. 'Our last harvest before he joined up. Do have it, my dear. It's one of my favourites. I had several prints made.'

'Thank you.' Edie looked numbly at the shining eyes she'd never seen, at the boyish curve of the cheek, the sweet, smiling mouth.

'Let's see if there's anything else here.' Helen sighed, loudly. 'Oh dear! I always think family snaps are so boring to an outsider, don't you?'

Mechanically, Edie looked at the photographs she handed her one by one.

'Let me tell you who they all are, shall I? That's Jane, Lewis's sister. And my husband, poor Bertie. These two are Jane's little boys, Michael and Peter. Aren't they tinkers? Mike's about the same age as your David, I imagine. Just a baby still. And that's Maureen, of course.' Again, the glassy laugh. 'Maureen seems to be on nearly all of them, doesn't she?'

'She's your other daughter?'

Helen's eyes widened. 'Maureen? No, dear. Lewis must have told you about Maureen. They've been friends all their lives. Childhood sweethearts!'

'Oh, yes,' Edie interrupted her hurriedly. 'I think he did mention her.'

'I'm sure of it. Maureen's people have the orchards next to ours. Between you and me, Edie, we always hoped ... Well, if they *did* make a match of it none of us would complain. *Or* be very surprised.'

Edie sat in silence, looking at the blurred image of the small, sweet-faced girl waving from her perch on a fallen branch. 'She looks nice,' she said at last.

'Oh, she is. An absolute gem. Only a month or two younger than Lewis. And brought up to the life, of course. Apple farming's in her blood. Like us.'

Calmly, Edie handed back the snaps. Helen's 'Keep Off' message beat against her brain like a sledge-hammer. She might be a clever woman, she thought, but she certainly wasn't subtle. She obviously knew exactly what the situation was, and was determined to put an end to their love affair. But Edie could be determined too, especially when Lewis's happiness was at stake.

'Helen,' she asked, 'will you let Lewis run the orchards when he goes home? Tell me if you think I should mind my own business.'

'Not at all.' Helen smiled. 'It's sweet of you to take an interest. But it all depends on tomorrow, doesn't it? At best the doctors are only hoping for sixty per cent recovery of vision. We could cope with that, I think. That shouldn't be a major problem.'

'But at worst?' Edie struggled to hide the agony she felt. 'What about if he's blind?'

Helen grimaced. 'It doesn't bear thinking about, does it?'

'But we . . . you've got to think about it. I know *he* does, all the time.'

Helen stood up and crossed to the window, standing with her back to Edie. 'We have an excellent farm manager at present,' she told her. 'A splendid man called Jimmy Trotter. Very capable and trustworthy. So nothing would change. He'd be happy to look after Greenways till I'm too old to care, and then we . . . we'd have to sell, I suppose. Jane doesn't want it, I know that. It's a terrible shame but—'

'But what about Lewis?' Edie was shouting now, desperate for reassurance. 'What will Lewis do?'

Slowly, Helen turned to look at her. This time there was no attempt to disguise her hostility. 'He's *my* son, Edie. *My* responsibility. I assure you, I'll look after him. Find him something to keep him occupied. I'll always be there to take care of him.'

Through the long reaches of the night Edie lay in bed, staring into the darkness, trying to think. Sleep was impossible. The house seemed to be suffocating her. She had to clear her head, get things worked out in her own mind. Lewis's future and her own, the lives of her children, and Marigold and Will and Joe – perhaps even of this poor girl Maureen, whom she hadn't even heard about till a few hours ago – all of them hung in the balance.

Silent as a shadow, warmly wrapped in her thick blue dressing gown, and carrying the patchwork quilt from the bed, she moved along the landing, pausing briefly to listen to the steady breathing of her children as she passed their bedroom doors. Then she slipped down the stairs and let herself out into the back garden. Stepping across the dewy grass she made her way to the wooden bench that stood beside the young cherry tree that had been planted by the builder on the day she and Will had bought the house. 'Nought but a sapling now,' the man had said, 'but you'll see, lass. Your grandbairns will be swinging from its boughs before you've hardly had time to turn around.'

She sat down, pulled her knees up to her chin, wrapped the quilt round her shoulders and turned her face towards the eastern sky. The night was just beginning to let go its hold. The blackness had given way, almost imperceptibly, to leaden grey. And then, like a flower opening, a gleam of coral light began to stretch and spread up and across the horizon. Almost at the same moment as she caught her first sight of the sun, a tiny wren, perched on the rain spout above her head, threw back its head and sang in the dawn.

Edie nodded wearily. Her mind was made up now. Her way clear. If Lewis's sight was saved she would never see him again. He would go home to his orchards, and for a while he would grieve. Eventually, perhaps when the war was over, Maureen would reach out to him and ease away his pain. But if he were blind, if his sight had been completely destroyed, then nothing on earth would keep her away from him. She would stay by his side for the rest of his life, follow him to the world's end, and no power on earth would prevent it. Lewis was a brave man, she knew that. He could live without her. He could live without his eyes. But he couldn't, wouldn't, live without both, because she wouldn't let him.

Early that evening, after sleep-walking through the day, she waited feverishly for Helen's return from the Newcastle Infirmary. She had bathed David and put him to bed, sent the girls off to play in Marigold's room, cleared away the tea things and washed them up before she heard the rattle of the garden gate. The minute she saw Helen's face she knew her own future.

'He can see! It's all right. He can see!' Helen shouted, running up the path. 'He can see, Edie. Can you believe it, he can *see!*' She put her arms round Edie and hugged her. 'He took one look at my face and said, "Mother, you're wearing too much lipstick, and you know how I hate that plum colour." I didn't dare hope, but . . .' Laughing and crying she let Edie lead her into the lounge and pour her a glass of Joe's best sherry. 'Oh, Edie, I'll have him home for Christmas!'

'That's really marvellous.' Edie smiled, struggling for self-control, wiping away her own tears. 'I'm so pleased for him. And for you, too. It's wonderful!'

'We're going home on Tuesday,' Helen told her. 'The doctors say there's no need to wait any longer. But he's longing to *see* you.' She laughed. 'You're so pretty, my dear, with all that lovely fair hair of yours. Of course, he had to ask me what you looked like! "She's got the bluest eyes imaginable," I told him. "Just you wait and see!" So, what about coming with me tomorrow? To say goodbye, I mean?'

Hurriedly Edie shook her head. 'Tomorrow? I'm sorry. I don't think I can manage that. I always seem to be so busy these days . . .' Her voice trailed away as she felt Helen's shrewd gaze upon her.

'But you two have been such friends.'

'Yes. Yes, we have.' She gave a little light laugh. 'But I'm afraid you'll have to say goodbye for me, Helen. Tell him I'd have loved to have seen him again, but I really can't find the time to go all the way to Newcastle. I have got a little present for him, though. I'll just go and get it, shall I?'

Dragging herself to her room, wrapping her arms tight around her body to stop herself from shaking to pieces, she sat down on her bed, and picked up the thin volume that lay ready. *Sonnets from the Portuguese*. Their favourite book. Weeks ago she'd bought it for him. To read to him. Now he would be able to read it himself.

On the flyleaf she wrote:

To my dear friend, Lewis, with my sincere wishes for a very happy life.

And she signed it,

Edie. (Edith Batey. MRS)
October 1940

She stood up, breathing deeply, smoothing down her hair as she tried to steady herself sufficiently to go downstairs and face Helen again. Then, just as she had her hand on the door, she stopped and turned back into the room. Rummaging in a drawer she found a stubby black pencil. With trembling hands she rustled through the book, and then she stopped and read one of the poems to herself, her lips moving as she captured the rhythm of the lines. When she had finished it she turned to the inside back cover and there she wrote the only love letter she was ever to write to Lewis Harrison. '2 2 9 1 4.'

Part Three

June 1960

My dear Maureen,

Forgive me, please, for rushing away from you with hardly a word of explanation. The truth is, I just can't find a way of explaining or even understanding what is happening at present. I do know now – though I didn't have an inkling of it until poor Jane blurted it out – that twenty years ago you loved Jonny Crozier and somehow my mother managed to persuade you to give him up and marry me instead. God knows what she told you. I suppose she convinced you that I was going to be a helpless invalid for the rest of my days. Whereas, in fact, I manage pretty well, don't I? With most things, anyway. Oh, my dear, to have to sacrifice your whole life and happiness for what any competent paid assistant could have done for me!

But . . . that's all history. What matters now, Maureen, is – the present. The present state of your heart, I mean. And of my own. I imagine you still love Jonny as much as ever you did and that that is the explanation of your strange behaviour last week, the fainting, the tears, the sleeplessness. Poor love, what you must have been going through! And how crass of me to get so excited and think we were going to have another child!

What I have to tell you now – the truly ironical part of this tale – is that while you were falling head over heels in love with Jonny (which you had every right to do, because we had made no promises to each other, had we? Hadn't even thought about a future together) while all that was happening for you, Maureen, I too was falling in love. I wonder if you ever guessed.

Her name was Edith Batey. I thought she had cast me off. That I had just imagined that she loved me. That perhaps she was merely sorry for me, because of my eyes. Now I have discovered that that *was not the case. I have not had one shred of contact with her since I came back to Greenways at the end of 1940. I don't even know if she is still alive, whether she still lives in Redbrae, whether her husband came back from the war, whether she even remembers my name. What I do know is that I must try to find her, Maureen. To see her. To lay the ghost, as it were.*

I ask nothing from you now, and expect nothing. You have given me more, a thousand times more, than should have been asked of you. If you feel that your future belongs with Jonny, I will understand. (I think – I hope! – that Sara is old enough to understand too.)

Soon, when we have both confronted our old selves, we will talk. I hope then that the way ahead will have become clear. Till then, my dearest dear, bear with me.

Lewis.

Lewis sat stiff and bolt upright, staring out of the window as the train rattled on its way towards the north. But he hardly saw the landscape, the fields and towns through which he travelled, or even noticed the other passengers. How extraordinary it all was, he thought. He still couldn't believe how quickly it had happened. He'd been working with Luke in the sunshine. He'd been aware that he was feeling happy. Since he'd discovered that Edie had *not* stopped loving him, had *not* abruptly rejected him, he'd felt himself invaded by a strange, languorous contentment, and it had somehow coloured his feelings towards himself, and towards Maureen. He'd begun to feel buoyed up and optimistic. He was sure that if he were more loving, more patient with her, somehow he'd break through that block of ice that seemed to be growing around her heart. They could make a new start, get to know each other all over again. That's what he'd been thinking when . . .

There was a little buzz of activity in the compartment as the inspector slid open the door, pushing his cap to the back of his head, peering at each one of them in turn. The pale woman in the seat opposite raised her eyes from her novel and smiled at him when he couldn't find his ticket, but he stared back at her as if she were a shadow. The man in the brown suit laid down his newspaper and said gloomily that he didn't suppose he was any good at the *Times* crossword, was he, but Lewis merely shook his head blankly. He was too tightly locked inside himself to be reached.

He took off his glasses and rubbed his tired eyes. One minute he'd been cutting the grass in the top orchard, a routine job that he always enjoyed. The next, Jane had been happily sipping away at her lemonade and letting the story all simply spill out, without a second thought. The revelation had turned his whole world topsy-turvy. For twenty years he'd thought that Edie didn't love him, and Maureen *did*. Wrong, on both counts. And he'd never even guessed. Poor Maureen must have gone on loving Jonny, thinking of Jonny, just the way he'd thought of Edie, imagined her day by day. Edie! She must be nearly fifty now, beginning to get old. Yet he still missed her . . . *ached* for her, and for all that they had been to each other.

He had spent five months in Redbrae after his plane had been shot down, that was all. During that tiny span of time his life had swung between the furthermost edge of despair and the most painful and delirious extreme of passion. It was as if the whole of human experience had been distilled, turned into an essence, so that afterwards everything seemed diluted in comparison. Even now, looking back at himself, remembering how he had loved Edie, he felt as if the breath had been squeezed from his body. His mouth was dry, his hands shaking. That one place, that particular person, had had the most profound effect upon him, had created the man he was *now*, and yet he had experienced it all in total darkness. He had seen Redbrae only through Edie's eyes, had seen *her* only through the tips of his fingers . . .

At Durham the train paused briefly and he gazed out across huddled roofs and chimney-pots towards the dominating outline of castle and cathedral, thrusting up from their river-wound promontory. And then they were pulling into Newcastle, and there was a shouting from the platform as the porters grabbed open the doors and held out their hands for luggage. Lewis jumped out without even noticing the pale woman's quiet 'Goodbye', and felt himself swept along by a headlong rush of passengers until he found the Sunderland train and collapsed into a corner seat. Within minutes they were moving out of the city and he gazed down at the great shipyards of the Tyne, at the bridges that looped across the river.

> I canna get tae ma luve
> If I should dee
> For the waters o' Tyne lie
> Between him an' me . . .

Lewis blinked with sudden pain as he heard Marigold Batey singing out to him across the chasm of years, her voice as fresh and clear as a raindrop. Edie's Sunday Suppers . . . Taffy Evans at the piano . . . seven-year-old Marigold singing all those old north-country songs of love and loss and longing. Why did it seem so much more real to him, in every single detail, than what he did last weekend?

He had been twenty-two years old when his plane had come down in a field in France, the only one of his crew to survive. They had taken off from the airfield in Lincolnshire with no idea, not the slightest premonition, that this was to be their final flight. He'd walked across the tarmac with his navigator, Toft Brinham.

'I meant to write to my wife last night,' Toft mumbled. 'And I never got round to it. Too busy trying to beat you at bridge.'

'Not to worry,' Lewis had told him, without a second thought. 'You can do it when we get back.'

The memory was fragmented. Distorted. He could recall a terrifying creaking noise he didn't recognise that travelled along the length of the aircraft. Then there was a sensation of intense heat, and wind, and someone, somewhere, began to scream uncontrollably, on and on. It had irritated him, the screaming. He'd wished it would stop, so that he could hear what else was happening, try to work out what to do. It was only later that he wondered if the screaming might have come from deep inside himself. And then he saw the flames licking up around the cockpit. He remembered thinking, quite calmly, 'This is the end. I'm going to die now.' He hadn't been frightened. There was no sensation of panic or confusion. His mind had been absolutely clear, and all his thoughts were of his mother. How would she survive this? To lose her only beloved son when she had already lost her husband. How would she get through it, so alone, so bereft? And then he must have lost consciousness because the next thing he remembered was bumping along a rutted road in what he imagined was an army lorry, his head cradled, with strange gentleness, against some sort of rough material that smelled of sweat and grass, perhaps, and soil. He liked it. It reminded him of the Kent countryside. Of working in the orchards in the heat of high summer.

117

'Don't worry, mate,' a voice said in a Cockney twang. 'We'll get you fixed up in a jiffy. Don't you worry about a thing.'

Lewis was surprised. Up till then he hadn't realised he had anything to worry about. He tried to open his eyes to look up at the man who was holding him . . . and realised that he couldn't. His eyes were somehow sealed. Sealed and sightless. It was in that moment that he began to wish – despite Helen's need of him, and her grief, and loneliness – he began to wish that he were dead.

For a long time the death wish remained with him, became his friend and constant companion. He was taken for a few days to a field hospital so that he could rest and have his burns assessed. It was there that he got his first taste of the cool, dispassionate, clinical kindness that was the normal method of dealing with wounded men. Medical staff were warned, one of the doctors told him, not to get involved. To suppress any emotion. Emotion, apparently, got in the way of efficient nursing, and there were so many needing their help.

The long, slow journey back to England was a nightmare. Having lost his sight, his other senses began to work overtime, and the cries of his fellow travellers and the stench of their sickness were an agony to him. But in a way it was an agony that he welcomed because it reinforced his certainty that he would be better dead.

At Redbrae station, for the first time since he'd fallen out of the sky, the old, remembered realities began to batter against his blindness. The heady perfume of flowers. The warmth of the sun on his face. The sound of a child, singing. The gentle voice of a woman who was neither cool nor clinical, and the touch of her hand. There, standing alone on the platform, he was reminded of what his life had been before the war. The calm, measured pattern of days and seasons, the close-spun web of friends and family, that like a fool he had taken for granted. He was reminded that, whatever happened, it could never, ever, be the same again. He longed for escape. Forgetfulness. Lethe. The word itself was a poem. 'In ease on Lethe's wharf'. Where on earth had *that* come from, he wondered. And then he checked himself. None of that mattered any longer. Words. Poetry. Books. It wouldn't be the same, reading them in Braille.

During the first weeks of his hospitalisation, first at Redbrae, then at Newcastle, and then back to Redbrae again, Lewis lived in a pit of despair. Not that he allowed the outside world to witness it. Somehow, that would be breaking the rules. 'Must put a brave face on things!' His mother's words came glimmering back to him. He'd absorbed her brittle brand of stoicism along with his daily apple juice. Besides, more than anything, he dreaded their pity. He'd heard the nurses whispering in the corridor outside. 'Terrible thing – the poor lad's not much more than a bairn!' Perhaps they'd imagined the thick swathe of bandages around his head made him deaf as well as blind. At least he was spared the pain of having to see it in their faces.

Then, out of the blue, leaving him feeling literally as if he'd been struck by a thunderbolt, his life exploded. Without intending to, driven by some compulsion he wasn't even aware of, he made love to Edie. He fell in love with Edie. And, more miraculous than that, Edie fell in love with him and transformed him overnight from a miserable, suicidal wretch into a young man with everything to live for. Who needed eyes, when Edie was there to do his seeing for him? To live through her, he discovered, was even better than living through himself. She saw things with such freshness, such clarity, responded to words, images, ideas so vividly, that for him they were re-created. She made him feel more . . . more significant than he had been before the war, full of courage and confidence and imagination and delight. He felt reborn.

Then, or so he'd thought, she had suddenly turned her face away from him. When the time came for his bandages to be removed, when it would at last be clear whether he could see, and how much he could see, all that he'd wanted was that she should be there to share it with him.

'You *must* bring Edie!' he'd reminded his mother. 'Don't forget, I've never even *seen* her. And if I can't see her, at least I'll have her here to hold my hand.'

But when the big moment came, Helen was at his bedside on her own, her eyes shining with tears beneath mascara-heavy lashes, her lips plum red as she leaned forward to kiss him.

'Will you bring Edie now?' he'd asked, trying to peer into the fog at the end of the room.

'Darling!' Helen remonstrated. 'I'm sorry. She had the children to see to . . .'

Lewis couldn't believe that she wasn't there. It was a joke, he thought. But a cruel one. He forced a little laugh. 'Good try! But I know that Mrs Briggs looks after them when Edie's not there. Please don't make me wait any longer, Mother.'

And then he saw his mother's expression and realised that she really was alone.

'I'm sorry,' she said sympathetically, reaching for his hand. 'I'm afraid she just couldn't make it, darling. Not today. But I know she'll be thrilled when I tell her our wonderful news.'

At once his brief euphoria evaporated. He closed his eyes. If he couldn't look at Edie, there was nothing much he wanted to look at.

In all these years he had never understood what had happened. Why she had changed towards him. One day, it seemed, they had just about settled it that as soon as he'd had his operation she would go with him to Greenways. That they would live there together with the three children, like a proper family. The next, he was blinking his eyes over a dismissive inscription in a book. 'With my sincere wishes for a very happy life.' And his mother was watching him, bright as a bird, her head on one side.

'A very sensible sort of woman, Edie!' she'd said. 'And so devoted to her family. She obviously misses that husband of hers dreadfully.'

'Do you think so?' Lewis stared at her numbly.

'I know so!' She gave a little peal of laughter. 'Edie and I have got to know each other very well this last week. We've talked and talked. She loves her voluntary work with the wounded – people like you, darling – but she says she'd give it all up tomorrow if only she could have Will back by her side.'

Lewis felt a sense of loneliness that pierced him like a physical pain. He'd thought that Edie loved him. But apparently he'd been nothing more than a temporary distraction, someone to fill in the empty hours while her husband was away. He felt icy cold. Betrayed. How was he going to get through the rest of his life without her? He didn't want another single day of it.

The train gave a piercing whistle and with a huge effort of will

Lewis dragged himself back from his memories and tried to focus his attention on what was going on around him. He still didn't know what had happened to make Edie change her mind about leaving Redbrae. Perhaps she had decided it was too cruel to Will. Perhaps she'd told Joe and he'd made things impossible for her. But at least he knew now that his mother had been wrong. Edie hadn't stopped loving him. And perhaps, in the end, that was all that mattered.

As he stared out of the carriage window, screwing up his eyes in the bright light, he saw that they were clattering across yet another great bridge, dashing high above the shipyards of yet another great river, and approaching Sunderland station. It was late afternoon, grey and still, as Lewis climbed up the steps from the platform. As soon as he stepped out into the street he felt the slap of air on his face, several degrees colder than the balmy Kent climate he was used to, and the screams of seagulls overhead reminded him that he was less than half a mile away from the North Sea.

All during the day, while he had been travelling northward, he had intended to go straight on to Redbrae, to Cherry Villas, to see if Edie still lived there, or, if not, to try to discover where he might find her. He wouldn't be happy till he had actually seen her, he told himself. Wouldn't be able to rest until at least he knew where she was. But as one of the station taxis slowed beside him, and the driver's face grinned up at him, he found himself changing his mind.

'Er, I – I'm looking for a comfortable hotel,' he said. 'Somewhere central. Is there one you could recommend? That you could take me to?'

The driver yanked on his handbrake, got out of his cab and stood beside him, appraising his well-cut suit, looking at the small overnight bag in his hand. 'You don't need a taxi, man,' he said amiably. 'The Palace is the place you want, and you're nearly there already. Just turn right past Binns – that's that big shop over there – and you'll see the Palace straight in front of you. It's only five minutes.'

'Thanks!' Lewis nodded. 'Sorry to do you out of a fare. Let me give—'

But the driver was already back in his seat, cheerfully banging the door shut. 'Why no, man. You don't need give me owt. All I've given you is a moment of me time, like, and that's free.'

Lewis smiled. The man's warmth, his sing-song voice ... Suddenly he felt as if he had come home. Tomorrow, he promised himself, tomorrow he'd find Edie again.

Next morning he dawdled over breakfast in the Palace's darkly panelled dining room. Carefully he tidied his neat, impersonal bedroom, even though he knew that the minute he left it a hotel chambermaid would come in and do it all over again. At the desk in the foyer he handed in his key and told the receptionist he hadn't decided yet how many nights he would be staying. He went outside and thought he'd have a stroll round the huge park that he'd seen from his bedroom window, go and admire the fountains, watch the old lady feeding the ducks. And then the clock on the town hall struck ten, and he knew he could delay the last leg of his journey no longer.

He returned to the railway station and bought a ticket for Redbrae. Half an hour later he had reached the little railway station beside the sea and climbed down on to the platform where Edie had first found him, lost, alone, and frightened in his darkness. He stared around, trying to take it all in. There was a little row of nondescript buildings, ticket office, parcels office, waiting room, and a long stretch of immaculate garden, with closely shaven grass, and beds of blowsy red paeonies in full flower. Separating the station from the road outside was a white-painted wooden fence, regular as a row of dentures. And beyond that, he could see the sea. He shook his head as if trying to wake himself from a dream. This is where it had begun. The band playing, the smell of roses hanging in the hot sunshine, the mug of sweet tea thrust into his hands, the rough texture of bandages itching against his cheek. And then Edie's voice, gentle, anxious. 'Can I help you?'

He walked to the station exit and handed over his ticket. 'Can you tell me how to get to Cherry Villas?' he asked the man at the gate. 'It's up through the village, on the way to ...'

The station master nodded. 'Why, man, I know where Cherry Villas is,' he said. 'It's quite a step from here. But not a bad walk on a day like this. Just come on out into the road and I'll show you the best way to go.'

As if in a trance, Lewis followed his directions, feeling Edie beside him every step of the way, hearing her voice in his ears, encouraging him, leading him to her side.

'You want to keep straight along Station Street, then cross the main road. Take care there, it's busy, you know – the traffic's terrible these days. Round the edge of the village green, up Redbrae Street, turn left and up the hill to where the road divides. Now, the right fork takes you to the hospital, but the left one leads straight into Cherry Villas. You can't miss it. All right, man?'

When he reached the street he walked along it slowly until he came to number 11, paused, then opened the little garden gate. It swung shut behind him with a metallic clunk of the catch, and Lewis shivered. That noise – he'd heard it so often before, exactly the same. It was as if time were flooding away from him, as remorselessly as the tide going out. He couldn't hold on to the here and now. Inside the gate he was paralysed, unable to force himself along the path. He'd been an idiot, he thought. He should never have come back. It was lunacy. He must get away. As quickly as he could. Before it was too late. He must go back to Greenways and stop behaving like a lovesick adolescent. He turned round, fumbling with the gate, wrenching at it desperately. And then he heard the front door open behind him.

He swung round and saw a woman standing there, a middle-aged woman, small, ordinary. As she looked at him her hand flew up to her mouth. He stood, it seemed for a lifetime, gazing at her. Her body was rounded and comfortable in a neat blue cotton dress printed with little white daisies. Her arms and legs were bare, and she wore old brown sandals on her feet. Her fair hair, streaked with grey, was pulled back from her face, which was lined but still pretty in a faded, unremarkable sort of way. It was her eyes that made her extraordinary. They were the sort of vivid blue that seems to demand extravagant comparisons. Like violets, he thought. Periwinkles. No – they were amethyst blue. Or the colour of lapis lazuli, perhaps . . .

At last, he was able to move. With two strides he covered the distance between them and without thinking what he was doing, lifted his hands towards her. 'May I?' he asked.

She nodded, shyly. And as he traced the contours of her face with his fingers, gently feeling the cheekbones, the tip of the nose, the little cleft in the middle of the top lip, the high line of the forehead where the hair sprang away from it, he knew without doubt that he had found Edie again. He gave a deep, shuddering sigh, lifted her hand to his face, closed his eyes and rubbed his cheek longingly against the curl of her fingers.

'Lewis!' she said. 'I thought I'd never see you again in my whole life.'

He laughed shakily. 'I came as soon as I got your message,' he told her. 'In the back of the book you gave me.'

'The book . . . ?'

Fumbling in his pocket, his fingers clumsy, he tugged out the slender volume, bound in green suede, and held it up to show her.

'Elizabeth Barrett Browning!' She gasped. 'But that – that was twenty years ago!'

'I know.' He saw the colour rush to her cheeks as she remembered the words she had contrived to send him. 'But I've just found it.'

'Oh, that's terrible! All this time. What have you been thinking about me?'

'I've been thinking that . . . perhaps you'd forgotten . . .'

'Oh, pet!' She smiled sadly. 'I could no more forget you than fly to the moon.'

She led him into her little kitchen and made him sit on a stool while she put the kettle on. At first, they groped for words, hardly knowing where to begin. Then, 'How's Maureen?' she asked him.

He looked at her. 'You know about Maureen?'

'Why yes.'

'But how?'

'Your mother told me all about her. When she was staying here. She showed me pictures of the two of you together. All the old family stories. She was a pretty girl, your Maureen.'

'We were school friends. She lived on the next farm. That's all there was to it – then.' His face changed, appalled at the sudden realisation that was hammering at his brain. 'So that's what happened! It was because of *her*, wasn't it? Not because of

David and Josie. Or even Will. It was because of Maureen that you didn't come to Greenways.'

She nodded, then hurried out of the kitchen. 'Stay there,' she called over her shoulder. 'I've got something to show you.'

When she came back she was carrying a large brown envelope. She opened it carefully and pulled out a handful of photographs. One was of Lewis, holding a basket of apples. The next was his wedding photograph. The third showed him cradling Sara in his arms at her christening, Maureen smiling by his side.

He could hardly believe the evidence of his eyes. 'How did you get these?'

'Helen sent them. She used to write me a letter every Christmas, tuck it inside her card.'

'How *could* she? What did she think she was doing?'

Edie shrugged. 'I think she was just trying to tell me in her own funny way that you were getting on all right.'

'I had no idea, Edie. I knew nothing about any of this.'

She smiled. 'I was really pleased about Sara, anyway. She must be almost grown up now.'

'No. She's only fifteen. Sixteen quite soon.'

'That's pretty grown-up, these days. What's she like? Does she take after you or Maureen?'

'What?' He stared at her blankly. 'I don't know. They say she's like my mother. And she loves her too. More than Maureen and me, I sometimes think. They've always been very close. Ever since she was a baby.'

Edie was thoughtful. 'That's what Helen was fighting for, wasn't it? For a grandchild she could call her very own. If we'd had a baby, Lewis . . .'

'Edie, don't.'

'We might have done, mightn't we?' She laughed. And then blushed. 'But our bairn would have had dirty old coal dust mixed in her veins, not pure apple juice.'

After they'd drunk their coffee, Edie washed out the mugs, suddenly brisk and busy. 'Just look at the time,' she said. 'I must get the dinner on. You'll stay and have some with us, won't you? It's nothing special, but there's plenty to go round.'

'Us? Joe, you mean?'

Edie shook her head. 'Joe died a few years ago. But Will comes home at midday. He's head teacher now, you know. He got the job when Lilian Taylor left to get married.'

'Will!' Lewis felt a wave of panic rising inside him. 'I can't face Will. Not yet.'

'Why not? You'll like him. Now you're here, you'll have to meet my husband.'

'Not yet, though. It's too soon. I'm not ready.' He stood up, brushing his fingers through his hair, trying to get a hold of himself. 'I'll come back this afternoon, shall I? We could go for a walk. Back to the dene. I'd love to *see* the dene, Edie.'

'I'm sorry, Lewis. I've got to go out this afternoon. I've got a class.'

'What sort of class? Can't you miss it for once?'

'No. I must go. It's an art group. A life class at the college. It's just once a week, and I—'

'I didn't know you were an artist. You never told me.'

'I wasn't. In those days. I've just been doing it for the last year or two. But now, it's the most important thing . . .'

She saw the hurt spread across his face like a bruise. He turned his head away from her.

'How long are you staying?' she asked him quietly.

'I don't know. I don't know anything, Edie. I just came, that's all. I had to. To see you.'

She laid her hand on his arm. 'Come back tomorrow. As early as you can. I'll tell Will to have school dinner for once, and then we can have the whole day to ourselves. To catch up with everything.'

'But what about the children?'

'Which children?'

'David and Josie.'

She laughed out loud, putting her arms round him and hugging him tight. 'Where *are* you, Lewis, pet? Away with the fairies. They aren't children any more. Josie's married now. She lives next door in Joe's house. Runs Joe's shop, too. And she's got children of her own. Did you realise that I was a grandmother? And David – he's gone down the pit. Not actually hewing coal, thank goodness. He's a fully qualified mining engineer. And he loves it. He got married in March, and he and Cherry have got a cottage in Brick Row. Not much of a place, you know, but it's given them a start.'

Lewis bent his head sadly. 'I'm being a fool, aren't I? Everything's changed.'

She shook her head, linked her arm through his and led him along the hall to the front door. 'Not everything,' she murmured. And kissed him gently on the cheek.

10

Her name was Edith Batey.

Maureen sat at the kitchen table with Lewis's letter spread out in front of her. She read it through again and again. She wasn't aware of the wasp, noisy around the rim of the marmalade jar, the toast half-eaten on her plate. Nor even aware that she was crying, deep shuddering sobs that made the coffee slide around in her mug. All those years ago Lewis had been in love. Still was, perhaps. And she'd never guessed it.

During that first summer of the war the world's business had flowed on around her as if she and Jonny were something apart. Aircraft thundered overhead. The nine o'clock news, listened to every evening like a holy rite, was full of gloom and ominous warnings. But they had seemed to live in their own magical country where nothing could touch them.

Until, one hot, sunny morning, she had picked up the telephone. Helen's voice was so choked and distorted that at first Maureen couldn't work out what she was trying to tell her. She just heard 'Lewis' again and again. The only sound the woman could articulate was the name of her son. 'Hold on, I'll be there,' Maureen said. As she ran through the orchard and scrambled across the wall, which still seemed the natural way to get from her own home to Greenways, her heart was hammering with dread. Lewis had been killed. Poor Helen. How would she survive it?

She found her crouched in a corner of the drawing room, huddled into herself. Tears had made runnels down her powdered cheeks, her lipstick was smudged, her face blotched and swollen. Maureen dropped on her knees and wrapped her strong arms around her. She dared not ask the question that beat at her brain. Silently, rhythmically, she rocked her as if she were a distraught child.

At last Helen managed to speak. 'His plane has been shot down,' she said. 'Over France.'

Maureen waited, terrified. Perhaps he was alive, then, but had been taken prisoner. She summoned up her courage. 'Tell me. Please.'

'He was the only survivor. His whole crew wiped out. All his friends.'

'He's alive!' Maureen felt dizzy with relief. 'Thank God.'

But Helen shook her head wildly. 'He's injured, Maureen. Head injuries. Quite dreadful. They just don't know yet. It's his eyes.'

The days had shuffled between hope and despair. As soon as the news came that Lewis was to have an operation, Helen rushed to Newcastle to be at his bedside, and stayed there until the doctors were satisfied that he could go back to Redbrae to rest and recover. There would be a long wait, she was warned, before they knew whether or not the surgeon had been successful. She must learn to be patient. She came home calm, and bent her will to the task of taking charge of things again, making sure that Jimmy Trotter had everything ready and prepared for the picking season which would soon be upon them. She rang the hospital every day. And every day she rang Maureen. It was as if she were trying to feed from her young strength.

'He asks about you all the time,' she told her with a light laugh. 'I'm his mother, but *you* are the one he's missing.' And then the laughter faded. 'We must be brave, Maureen. Pray that he will see again.' The threat of his blindness hung over them both like a sword.

Gradually the pattern of Maureen's life began to change. She made sure that at least part of every day was set aside for Helen. 'Darling, try to understand,' she'd begged Jonny, when yet again she'd been too stretched to go out with him. 'We have all the rest of our lives. Just for the time being, I have to help Helen.'

'I know, but—'

'There are no buts. She's always been a second mother to me.

Now I have to be a second daughter. Why don't *you* come and see her sometime?'

But then they laughed, both of them, because they knew that that wouldn't do at all. Helen had never taken to Jonny, right from the first day when Lewis had introduced him, shining bright and handsome in his white flannels, tennis racquet swinging from his hand. Now she simply ignored him. Pretended he didn't exist. If Maureen mentioned his name she gave her a reproachful look and instantly changed the subject.

Maureen knew that soon she would have to explain about her and Jonny, make her understand how much he meant to her before they actually bought the engagement ring. But it was still too early. When they knew for sure what the future held for Lewis, when the doctors told Helen she could bring him home, then it would be the right time. Not before.

It was a fine, crisp October morning and Maureen was alone in the packing shed, scrubbing down the long bench. It felt strangely quiet now that the pickers had all gone but she always loved these autumn days when the harvest was gathered in and the crown of the year's work achieved. Suddenly her thoughts were disturbed by her mother's voice, calling from the top of the path. 'Telephone, darling. It's Helen. Urgent.'

She raced indoors and snatched up the phone, hastily drying her hands on her overall. She could almost feel the excitement tingling in Helen's voice.

'Wonderful news,' she cried. 'Do come round, Maureen, so we can talk about it.'

'Can't you tell me now? I'm in the middle of—'

'Please. I need you here. Don't let me down.'

Helen was waiting for her at the front door of Greenways. She was bubbling with impatience, jumping on and off the step like a little girl about to go to a party. She took both of Maureen's hands in her own and dragged her inside. 'I've just heard,' she told her. 'He's to have the bandages off next week. And then he'll be coming home. Isn't that marvellous?'

Maureen gazed at the brightness in her face. 'And he's going to be able to see?'

'Oh, we still don't know that. Not until the day. But I've

been working it all out. Whatever happens, we can manage, you know. If we organise things between us.'

Between us? For a moment Maureen thought Helen was talking about herself and Jimmy Trotter, but as the words flowed on she realised that it was she, and not Jimmy Trotter, who was being lined up as the other half of the partnership.

Helen didn't seem to notice the bewilderment that spread across her face. 'If Lew is blind,' she surged on, '– oh, God! let it not happen, but we *must* prepare ourselves – if he's blind we can divide it between us, can't we, working the orchards and looking after him? Do it fifty-fifty? I can't tell you how marvellous it is, having you to share it all with. At first, until we get into the swing of things, we'll have to make him the very *centre*, work out our lives around him. But later on—'

'Helen!' At last Maureen managed to interrupt her. 'Of course I'll do all I can to help, but I don't think I can promise as much as that.'

Helen stared at her. 'What do you mean?'

'You see, I have my own work.'

'Of course.'

'And – my own life.'

The brown eyes widened. 'Don't keep saying "my" like that. Surely you and Lewis . . .'

Maureen shook her head, feeling the panic mounting within her. 'I don't know what you're driving at.'

'But I always thought, you and he . . . I mean, he didn't exactly spell it out. He didn't *need* to. But surely the understanding was that when the war was over and things got back to normal, you and he would name the—'

'No!' Maureen heard her own voice shouting. 'You've got it quite wrong, Helen. There was never any "understanding" between Lewis and me.'

For a moment tears seemed to tremble in Helen's eyes. Then her face turned white and rigid. 'I can't believe this,' she said coldly. 'That you would turn your back on my poor son, after all you've been to each other, just because he's been sent home from the Front as . . . damaged goods. How could you?'

'It's got nothing to do with that,' Maureen cried. 'You mustn't even think such things.'

'What *is* it to do with, then?'

'It's to do with me being in love with Jonny Crozier. It's to do with us being lovers. It's because I worship him body and soul and I'm going to marry him in the spring.'

The words hovered on her tongue. Of course she should have said them. But she didn't. She couldn't bring herself to be so brutal. Instead she quietly took her leave, trying not to look at Helen, not to think about the contempt etched on her face, and hurried out into the fresh air.

For days she got through her chores like an automaton while her mind worked overtime. She kept her distance from Helen, and was relieved that Helen didn't make any attempt to contact her. She told Jonny that she was poorly, had picked up some bug or other and thought it would be safer if he didn't visit her, but she promised to ring him the moment she was feeling better. She felt very alone. She longed to talk to someone, to see it all through other eyes that were more objective, more clear-sighted than her own. She considered Jane, but Jane always echoed Helen's viewpoint and was bound to say her responsibility lay with Lewis. Anyway, with a husband like Robert, Jane was probably a bit of a cynic when it came to passion. And besides, she'd already warned her off Jonny in no uncertain terms. Phylly Bowman was another possibility but Jonny was her first cousin, whether she approved of him or not, so she could hardly be trusted to take an unbiased stance. In the end, lonely and confused, Maureen tried to talk to her mother.

'Darling! You do look peaky,' Nancy said, as Maureen sat down beside her. 'I've told you, you work too hard.' She made it sound like an accusation, as if her daughter spent every daylight hour in the orchards just to provoke her.

'There is a war on, Mother.'

'I'm well aware of that, Maureen. All the same, I'd like to see you enjoying yourself once in a while. When is your nice Jonny coming to see us again? He does brighten us all up, doesn't he?'

Maureen smiled. 'He'll be round soon, I imagine.'

'I'll look forward to that. He's so good with Daddy.'

'It was really Lewis I wanted to talk to you about.' She took a deep breath, trying to steady her voice. 'It's possible, you know, that . . . he's going to be blind. And Helen thinks that I should . . . that it's up to me, in a way . . . to look after him.'

'Blind! Oh, yes. I remember.' Nancy was shocked. 'Poor dear Lewis! We must all do what we can to help, darling.'

'Yes, of course. I *will* help. The problem is that Helen seems to think that I . . . well, that Lewis and I . . . ought to get . . .'

Before she could bring herself actually to say the word she saw that Nancy was not listening. Nancy was not really thinking about Lewis at all. And certainly, not about her.

'Daddy's sight is going too, you know,' she murmured. 'It's a terrible affliction. But he's so patient about it, poor love.'

Maureen nodded and gently patted her shoulder. 'Yes, Mother. I know he is.'

She realised that Nancy was quite incapable of making any distinction between a young man of twenty-two, with his whole life in tatters, and her octogenarian husband who was now sliding into a sad twilight. That it was ridiculous to expect her to be able to grasp the dichotomy by which she was obsessed, between physical love and self-fulfilment on the one hand, and friendship and loyalty on the other. There *was* no one else, she decided. She had to rely on herself. It was her life, and she had to work out how to live it.

Helen telephoned her from the hospital, her voice taut and controlled. 'I thought I should let you know,' she said crisply, 'that the bandages have been removed and Lewis can . . . he is not completely blind. He can distinguish shapes. And colours. He's putting a brave face on things.'

'I see,' Maureen replied. 'Thank you for letting me know.'

'We'll be home on Tuesday. Oh, there's the pips. I'm running out of money . . .'

'Thank you,' Maureen repeated dully.

'Just one thing.' Helen's voice sang down the line. 'He said I was to give you his love.'

As soon as Helen rang off, Maureen picked up the phone again and gave the operator the number of Jonny's surgery.

'Darling! Are you better now?' he asked.

'Yes. I think so.'

'Marvellous. I'm afraid I have a patient with me at the moment.'

'I'm sorry. It's a bad time. Shall I call later?'

'No.' She heard the laughter in his voice. 'I don't think she'll mind. She's very beautiful. And very dumb. A pedigree chinchilla!'

Maureen swallowed down a sob. 'Are you free tonight?'

'Of course I am. Go to the flicks? *The Lady Vanishes* is on at the Regent.'

'No. Please. Just a drive.'

'What? In the dark?'

'In the dark. Yes. See you about eight.'

They made love clamped awkwardly together in the back seat of Jonny's battered old Ford. It was a messy business, frantic and mechanical.

While he was still able to, Jonny looked down into Maureen's desperate face. 'Hey, is this really what you want?'

She nodded, clutching at him. 'Go on. Go on. Don't stop.'

At last she came to a shuddering climax, felt his body convulse almost instantaneously, and gripped her hands around the back of his neck. She breathed in deeply, registering the familiar smell of leather seats, woollen rug, wet dogs and antiseptic, and knew that she would remember it in the long years ahead, whenever she thought of Jonny. Grim-faced she struggled back into her clothes, pulled down her skirt, dabbed awkwardly at her hair.

'What is all this about?' Jonny asked, watching her carefully. 'You don't usually treat me like a stud.'

She stared through the window, trying to make out the shape of the horse-chestnut tree, black against the moonlight, that spread its branches over the car. 'I'm sorry. It was the last time, Jonny.'

He laughed easily. 'Oh, I wouldn't say it was as bad as that!' And then he realised that she was serious.

'I've decided to marry Lewis Harrison,' she told him. She glanced at his face, then turned away again quickly.

'But you *can't!*' he exploded. 'You love me. You know you do.'

'Love? Oh, yes. But Lewis was always my best friend. Way

back, when we were at the infant school. And even before that we used to play together, you know. Always.'

He tried to stop her gabbled words with a kiss, but she pushed him away angrily.

'You can't turn your back on your best friend, can you?' she demanded. 'Not when he needs you. Not when he's almost blind.'

'Maureen! This is just romantic nonsense. *I* need you. You know I do.' He took hold of her, forced her to look at him. 'Please! Lewis has had a rough time, I know. And things are going to be difficult for him. I understand how you feel. But don't throw our happiness away. *Please!*'

'I'm sorry, Jonny.' She forced herself to shrug off his pain. 'Happiness is not the only thing.'

'Darling!'

'Don't try to make me change my mind. I've quite decided.' And then she got out of the car and walked home alone, numb and blind with tears.

It was to be twenty years before she saw Jonny again, standing there so untouched by time, at Phylly Bowman's May-time party.

11

Perched high on a grassy bank, Will Batey gazed down into Redbrae Gorge and took a bite out of his pork pie. Edie didn't want him to go home for his dinner, he knew that. But he didn't want to have it at school either. If the staff found out that he was on the premises there would be one problem after another to deal with. What did he suggest they could do about little Jenny Pickett who still sat and cried every day because she wanted her mammy? Could he please deal with Sandy Motson who would insist on peeing against the lavatory wall and making all the girls scream and giggle? And did he know that someone kept on cutting out the pictures in the books in the library corner?

Yes, Will sighed, he *did* know. All those things and a few dozen others. And he didn't really care very much. Not today, anyway. Today he had other things on his mind. He looked around thoughtfully. Beneath his feet the land fell away, three hundred feet or more, down to the stream that ran along the bottom of the valley until it gushed out on to the sands. Stunted hawthorn bushes sprouted from the precipitous banks and leaned out, jutting up towards the sky. Weaving around them, through tussocks of skimpy, wind-bitten grass, narrow tracks led downwards from the clifftop path, gouged out by the heels and trouser-seats of generations of small boys as they defied gravity and made the giddy descent. As a dare, usually. As a proof that they weren't 'scaredy'. He'd done it himself often enough, and felt Joe's hand across his backside whenever he got found out.

He laughed out loud, remembering his father. Wherever he looked, there were memories of him, his stories echoing through his head.

'See that cave, kidder? Other side o' the gorge? Straight up so sharp you'd think only the seagulls could get to it?'

'Where? Where? Show me, Dad.'

'Ower *there*, lad. You can see the black mouth of it, beside that great boulder. When I was your age, there was a family living there. Raised a brood o' bairns, and every one as fit as a flea. They reckon it was the spring water that kept them healthy. Full of salts and minerals. Nature's own tonic wine.'

Will shook his head. It had always been one of Joe's cherished plans – he'd bottle up Redbrae water, give it a fancy name, trick it out with a classy label, then sell it to a grateful world. 'There's bound to be a bob or two in that, lad.'

Poor Joe and his schemes! He must have had a hundred. Will swallowed down the last mouthful of pie, crumpled up the brown paper bag and shoved it in his pocket. Then he looked at his watch, unfolded his long legs, scrambled to his feet and began to make his way back towards school. The trouble was, he had the uncomfortable feeling that he was beginning to turn a bit like his father. A dreamer of dreams. A teller of tales. And, perhaps, a bit of a loser too.

Half-way back towards the village, loping along the coast road, Will saw Tommy Briggs coming towards him, his beautiful red setter pulling on the end of its lead.

'Tommy!' Will said. 'Great day for a walk.'

'A trot, more like it,' Tommy grinned. 'You playing truant, Will?'

'Wish I dared. The Head 'ud lather me.'

They nodded at each other amiably and went their separate ways. Will liked Tommy. They'd gone to school together, played football in the same team. Tommy's mam, Ada, lived next door to him and Edie. Tommy's wife, Faith, used to work in Batey's – used to just about run Batey's till Josie and George took over. It was people like Tommy, Will thought, linked to him in so many different ways, that made him think of Redbrae as a special sort of place. The village, the school, had always been his whole world. He'd spent all his life there, apart from the war. It was the war that had made him realise how special it was. His war . . . flying training in Canada, service in the Middle East, and then . . . and then . . . Changi.

He stopped walking. His hands had begun to shake, he realised. They were clammy cold, sweating. He cursed softly beneath his breath. All these years, and even that name could still reduce him to this trembling apology for a man. He fumbled in his pocket, pulled out a handkerchief and scrubbed at his palms. He must push all that business out of his mind. It was over. Not forgotten. Never that. But over. Finished. All thanks to Edie.

He began to walk on, his stride steady now, his eyes raised from the ground. Edie had brought him back to life. When he'd thought there was no hope, no point. When humanity seemed to have disintegrated in a sea of pain and degradation and humiliation. When he'd thought he'd never get rid of the stench of it, the gorge rising, the self-disgust. Then Edie's clear, luminous face had swum towards him through his nightmares. 'I'm here, pet.' Her eyes willing him to survive, to learn to walk upright again. To dare to turn his back on a stranger. 'Hold my hand,' she'd whispered. 'You're safe here. You're with me.'

But now, Will thought, he must stop brooding on the past and face up to what was happening today. Try to imagine what Edie was thinking, feeling. Try to imagine the man beside her.

'Lewis Harrison,' she'd told him. 'You know. He was up at the hospital for a few months in nineteen forty. His eyes had been burned and I read to him sometimes. His mother used to send us a Christmas card – don't you remember? From Kent. They grew apples there.'

No, Will didn't remember the Christmas cards from Kent. But he remembered Edie in his arms, one quiet Sunday morning, turning towards him, her face aglow. 'There was a ghost, Will. A poor, blind ghost. But he's gone now, my love.'

Well, Will thought grimly, the ghost had come back to haunt him. Real, now. Live flesh and blood. And he'd seen Edie this morning, her face puzzled, staring at herself in the dressing-table mirror as if she were trying to work out who she was. It had frightened him.

He heard the school bell clang out and automatically he hurried towards the gates. Without Edie, he thought, there'd be nothing. He'd loved her ever since he'd first set eyes on her in that funny old flower shop where she'd worked. And *only* her, always. It was as simple as that. He sprinted across the playground, let himself through the big black front door, and pulled it shut behind him. The minute he was over the threshold, the school secretary was there, waiting to pounce. 'Mr Batey!' she announced. 'I have a parent waiting to see you. A complaint, I'm afraid.'

'Don't tell me,' he groaned. 'Not Sandy Motson again!'

Miss Scott pursed her lips and gave him a brief nod. 'Mrs Robson,' she called into the office, 'Mr Batey will see you now. This way, please.'

Will adjusted the expression on his face, squared his shoulders, stretched out his hand to Mrs Robson, and felt the school world settle around him again like a thick old flannel work-shirt.

'I don't believe it! Little Marigold is Mari Metcalfe!' Lewis stared at the glossy stage portrait and Edie, coming into the room with a tray in her hand, catching him suddenly unawares like that, chuckled at the expression on his face.

It had been a good day, she thought. She'd been dreading it in a way, being alone again with Lewis after all this time. She could see that for him the journey was not over. He was still struggling along, trying to find his way. But for her – oh, she'd reached journey's end years ago. She smiled slightly, thinking of this morning's walk through the village. He'd wanted to see it *all*, he'd said. The school, the church, the war memorial, the beach, the hospital, the dene. Especially the dene. What he hadn't bargained for was that the people in the village would want to see *him*.

'Why aye, Edie lass,' Taddy Blackwell had greeted her, striding up Redbrae Street. 'Off for a walk, are you?'

And then it had been Sergeant Robson riding past on his bike. 'Hello there, Edie. Too good to stay indoors?'

And after that there was Rita Hunter, slowing down the butcher's van and poking her head out of the window, and poor Teddy Laing smiling his endless smile, and old Mrs Howis, hobbling painfully towards young Dr Scott's surgery. All of them seemed to want to pause for a chat with Edie.

'I don't believe it!' exclaimed Lewis, after they'd been delayed yet again and required to admire Dolly Thomas's new baby, sleeping pink as a rosebud in her pram. 'How do you ever get anywhere?'

'It's not always like this,' Edie told him.

'So why today? Is it the weather or something? The sunshine gone to their heads?'

'No.' Edie grinned. 'Not the weather. It's you.' Lewis's face was a study. 'Edie Batey out for a walk! At eleven in the morning. With a man. A *strange* man. And poor Will hard at work in his classroom earning the daily bread! That's what it's all about, Lewis.'

'Why don't they mind their own business?'

'It *is* their own business,' Edie told him. 'That's Redbrae for you. We all like to know what's going on.'

For the rest of their walk Lewis moved along by her side as if in a trance. It seemed as if he could hardly bring himself to speak. Every now and then Edie stole a glance at his face. He looked pale and intent. From behind his glasses his eyes stared at the huge beach with its tawny sands and crumbling clay cliffs. When they walked along the bottom of the gorge he gazed up at the overhanging banks, watching the seagulls as they wheeled and screamed overhead. After they'd crossed the railway line they ignored the signs that read 'Trespassers Will Be Prosecuted' and cut across high fertile fields till, at last, they slithered down a steep hill into the dene. Smiling like an excited child, she led him along by the side of the stream, which had been their favourite walk. The place was still remote, secret. A little lost landscape, gleaming now with sheets of buttercups and moon daisies, loud with the sound of water.

She turned to him, curious. 'Well?' she asked. 'What do you think about it, Lewis? Is this what you imagined?' He couldn't speak. He shook his head, took off his spectacles and rubbed one hand across his eyes. She saw the glitter of tears. 'Come on, pet.' Gently, she took his hand. 'Enough for one day, eh? We'll walk back past the hospital and then I'll get you something to eat, shall I?'

He laughed shakily. 'I'm sorry to be such a fool, Edie. It's all so . . . It brings it all back. That smell . . . what is it?'

'Wild garlic, growing by the path.'

'Yes! I remember it. And the sound of the water, and . . .' His voice trailed forlornly away. 'I can hardly bear it.'

In her kitchen she poured him a glass of brandy. 'Drink this,' she said. 'You'll feel better.' She took a lettuce and tomatoes out of the fridge, lifted down a bowl of brown eggs from the pantry shelf, sliced crusty bread on a white wooden board. 'Omelette OK?'

He nodded. 'Thank you.' He picked up a tomato and looked at it thoughtfully. 'I make a pretty fine tomato salad,' he told her. 'Sara showed me. Have you got some basil?'

'Fraid not. But my herb garden, such as it is, is just outside the door there.'

They worked side by side. She swirled creamy eggs into sizzling butter. He chopped chives and parsley, drizzled oil and vinegar over sliced tomatoes. Then they carried their plates out into the garden and sat on the bench beneath the cherry tree, quiet and comfortable together, shaded from the high sun.

'Mmm. Lovely.' She stood up, brushing crumbs from her lap. 'I'll make us some coffee, shall I?'

'Let me help.'

'No need. Why don't you go into the sitting room? I've put out some photograph albums for you to look at.'

When she joined him there she found him staring incredulously at Marigold's face. 'Mari Metcalfe!' he repeated still amazed. 'But she's *famous*! Maureen and I actually had tickets for *The Dancing Years* but then Sara got measles or something. It's extraordinary. Isn't it?'

'I suppose it is, really,' Edie agreed. She looked over his shoulder as he sat on the sofa, glancing through the albums. 'You always imagine these starry names come from another world, don't you? Not an ordinary sort of place like Redbrae.'

'I remember Marigold singing,' Lewis told her, 'that first day on the platform when we arrived. After all that nightmare it was like – like a long, cool, wonderful drink.'

'Well, that's all over now since she got married. Simon runs a theatre in Surrey. So she still acts a bit and sings a bit. But she's given up her career for him, really. She seems very happy.'

'Good. I'm glad of that.'

'I'll tell you someone else who's happy. Lilian Taylor. Do you remember her?'

'The school teacher, you mean?'

'Yes. She's Mrs Harry Cargill now.'

'That Fascist! I thought he went to gaol.'

'He did. But she waited for him.' She laughed. 'Reclaimed him by love,' Joe said, but he always was an old softy at heart. Anyway, after the war they got married and opened a craft workshop making the most wonderful wooden toys and they're doing well. I went to their—'

Suddenly Lewis closed the album on his lap, twisted round and laid his finger on her lips. 'Sshh!' he said.

'Why? What's the matter?' Her face was suddenly wary.

'You *know* what's the matter. We've talked about everybody. At length. Haven't we? But what about *you*, Edie? You haven't told me anything about *you*.'

'I would have done. While we were out for our walk.'

He shook his head. 'I couldn't listen then. Couldn't take anything in. It was all too . . .'

'I know.' She smiled. 'But there's not much to tell, really. I don't help out in Batey's, now that Josie and George Timmins are there. That's why I've taken up the art classes. It's nothing very special, you know, but I enjoy it. I do portraits mostly. In charcoal.' She gave a sudden spurt of laughter, and laid the palms of her hands at either side of his face. 'I'd like to draw you, Lewis. I never saw your face properly until yesterday.'

He moaned, put out his arms to her, pulled her towards him. 'I still feel the same, Edie. I can't help it. This morning – in the dene – it was as if I'd never left.'

But at once she sprang away from him. 'We have all moved on, Lewis,' she said.

'Not me.'

'Of course you have!' Her voice was fierce. 'You and Maureen all these years. Working together. Bringing up a child. You've made something really good of your lives.'

'Please! Edie.' All he wanted was to feel her body warm and gentle beside him.

But she was relentless. 'And Sara. You – you glow when you talk about her. She's like a – a prize.'

He shook his head, desperate to make her understand. 'But *you*. I feel the same about *you*. Can't you remember how it was?'

She nodded, smiling sadly. 'The most exciting time of my

life. I felt as if . . . as if all the lights had been switched on.'

'Well, then—'

'Listen, pet.' Her voice was low. 'When I first met you, things were very bad. The war and everything. Suddenly I had Marigold to look after, as well as my own bairns. I used to get scared – nothing but the sirens night after night, and Joe out in the streets, leaving me to look after everything. And I was missing Will. Frightened that he'd not come back. Frightened that he'd come back different. Then – you arrived.'

'Edie,' he murmured roughly, reaching for her, 'I love you.'

She lifted her hands, entreating him to be quiet, to let her have her say. 'You were . . . I don't know . . . I was so mixed up. Part of me thought it was like having Will back again. You were in the Air Force too, a flyer like him. And you loved poetry, books and reading, just the way he did. But you were so young. And blind. That poor bandaged head of yours! I wanted to look after you. Mother you. Like our David. And then . . . then you made love to me. Husband. Child. Lover. I was possessed.'

His face was shining. 'That's it. That's the way it was – *is* – for me, Edie. That's why I want us to start again. Together. The way it should have been.'

She shook her head. 'Don't you see? It was wartime. Dream-time. Not real.'

'You can't say that. It was the most real thing—'

'When Will came home . . . He'd had a terrible time, you know. After you'd gone I heard . . . One night, there was a telegram. They said his plane had been shot down in the jungle. He was reported missing. I felt . . . I could hardly live with myself . . . thinking that . . . while all those awful things were happening to him, you and I had been together in this very room! I couldn't bear it, Lewis. At first I was convinced that he was dead. That I'd never get the chance to make it up to him. Then, months and months afterwards, the Red Cross got in touch. They'd found him, they said. He was in – in Changi prison camp.'

'I – I'm sorry. I didn't know.'

'When he got home . . . it was just before Christmas nineteen forty-five. It was horrible. I can't tell you. I tried so hard, *too* hard, to make things right for him. And he tried too – poor Will!

– he tried to pretend that he was fine. Really well. Getting along nicely, thank you. But inside we were both living in hell.'

'You didn't tell him? About you and me?'

'Of course not. That wasn't important.'

Lewis winced.

'It was just as if we were bereaved, both of us, mourning for the people we'd been before the war. We felt so . . . so lost. Sad. And it went on for years. I thought that we'd never get over it. That this was it for the rest of our lives. Strangers, sharing bed and board.'

Suddenly, her face gleamed, her eyes seemed to deepen into a more intense blue. Lewis, watching, was moved almost to tears again by the transformation.

'And then,' she went on, 'one morning – it was a Sunday, I remember. Years later, the girls were almost grown-up. I'd gone downstairs to make us a cup of tea. August, holiday weather, and Josie and George had taken David off to Seaburn for a day on the beach, so we had the house to ourselves for a change. It's all so clear to me, Lewis, like watching a film. I put the tea on a tray, my little set with the poppies on, cups and teapot and everything, and I carried it upstairs. Everything ordinary. Humdrum. He was sleeping. The sun shining in on him. I didn't even know what was happening to me. But from that moment, Lewis, everything just seemed to slip into place again.'

She stood just inside the bedroom door and looked down at Will as he lay sleeping. His hair was pure white now, his face deeply etched, making him look much older than a man in his mid-forties. But his body was still strong, lean and muscular. He slept naked because of the August heat, and the top sheet had slithered towards the floor, leaving his back unprotected. Quietly she stepped towards the bed, leaning over him, forcing herself to look at his back, to think about what it meant. From just below his neck, down towards the narrowing of his waist, it was thickly ridged with horizontal scars. Highlighted by the sunshine, the old, healed lesions were like the rungs of a step ladder, only wider, spreading relentlessly from one side to the other.

In all these years Will had never mentioned them, never explained them, although he had never tried to hide them from her either. But Edie had learned the story they told from one of Will's friends, a Changi survivor like himself.

'You see, they whipped him,' he'd explained. 'One of the men had stolen an egg. One measly egg. He was trying to smuggle it across to the children in the other camp. And the guards wanted Will to tell them who had taken it.'

'Did Will know?'

'He knew everything, your husband. When anybody did anything they told Will. Don't ask me why. He was like a father confessor to us all. That's the reason the Nips hated him so much.'

'Did he tell them? About the egg?'

'Just look at his back, Mrs Batey. Does that look like a man who gives in under torture?'

Now, staring again at the flagellated body, Edie felt her own flesh melt in tenderness. Gentle Will. This was the man who spent his life with children, coaxing them to learn, and to read, playing football with them; weaving them magic and stories; teaching them how to live decent, ordinary lives. He captured them with kindness. He never raised his voice, or slapped their hands, or threatened them with punishment. Yet this was the man who had been strapped face down on a wooden frame while the skin had been systematically ripped from his back in bleeding strips. Not once, but again and again and again.

Silently, she slipped out of her dressing gown, and tugged at the ribbon round the neck of her nightdress until it fell from her shoulders. Then she lay down by Will's side and wound him closely in her arms. He opened drowsy eyes and gazed at her.

'I do love you, Will,' she murmured. Peace washed over her. The agonies of her guilt receded and left her invaded by joy. At last, she thought, the long sad years of separation were over.

Will smiled at her wonderingly, recognising at once the change in her face. 'You've come back to me, bonny lass!'

She nodded, wordless.

'Yes!' He sighed. 'We've both had to live with our ghosts, Edie. I just couldn't talk about mine. And I knew you didn't want me to interfere with yours.'

'I'm sorry,' she whispered. 'There was a ghost. A poor, blindfold ghost, sitting four-square between us. But it's gone, my love. More than ten years, but it's gone at last.' And she kissed him.

Will laughed. 'Cause for celebration,' he said, as he gathered her hungrily into his arms.

And after they'd made love, at the same time old lovers and new lovers together, they lay, hands clasped, and gazed at each other in an ecstasy of rediscovery.

As Edie raised her eyes, and fixed her calm blue gaze upon him, Lewis felt his heart pound as if he were a guilty man. An intruder upon their most intimate life, voyeur at the bedroom door. At once he knew that in some strange way she had broken the chains in which his memories had held him for so long.

He shook his head. 'What was it all about, then? Us, I mean?' he asked her humbly. 'All that passion? That love and longing? What was it all for?'

'Oh, Lewis! Don't ask. All I know is that I'll never regret it. Not a minute of it.'

'Won't you?'

'Of *course* not! But now, let it pass, love. Let it go.'

A tremor ran through his body. 'Are you sending me away?'

'No. Please. Wait to see Will, at least. He's looking forward to meeting you.'

Lewis shook his head. 'Don't ask it.'

'Why not? You would like him.'

'I know I would. I know it, Edie. But I think I should go.' He felt numb. He looked down at her grave face and knew that she was suffering too. And then, through his grief, like a pale glimmer of dawn, he felt the beginning of something that was almost like relief. He was suddenly very tired. He must go home, he thought. Enquire at the station when there would be a train. He must get back to Greenways. Maureen would be wondering . . .

Edie put out her hand to him. 'I'm very glad you came,' she said. '*Very* glad.'

'Me too.' Gently he bent and kissed her forehead. 'Thank you, Edie. For everything.'

'You still here, Mr Batey?' Mrs Wilson was amazed. 'Nearly five o'clock. Your poor wife will be looking for you.'

Will was taking his time about going home. Usually he couldn't wait to slip out of the building, calling a cheerful goodnight to the cleaners as they piled chairs on top of desks and laboriously began to sweep every floor. But today he kept finding extra jobs to keep him busy. He raised his eyebrows at Mrs Wilson's indignant face as she shuffled at his doorway, a Woodbine clamped to her lower lip, a bucket clenched in her rough, red hand.

'Is that the time?' he exclaimed. 'I will be in trouble if I don't make a move. Dear me! We've got a visitor too.' Reluctantly he scooped up a pile of blue exercise books and stacked them on a shelf. 'Better finish these tomorrow, I suppose.'

For the first time, the road that led from the school to Cherry Villas wearied him. He trudged up the hill, feeling the weight of his fifty-three years heavy on his shoulders. The late-afternoon sun glinted from every window. Its brilliance made the little colliery houses look drab, the streets mean and dirty. He took off his tie, unbuttoned his shirt collar, pushed his hand through his hair. June. Midsummer. And he was old and worn out. He reached his garden gate, and pushed it open, slipped his key into the lock of the front door, let himself inside. He felt ludicrously nervous, a stranger in his own house.

'Hello!' he called. 'I'm home.'

At once he heard Edie's answering voice. 'In the sitting room, pet.'

Will paused and braced himself, arranging his face for a cordial welcome to Lewis. He found Edie alone. She was sitting on a low chair by the window, her sketch pad on her lap. She laid it down at once and reached out her hand to him, her face serene.

'You look worn out,' she said. 'Come and sit down. The kettle's been boiled.'

'Where's Lewis?' he asked. 'I'm sorry I'm late. I got—'

'Lewis has gone,' she told him.

'What do you mean? I thought he'd be eating with us. You baked specially.'

She shook her head, smiling. 'He decided to go.'

'When am I going to meet him, then? Coming back tomorrow, is he?'

'I don't think so. He just wanted to have a chat about old times,

really. But it's funny, isn't it? After all these years, there was just
. . . suddenly, there was nothing more to say.' She stood up, and
kissed him lightly.

'What have you been drawing?' he asked, stooping to pick up
her pad from the floor. And as he lifted the top page, his own face
gazed out at him, radiant and strong, the eyes alight, the mouth
smiling. He looked closer and saw that she had written his name
and a date in the bottom right-hand corner. 'Will Batey, August
9th, 1953.'

She was watching him closely, her head on one side. 'I've been
doing it from memory,' she said.

He nodded, his eyes fixed on her. 'I remember too. Sunday
morning. The kids had gone to the beach. You brought us tea,
in the poppy cups.'

She laughed, blushed suddenly and bent her head.

'But why?' he asked her. 'Why are you doing this today?'

She shrugged. 'I just suddenly wanted to. A sort of . . . love
letter, I suppose. From me to you.'

12 ∫

Lewis opened his eyes slowly, reluctantly. Moved his arms and legs. Clenched his toes and fingers. Then he relaxed and tried to think. Where was he, he wondered. What time was it? Was this a dream, and if so, why did it hurt so much? He looked around cautiously, peering about him, trying not to move his throbbing head. Everything . . . white. He was lying in a white bed, in a quiet, white room. A room he'd never seen before. He frowned, trying to remember. Then, feeling as if he were being borne along on a relentless river, he closed his eyes again, and slept. When he woke again a woman's face was peering down at him. A square, friendly looking face, darkly freckled, with gingery eyebrows and a wide mouth.

'Mr Harrison?' The mouth opened and spoke to him. Knew his name. 'Are you feeling a bit better, pet?' The eyebrows rose, formed two ginger crescent moons.

Despite himself, Lewis smiled. 'My head aches. Haven't got a hangover, have I?'

'Why no, man. You've had an accident. Got yourself run over. Can't you remember?'

Lewis shook his head, then gave a grunt of pain.

'You just lie still,' the woman told him, 'and I'll fetch the doctor.'

'Just tell me first, where am I?'

She stared. 'Why you're in the hospital, of course. Sunderland General. Didn't you even know that?'

Dr Norris loomed over him, looked at the notes clipped to the bottom of the bed, then sat down by his side. 'Well, Mr Harrison,' he said, 'it seems you've had a lucky escape.'

'What happened?' Lewis asked him.

'That's exactly what we've been trying to find out. Apparently you walked straight out into the road, bang in front of an approaching car. Teatime yesterday. At the cross-roads between the railway station and the Palace. The driver hadn't a chance. He said you seemed to be looking right at him, but just kept on going.'

Lewis groaned. 'The station! I remember. I'd just been checking up on the next London train. I was on my way back to the hotel.'

'You had your mind on other things?'

'Yes.' Lewis gave a brief laugh. 'I did, as it happens. But that wasn't the problem. It's my sight. Often I don't see things at the side.'

'Ah! So that's it!' Dr Norris leaned towards him and peered closely at his eyes, then handed him his glasses which were sitting on the bedside locker, still miraculously intact. 'When did this happen?'

'Twenty years ago. The war. My plane was shot down.'

'Right. So this is your second lucky escape. Well, can I beg you to take extra care in future? It seems to me you're in danger of using up your good luck. Anyway, this time you're fine. We don't expect any after-effects.'

Lewis smiled. 'So I can go home, then?'

'All in good time. We'll need to keep an eye on you for a couple of days or so, I think. Just to be on the safe side. Is there someone we can get in touch with?'

'Not really. Just the hotel, perhaps. Let them know I'll be back for my luggage.'

'What about your wife? Family? We found your name in your notebook, but no address or anything, so we haven't been able to contact—'

'Oh, no!' Lewis was adamant. 'There's no need. I live in Kent but my wife's on holiday anyway. With my daughter.' The lie slipped out even before he knew he was going to tell it. He didn't want to complicate things for Maureen any more than he had already. She'd be busy enough trying to get her own life in order without having to worry about him, he thought. Much better if she didn't know, otherwise she'd feel she ought to catch the next train. 'I'd just come up to see one or two friends from the old days,' he explained.

'Old days?'

'I was here during the war. Redbrae Emergency Hospital, then Newcastle Eye Infirmary.'

'And now Sunderland!' Dr Norris laughed. 'We obviously look after you too well. You can't keep away from the wards. Well, what about giving me your friends' number, then? They might like to come and visit you. Bring you the odd grape. Not much fun being in hospital with no visitors, is it?'

For a moment Lewis lay still, his eyes closed. How strange it would be, he thought, how marvellous, to have Edie by his hospital bed again. Just the way it used to be. Her face seemed to float in front of him, so close, so potent, that he almost felt he could reach out and touch her cheek. But then, resolutely, he pushed the idea away from him.

'Thanks,' he said. 'But I don't think so. We're not that close any longer. Just old acquaintances, really.'

The doctor stood up and gave him a wry grin. 'Funny, isn't it, the way these things turn out? Just like on holiday. One day you're swearing you'll be friends till the day you die. The next, you're passing strangers.'

Lewis nodded dumbly.

'Well, Mr Harrison, I suggest you try to get as much bed rest as possible. I'll take another look at you tomorrow, but I imagine we'll be able to pack you off home by the weekend. I don't suppose there's anything that can't keep till then.'

Late on Saturday afternoon the women of the Harrison family were all gathered together in the front bedroom of Penny Cottage. It looked like a tableau from a West End play. Helen lay motionless upon her narrow bed, her back propped against a mound of pillows, frosty white and trimmed with lace. Sara perched close beside her on the coverlet, holding her hand. At one side stood Maureen, calm and quiet. At the other, Jane fidgeted about. She leaned forward as if she would like to plump up the pillows, then thought better of it. She examined the bedside table, checking the glass of water and the box of pills, and then she gazed at the delphiniums, burning blue in their urn on the broad window-sill.

Keeping a respectful distance, Mrs Sammes loomed at the bedroom door. She cleared her throat. 'Well, then. I'll just pop downstairs and put the kettle on, shall I?' Her words broke the spell of silence.

Maureen nodded, smiling at her. 'That would be very kind of you, Mrs Sammes.' Then she turned back to Helen. With her face cleansed of its make-up, grey hair pressed down damply against her scalp, she looked, for the first time, like a frail old woman. 'What a fright you gave us,' Maureen said. 'How are you feeling now?'

'I'm all right, dear,' Helen told her. 'A bit weak and wobbly, that's all.'

'I *knew* we should have got the doctor in,' Jane said. 'When you began to get those headaches. I knew you weren't well. I told Lewis. I went over to see him specially. He said I wasn't to fuss!'

'Where *is* Lewis?' Helen asked vaguely.

Maureen seemed not to hear her. 'What exactly happened? Can you remember?'

Helen frowned. 'No. I'm sorry. I was getting changed. I was looking in my box for a brooch I wanted. The moonstone, set in silver. You know the one. It looks perfect with my grey dress. Bertie bought it for me, when—'

'Mother!' Jane exclaimed.

'Then I just felt . . . I don't know how to describe it. A bit woozy. Light-headed.' She attempted a little joke. 'I suppose you all think I'd been hitting the bottle, but it was far too early for that. The next thing I knew, I was in bed. Mrs Sammes was wringing her hands and crying, "Woe! Woe!" the way she does. And Dr Redwood was here.' Despite her brave attempt to make light of it, she could not conceal the fear in her eyes. 'What did he say?'

'He's very worried about you,' Jane scolded. 'We all are. When poor Mrs Sammes came in and found you stretched out cold on the floor she thought you were dead.'

Maureen shook her head quickly. 'The doctor's a bit concerned, that's all. You just had a little turn, he says. Your blood pressure is slightly up. So you're to stay quietly in bed, and rest, and take your pills, and he'll come back and see you tomorrow.'

In fact, that wasn't quite what Dr Redwood had said but he had been adamant that Helen should not be worried or upset. 'A spasm' was how he'd described her black-out, as Maureen had walked with him to his car. 'In medical terms, "a cerebro-vascular accident". But they're very common, you know, Mrs Harrison. Sometimes they're just a little warning sign that something isn't quite right.' He'd patted her arm reassuringly. 'I don't think you need to be too anxious about your mother-in-law. She's always been as tough as old boots. But there should be someone with her, just for a day or two. You won't be leaving her on her own, will you?'

A tiny trace of colour was beginning to return to Helen's cheeks. She looked from one face to the other, squeezed Sara's warm hand. 'Well, it's very sweet of you all to rush to my bedside like this. I'm flattered.'

'I'm going to stay with you tonight, Mother,' Jane promised. 'And Robert will be along later. He sends his love and says that you're to be a good girl and do what you're told.'

Helen smiled faintly. 'Dear Robert!' She looked at Maureen. 'When is Lewis coming?'

Maureen's face was expressionless. 'I'm afraid he's away for a day or two.'

'Away. Where?' Helen looked surprised.

'In . . . in Birmingham.'

'No, he's not!' Sara exploded, staring at her mother. 'He's in Sunderland.'

Helen's hand flew to her mouth, and Jane glanced quickly from Sara to Maureen. 'Lewis is in Sunderland?' she repeated.

'Of course he's not, Jane.' Maureen's eyes flashed at Sara, sending her urgent warning signals. 'Sara's got it wrong. Why ever would he be in Sunderland? He's gone to Birmingham. There's a weekend conference, a new fruit-marketing initiative they're talking about. He thought it might be useful.'

Helen nodded quietly. 'Of course. So there is. I think I remember reading about it.' Wearily she closed her eyes again.

'I'd better take Sara home now,' Maureen said, dropping a light kiss on Helen's forehead. 'I'll be back tomorrow morning, Jane. And you'll keep in touch, won't you?'

As soon as the car pulled away from the cottage Maureen

turned on Sara in a fury. '*Why* did you have to go and say that?' she demanded. 'About Sunderland?'

'Because it's *true*! Isn't it?'

Maureen was silent.

'I *know* Dad's in Sunderland,' Sara said. 'I saw the postmark on that letter he sent you.'

'Oh, you did, did you? And I suppose you read what was inside too.'

'No, I did *not*,' Sara flared. 'I am not in the habit of reading other people's letters.'

'Well, that's something anyway. You just content yourself with examining their envelopes.'

'I didn't think there was any law against it.'

'No.' Maureen drove in silence for a minute or two. 'I'm sorry, Sara. I shouldn't have said that. But you've never spoken to me like this before.'

'You've never behaved like this before. And what I want to know is – what is Dad doing in Sunderland?'

'I don't really think it's any of your business.'

'None of my business! He is my father, for God's sake!'

'Sara! Don't talk like that.'

'Why shouldn't I talk like that? Why shouldn't I swear if I want to? I'm sick of you two. The pair of you. You really get on my nerves these days.'

Maureen was so appalled by Sara's outburst that she pulled over to the side of the road and switched off the engine. 'What on earth is the matter with you?' she asked.

'You're the matter. You and Dad. It's been going on for weeks now, hasn't it?'

'What has? What exactly are you talking about?'

'You really want me to tell you, do you?'

'Of course I do.'

'All right, then.' Sara looked at her grimly and held up her left hand to help emphasise the charges she wished to bring. 'Firstly,' she said, tapping her little finger, 'after the Blossom Procession, you absolutely refused to take care of Gran. Didn't you? You had more important things to do, you told us. And look at her now. She might be *dying*, and it's all your fault.'

'I don't think—'

'Please don't interrupt. You said you wanted to know.'

'Sorry.'

'Secondly, you started drooping round the house like a – a lovesick moose.'

'Sara!'

'That's *just* what you looked like. A miserable old moose, with your face all droopy and your mouth turned down. Thirdly,' the middle finger received a sharp tap, 'Dad suddenly starts going berserk, throwing books all over the office, including the wastepaper basket, and muttering about "secret messages" and all that pathetic schoolboy rubbish. Fourthly, he just ups and offs, and you say he's decided to go to Birmingham, just like that, without any warning, when you know very well he never goes *anywhere* on his own.'

'Have you finished now?'

'No, I have not,' Sara shouted. 'Fifthly,' she hit her thumb in final triumph, 'fifthly, when I have proof positive that he's jolly well not in Birmingham, that he's gone off to Sunderland, for some God-forsaken reason, *you* make out that I'm a liar. In front of Gran and Auntie Jane. How could you? You know very well that it's not me that's telling lies, Mum. There's something going on, I know there is, but of course nobody bothers to tell me anything.'

'Sara. Darling.' Maureen stretched out to take the girl's hand, but she jerked it away from her. 'Lewis and I have been a bit upset recently, I admit it. All over something that happened years and years ago, long before you were even thought of. But—'

'*What?* What happened years and years ago?'

'I can't tell you that. It's nothing to do with you.'

'Of course it's to do with me. You're my parents, aren't you? He had no right to go off like that. What's going to happen to us?' Her voice rose. 'I always thought you loved each other. Gran thought you did, anyway. She always said—'

'We *do*, but—'

'You see, you never give me a straight answer. I don't think you've even told Dad that Gran's ill, or he'd be on his way back by now. He'd want to be with her.'

'I can't tell Dad.' Maureen shook her head. 'I don't know where he is.'

'Yes, you do. He's in Sunderland.'

'Listen, Sara. He posted a letter to me, from somewhere in the Sunderland area, last weekend. But there was no address on it and I haven't heard from him since. So, I do not know where your father is and that is the truth.'

Sara stared at her miserably. 'What are we going to do, then? What if Gran is really ill?'

Maureen reached out her hand again and felt a surge of relief as this time Sara clasped it and held it tight. 'I don't think she is, darling. I think it was just a little faint.'

'But what if . . . ?'

'If the worst happens, we'll find ways and means, I'm sure. But for now, I think we should just go home and be patient. Please, can we be friends again?'

Sara shrugged. 'I suppose so,' she mumbled.

Maureen switched on the engine and checked her rear-view mirror. 'I hope you feel a bit better for getting that little lot off your chest.'

'Mum.'

'Oh, darling, not "sixthly", *please*! I don't think I'm strong enough.'

Sara gave a subdued giggle. 'I didn't really mean the bit – the bit about you looking like an old moose. Sorry.'

Maureen raised her eyebrows. 'Well, that's a relief, anyway. I suppose I must be grateful for small mercies.'

Lewis paid off the taxi-driver, slotted his key into the lock of the front door, and stepped inside into the cool, flagged hallway of Greenways. He breathed in the fragrance of the big bowl of sweet peas that stood on the circular table, looked briefly at the pile of letters standing beside it.

'Hello!' he called. 'I'm back!'

He felt oddly excited, as if he'd come home after a long absence in a far-off place. The house was steeped in silence. He looked at his watch. Just after six. Maureen's car wasn't in the courtyard, so he supposed she might have gone into Donchurch, or to Tillerton to see his mother. But Sara might be somewhere about. Up in her room perhaps.

'Hello!' he called again.

Perhaps he should have rung to let them know he was on his way. He'd thought about it, but decided against it. He'd wanted to surprise them. To make it a sort of . . . unexpected reunion. He ran upstairs and looked first inside the study, then into the bedrooms. Sara's room was in even more than its usual chaos, every drawer open, gramophone records on the chairs, clothes all over the floor. He grinned. This was Sara's way. She lived her life like a whirlwind. He retraced his steps downstairs, poured himself a drink and carried it out through the french windows on to the terrace. One small whisky, he thought, then he'd go and look at the orchards. He was eager to see how Luke had been getting on, how he'd managed with the work he'd left him. Only a few weeks now, and they'd be getting under way with the apple-picking. Gathering in the rich harvest.

He'd just settled himself into a chair, legs stretched out in front of him, feeling the whisky relax his body after the strains of the long journey, when he heard someone moving inside the house. Hurrying back into the drawing room, he saw Sara silhouetted in the doorway.

He held out his arms to her. 'Hi! I'm home.'

Sara didn't move. Her body was rigid. Her face a white mask. 'Where've you *been*?' she hissed. 'You should have been *here*. With *us*.'

He went towards her. 'I'm sorry, sweetheart.'

'You just went off and left us. And now she's ill. She's been asking for you.'

'Who? What do you mean?' he cried. 'Your mother? Where is she?' And then he saw Maureen, standing behind Sara, her face in shadow.

'Not me. Helen,' she said. 'But don't worry. She's going to be all right. Come on, I'll drive you over there straight away.'

Late that evening, Lewis and Maureen sat together, face to face at their kitchen table, as strange and awkward as if they had just met.

Lewis said, 'When Sara came in, I thought she was talking about you, Maureen. I thought . . . my going off like that . . . and Jonny Crozier and everything . . . all these wasted years . . . I thought perhaps you had . . .'

She smiled bleakly. 'Taken an overdose or something? Not my style. That's the temptation, but never the answer.'

'Maureen! Don't. Please!'

'Doesn't everybody feel like that sometimes?'

'I don't know.'

She gazed at him, her head on one side, considering. 'You surprise me, Lewis. But, anyway, it's not my role, is it? I've been cast as the sensible one who just soldiers on. I'm not even allowed to cry in the night just once in a while.'

'No. But I didn't know, you see.'

'We all missed you, Lewis. You just went bolting off and it was quite frightening, not having a phone number or anything. A whole week and you never even rang. Where've you been? I mean, what's been happening?'

'I had . . . a little accident. Stupid.'

'What sort of accident?'

'It was nothing. Really.'

'Please. Tell me. Talk to me, Lewis.'

'It's not even worth talking about. It just held me up – up there – longer than I intended. I meant to be on my way back days ago.'

'What about Edie? You did see her, I suppose?'

He nodded, his eyes on her face. 'Edie and I said goodbye. Properly, this time.'

'I see.' Her voice was little more than a whisper. 'And how do you feel about that?'

'All right.' He smiled, relieved. 'I really feel that everything's . . . all right.'

'I'm glad, Lewis. Glad that you went. And that it worked out for you.' She bent her head. 'But I'm afraid everything's definitely *not* all right round here.'

'What do you mean? Mother? Is there something you haven't told . . . ?'

'Not Mother. Sara. She's very angry. With both of us.'

'But why?'

'Because she couldn't understand what was happening. She kept trying to tell me about some poetry book.'

'*The Sonnets.*'

'*From the Portuguese*? That's right.'

'Yes. There was a message in it. From Edie. I didn't know it was there, but Sara found it, you see. It was a sort of code.' His face clouded. 'Maureen, you didn't tell her, did you? All that stuff in the letter I wrote on the train, about Edie and Jonny and everything?'

'Of course I didn't. What do you take me for? But I had my own problems, Lewis. Perhaps I didn't pay her as much attention as I should.'

'Perhaps we never do. That's why she always goes to my mother. I'm going to have to speak to Mother, aren't I? The things she's done. To all of us.'

'I don't think so. What's the point?'

'I *must*!'

Maureen shook her head anxiously. 'Not yet, anyway. She's not strong enough. Dr Redwood says she's not to be worried.'

'No. But when she's better. I must just speak to her, Maureen. She's made such a mess of things. All our *lives* . . .'

Lewis stood up and pushed back his chair roughly, making it grate across the tiled floor. He walked to the window and stood looking out into the dark garden. 'I don't even know any more, I daren't even ask, how things stand between you and me.'

Maureen sat at the table, her eyes lingering on his drooped head, the forlorn curve of his back, the big hands hanging limply by his sides. Then, slowly, she got up and went to him. Standing behind him she twined her arms around his waist, and laid cheek sadly against his shoulder.

Helen's room seemed to be brimming over with sunshine and flowers. Lewis found her sitting up in bed, with a copy of *Good Housekeeping* in her hand and her new library book resting invitingly on the table by her side. But, for the moment, all her attention and delight were focused on him.

'You're looking very much better, Mother.' He bent and kissed her.

'I feel much better.' She smiled. 'In fact, I feel a fraud. I should be up and about.'

'Not yet. It's only a few days since it happened . . .'

'It seems *ages*!'

'. . . and Dr Redwood says you're to stay there for at least a week.'

'All right. All right.' She pulled the face of a naughty child. 'Don't lecture me, darling.' She patted the coverlet beside her. 'Come here and tell me all the news. I don't know when I last had you all to myself like this.'

Obediently Lewis stepped forward and sat down beside her. 'As it happens, I do want to talk to you,' he said gravely.

At once her expression changed. 'Oh dear, you're looking awfully solemn. I hope you're not going to be cross.'

'I've been up to see Edie. Edith Batey. You remember Edie, I'm sure.'

She didn't answer. She began to rummage in the pocket of her bedjacket for a handkerchief.

'You don't seem to be surprised,' he said.

'No. Sara told me.'

'Sara told you what?' He could barely suppress his astonishment.

'Sara said you'd been to Sunderland. Maureen tried to cover up for you, but I knew exactly what you'd been doing there.'

For a moment Lewis faltered, trying to work out what had passed between the three of them. Then he decided not to be deflected and pressed on with the little speech he had worked out days ago and had been saving up until Helen seemed well again. 'Edie told me that when you stayed with her at Cherry Villas, just before my bandages were removed, you led her to believe that I was engaged to be married to Maureen.'

Helen looked vague. 'Did I? I don't remember. It's all so long ago.'

'You surprise me. Usually it's the things that happened long ago that you remember best.'

She flinched at the cruelty of his barb. 'Perhaps,' she said, 'Edie jumped to that conclusion just from the way I talked.'

'From the way you talked!' Lewis was incredulous. 'But how *could* you have talked that way when you knew full well that Maureen was in love with Jonny Crozier?'

Helen crumpled her delicate lace handkerchief into a tight ball. 'Who told you that? Was it Maureen? I thought she might, when that dreadful man came back here. All that horrible bleached hair. Ugh!' She shuddered with distaste.

'Not Maureen. Maureen has never so much as mentioned his name.' He stood up, straightened his back and gazed out at the finger spire of St Michael's, pointing up towards the clear sky.

'Who, then?' Helen demanded.

'*Who* is not important, Mother. What I want to know is *why*? Why did you do all those dreadful things? Whatever got into you?'

'I don't know what you mean.'

'I think you do.'

She shrugged. 'Whatever I did, I did for *you*,' she said. 'You needed a wife to look after you. And you were always so good together, you and Maureen. I used to watch you, listen to you laughing.' Her tone changed, became almost pleading. 'And it's all worked out so well, hasn't it? Bringing the orchards together, running them as one. A perfect partnership in every way. I knew it would be.'

Lewis stared at her curiously as if he were seeing her for the first time. Her skin looked as fine as carved ivory, her eyes dark brown like his own, her chin jutting and determined.

She flushed under his scrutiny. 'I've always felt so happy about the pair of you.' Her voice was light, almost childlike. 'It's been such a *good* marriage.'

He could hardly believe that she would be so obstinate, refuse even to contemplate the possibility that she might have been wrong. 'I found her on her *knees*, Mother,' he said. 'The night after she met him again. Maureen on her knees and crying as if her heart would break. Does that sound like a good marriage?'

'Well, it's not my fault,' Helen retorted. 'I did my best. I had to do something to get you away from that Edith woman.'

'But why? How dare you?'

'You were completely infatuated with her. Don't you remember? And it would have been a *disaster*, Lewis. For you, for the business. For *all* of us.' He couldn't bring himself to speak, could hardly bear to listen, but she forged ahead remorselessly. 'A woman like that, from a colliery village. A shop assistant! I don't know what got into you. What could she know of the life we lived here? Quite apart from the fact that she was older than you. And married, for heaven's sake, with children. I just couldn't believe that you would be so idiotic. I put it down to your plane crash, of course. Clouding your judgement. Anyone could see that she was totally unsuitable.'

'You bullied poor Maureen into marrying me, just to get me away from Edie?'

She lifted her head and looked at him defiantly. 'Yes. If you like. I suppose I did.'

Suddenly Lewis was beside himself with anger. He forgot about Helen's fainting fit. Forgot Dr Redwood's warning that she must be quiet and tranquil. All he could think of was his own pain. He turned on his mother in a rage. 'I loved Edie,' he stormed. 'Adored her. The only thing I wanted in the whole world was to have her here with me. And the children too. It was my idea of heaven on earth.' He pounded his fist against the bedroom wall, relishing the sensation of its hard strength bruising his skin. 'For twenty years I've had to live with this,' he shouted. 'Every single day – imagining that she'd never loved me, that she'd just been . . . amusing herself. That's what you made me think. You did it deliberately. What a poisonous thing! "All she wants is to have Will back by her side," you said. I can still *hear* you saying it.'

Helen was terrified by his fury. 'Darling! I thought I was acting for the best. You've got to believe me.' She held out her arms to him imploringly.

'No!' And then his voice dropped. He felt drained and exhausted. 'It was a cruel thing to do, Mother,' he told her. 'Stupid and greedy and cruel. Four lives ruined because of your meddling.' Slowly he walked towards the door.

'Don't say that, Lewis,' she begged, trying to crawl out of bed and hold on to him. 'I did it all for you. Please, don't go away and leave me like this. Stay a little longer.'

'I'll send Sara up,' he said curtly. 'I don't want to talk to you any more.'

Sara took his place at Helen's bedside while Lewis paced the little rooms below, marched about the garden, tried to read and threw aside his book in disgust. His whole life had been a sham, he thought. Nothing in it was what it had seemed. All the women he had loved – Helen, Edie, Maureen and even Sara – every single relationship had been based on the shifting sands of misunderstanding or manipulation. Nothing seemed reliable or trustworthy any more.

'Dad! Dad!' Sara's terrified shout cut through his thoughts. 'Dad! Come quickly.'

He leapt up the narrow staircase and through the open door.

'I thought she'd fallen asleep,' Sara said, 'But look! I'm frightened.'

Lewis stood at the side of the bed, gazing down at Helen. Her head had fallen awkwardly to one side. Her eyes were closed, her mouth sagged open. And her breathing rasped around the room, harsh and ragged. 'Call Dr Redwood,' he said. 'Quickly. Tell him it's urgent.'

Sara had already reached the bottom of the stairs and was stretching out her hand towards the telephone.

'And then you'd better ring Mum and Jane,' he shouted after her. 'Say they should come at once.'

Helen died an hour later, without regaining consciousness. Sara neither shed a tear nor spoke one word. When Lewis tried to put his arms around her she pushed him fiercely away. Wrapping her grief around her like a cloak, she walked home alone by the edge of the river. She was blind to the beauty of the summer's evening. She did not see the swallows that skimmed and dipped across the water. When she reached Greenways she went slowly upstairs, then she shut herself into her bedroom to meet her grief in private.

Part Four

July 1960

'Dear friends, we meet today – in this beautiful church of St Michael and All Angels, just a stone's throw away from Penny Cottage – not to mourn the death, but to rejoice in the life of Helen Harrison.

'Helen has been a member of this parish for over fifty years, ever since her beloved Bertie brought her here, as his young bride, to Greenways. Theirs was a good, happy and blessed marriage. But when Bertie died, at a tragically early age, Helen did not submerge herself in grief. It would have been so easy. But, for the sake of her children, Jane and Lewis, she bravely surged ahead, looking after her young family with selfless devotion and at the same time working to build up the orchards into a thriving business, just for them. These two powerful strands – her family, and their orchards – have always wound together to form the strong, central thread of Helen's life, a bright rainbow thread of colour and beauty.

'To Jane and Robert, and their sons, Peter and Michael, of whom she was so proud, and to Lewis and Maureen, with whom she worked side by side among the apple trees for so many years, we extend our heartfelt sympathy at this sad time.

'But I would like to say a special word about Helen's granddaughter, Sara. I often spent a quiet half-hour with Helen in her pretty little sitting room or in her lovely garden as we drank tea together, or sometimes, even, a small glass of her excellent sherry! Usually, wherever our conversation began, it ended with Sara. She was, Helen told me – with that little glint of humour which she never lost – the very apple of her eye. Theirs was that special relationship that sometimes blossoms and fruits between grandmother and granddaughter – one of mutual devotion, admiration and understanding. Sara, more than anyone, I believe, is going to miss Helen's vibrant *presence. And so, my friends, it is to Sara in particular that I ask you now to extend your loving and prayerful thoughts, which I trust will comfort and support her in the months to come.*

'And now let us sing together, not a funeral dirge, but that splendid hymn of a rich harvest safely garnered—

> *'God the Father! Whose creation*
> *Gives to flowers and fruits their birth . . .'*

13

Perched gingerly on the edge of the rose brocade sofa in the drawing room at Greenways, sweating in the heat of the overcast July afternoon, Police Sergeant Donald Trespin ran his finger round the inside of his collar and gazed sadly at the notebook he held in his big red hand. Then he cleared his throat, raised his eyes and met the accusing stare of Maureen and Lewis. 'I'm afraid there's still no news of your daughter,' he told them.

Impatiently Maureen pushed back a lock of black hair that had fallen over her brow. 'But she's been away for ages. Days and days. You must have some lead?'

'Ten,' the policeman said in his slow voice. 'Ten days.'

'She could be *dead*!' Lewis exclaimed. 'What on earth are you doing about it?'

'Quite a lot, sir. But as I explained before, it's very difficult. There's not much you can do when a sixteen-year-old is determined to leave home.'

'But Sara's just not the type to go wandering off.'

'There is no type, Mr Harrison. In my experience, almost every one of us has the urge to leave home at some time or another.'

'But you see Sara's always been ... quite young for her age. Unsophisticated, I mean.' Maureen found herself almost pleading with the officer. 'Perhaps we've protected her too much. But she loves Greenways, and country life ... and the orchards and everything. It's all she's ever wanted.'

Sergeant Trespin nodded abruptly, his blue eyes narrow and red-rimmed as if he hadn't slept. 'But things have changed recently, haven't they? There's been a death in the family.'

'My mother,' Lewis said. 'Yes. Sara adored her. They were always very close. Almost from the day Sara was born.'

'Right. And have you got anything to add to that?'

'What do you mean – add? Old ladies die. But isn't that enough to upset a sensitive teenager?'

'No family rows? Arguments? Fallings out?'

'Of course not.'

'Lewis!' Maureen prompted him quietly.

Lewis shifted uncomfortably in his armchair. 'Well, I did have a – a confrontation, if you like, with my mother. Just a few hours before she died, in fact. And perhaps Sara got it into her head that the two things were connected. That it was because of the row. But she was wrong,' he insisted. 'My mother was very ill. We didn't realise it, but Dr Redwood said afterwards that she'd been living on borrowed time.'

Sergeant Trespin bent his grey head and wrote, slowly and with great deliberation, in his little notebook. 'Would you mind telling me what the . . . confrontation was about, sir? The one you had with your mother?'

'Oh, something that happened twenty years ago. Before I was married, even. Long before Sara was born. And it was just . . . a private matter between my wife, my mother and myself. Sara knew nothing about it.'

'Didn't she?' The sergeant put his head on one side and pursed up his lips as if he were going to whistle.

'No. Just old, old family history that has nothing to do with anything.'

'I see. But these things do have a habit of coming back to haunt us, don't they? And you still have no idea at all of where she might have gone?'

'None,' Lewis said desperately. 'We've told you.'

'We're a very small family,' Maureen explained. 'There's only Lewis's sister and her husband, and they're as puzzled as we are.'

'Mm. That would be . . .' the sergeant jabbed at his notebook with a stubby forefinger '. . . Mr and Mrs Prescott, from Donchurch. The bank manager. Yes. We've talked to the sons too. Michael and Peter Prescott. No lead there. What about Sara's friends? Boyfriends?'

Maureen shook her head. 'No one special. There was always a gang of them. She hardly brought anyone home. We're a bit remote here, you see. Off the beaten track. All that business of having to ferry them around everywhere. My husband doesn't drive. And we're usually so busy . . .' Her voice trailed off disconsolately.

'We have talked to her head teacher,' Lewis said. 'And her form teacher too. She's been marvellous. Had the whole class in, one by one. They all say the same thing – Sara was just devastated when my mother died. The shock and everything.'

Sergeant Trespin was deeply involved with his notebook again. 'Yes. But it seems that she did talk to one or two of her friends. Told them about . . . the confrontation you had with your mother, in point of fact.'

Lewis looked alarmed.

'Let me see. David Walters mentioned it. Yes. And . . . and Alexina Bowman . . .'

'Phylly's youngest, you mean?' Maureen asked. 'But Sara hardly knows Alex. They're not special friends or anything.'

The sergeant nodded. 'They were doubles partners. School tennis. So, we still have no idea where she might have gone, except that a taxi driver dropped her off at Donchurch railway station hours before there was a train due in going anywhere. Not a lot of help. Next problem – do we know how she's managing for money?'

Lewis said, 'She has got enough. For the time being, anyway. She's taken her savings book, and she had quite a lot in it.'

'Did she?'

'My mother made her a regular allowance, you see. And Sara often worked for us, in the orchards. Weekends, after school, holidays. We always paid her the going rate.'

'I see. So she can support herself for a while.'

Maureen's eyes began to brim with tears.

'That's good,' the policeman assured her. 'It's the kids who don't have any money that get into trouble – thieving, falling into bad company.

'For goodness sake! This is our child you're talking about.' Lewis took Maureen's hand and held it tightly.

'Each and every one of them is somebody's child, sir.' Abruptly,

Sergeant Trespin closed his notebook, buttoned it safely into the top pocket of his tunic, and levered himself up from the corner of the sofa. 'We're doing as much as we possibly can, Mr Harrison. Sara's photograph has been distributed, and all our men are keeping their eyes peeled. And we make regular checks on all hospitals and mortuaries as a matter of course.'

Lewis felt Maureen's hand tremble within his own. 'Thank you,' he said. 'Please forgive me if I've been rude. It's just . . . this is a terrible time for us. Terrible.'

'I know, sir. But my feeling is, you should be very hopeful. From all I hear, your daughter is a bright girl. Self-confident. Capable. Well able to look after herself.'

'But she *is* just turned sixteen,' Maureen reminded him, 'and she's never been away on her own before, not even on holiday. She doesn't know what it's like . . .'

'Maybe. But she knew exactly what she was doing, didn't she? She took enough clothes, and enough money. Waited till she had the place to herself, then calmly tidied her bedroom, called herself a taxi, and walked out. All very well organised.'

'We'd had to go over to see my mother's solicitors,' Lewis told him. 'The will and everything. Papers to sign.'

Maureen nodded. 'Otherwise we'd never have left her on her own. But she said – she didn't want to come with us.'

'As I say,' Sergeant Trespin concluded, 'all carefully planned. She's very much in charge of things. I think there's every indication that Sara will let you know where she is and what she's up to just as soon as she's good and ready. But not before.'

The battered blue VW Beetle was crawling painfully along a narrow road that seemed to climb out of the valley and up, straight into the clouds. Crouched in the driver's seat, Tina Johnson clutched the steering wheel and gazed doggedly ahead. By her side, peering around her with the rapture of a devout pilgrim, sat her twin sister, Mrs Rusty Rollins. Tina and Rusty were the image of each other, raw-boned and wiry, with pale, tea-leaf freckled faces, marmalade-coloured hair and big wide smiles that reached right up to their ears. At last, after weeks of skivvying in London hotels to top up their funds, they were 'doing the UK'. They'd bought themselves an old banger of a car which, they were assured, would get them from Land's End to John o'Groats without so much as a hiccup, and now they were bent on visiting all the places they'd read about and dreamed about in that last long winter in Sydney when they'd conceived the thrilling idea of selling their house, cashing in their savings and seeing the world before they were too old. They were going to be sixty soon. They dared not put it off much longer.

It was just over a week since they'd started their journey but already they'd managed to visit Devon and Cornwall, Stratford-upon-Avon and the Lake District. Now they were on the way to their own Holy Grail, the Roman Wall.

'Isn't this just amazing!' exclaimed Rusty, hanging out of the window in a trance of delight as they drove through stretches of moorland just beginning to turn into a rosy haze as the heather came into bloom.

'It's all right for you!' Tina put her foot on the accelerator and the Beetle coughed reproachfully. 'I'm far too busy driving this wreck to enjoy the countryside.'

'Tina!' Rusty turned towards her sister. 'You know very well that you like to do the driving. Every time I offer—'

'I know! I know!' Tina clucked. 'Just don't expect me to go into raptures about the blooming heather, that's all.'

Squashed into the back seat, barricaded by a mound of battered suitcases and overflowing carrier bags, Sara gave an explosive giggle. She loved listening to the amiable bickering that Tina and Rusty managed to keep up for miles on end without drawing breath. She was beginning to feel almost happy again. She was laughing – for the first time since her grandmother had died. And it was all due to these two Australian women, she thought, tough and rough, and with hearts as big as the Albert Memorial.

She'd met them on her first night in London, when she'd just run away from Greenways and taken refuge in the Leonora Guest House in Gower Street. The Leonora was a shabby, down-at-heel sort of place that smelled of cooked cabbage and washing-up and disinfectant even in the middle of the afternoon. Its great attraction was that it was both central and cheap. It was run by a Welsh family, two sisters and their brother, middle-aged and unsmiling. They all wore dark clothes and scurried silently around the house with neat pattering movements. But when they were working in the kitchen they sang hymns, in Welsh, their voices lifted in perfect harmony that surged around the quiet, listening rooms. Little singing Welsh mice, thought Sara, and wished Davey were there to share it with her. She felt very alone. It had been difficult going in to supper by herself and she had sat uncomfortably at her single table, not knowing where to look, studying the beige-coloured wallpaper, gazing through the grimy net curtains at the backyard. Then suddenly Tina had smiled at her across the room, lighting up the space between.

'We were wondering if you'd like to join us, dearie,' she'd offered.

And Rusty had joined in, 'It would be a real pleasure.'

By the end of the evening, curled up in the basket chair in their bedroom, sipping at the illicit cocoa that Tina had managed to brew up, Sara felt that she had known them, and liked them, all her life. So when, a few days later, they asked her if she might consider going with them on their travels, it didn't take her long to make up her mind. She had intended to get a job in a shop or coffee bar. 'SMART GIRL WANTED' signs seemed to shine out from every window. But Tina and Rusty were set against the idea.

'You're much too clever for that sort of thing,' Tina had said. 'Slave labour, that's what it is. The worse the work, the smaller the pay. That's the truth of it, isn't it, Rusty?'

Rusty had nodded her head gloomily. 'Too pretty too! Those men out there – like tom cats! Can't keep their hands to themselves. *Nor* anything else.' She'd rolled her eyes in warning. 'Believe me. A young girl like you on her own in the city. Tina and me – we'd never have a moment's peace, worrying about you. And what your *mother* would think.'

'Please!' Sara held up her hands for mercy. 'Do *not* bring my mother into this.'

'But have you written yet? Or phoned?' Rusty demanded. 'If I didn't know where *my* girl was – even though she's married now with a husband to look after her – even so, I'd—'

'I will. I *will* write. Promise.'

'When?'

'Soon.'

Tina smiled at her. 'That's good, dearie. And you'll come on holiday with us too?'

'I'm not sure. I can't decide.'

'Tina and I will pay for the petrol, of course,' Rusty assured her. 'That's only fair. And the rest we'll split three ways – food and room and everything. So it will be much cheaper than staying on in this old place. And we'll have a great time. Won't we, Tina?'

'Course we will. Always do.'

And they'd been right, Sara decided, watching the countryside pass by her window, the sheep that stood neck-high among the bracken, staring at the car with their calm, peaty eyes. She'd turned into a nomad. Only a few months ago she could imagine nothing better than spending her whole life among the apple orchards. Now, she thought, she could travel the roads for months and never feel the slightest pang of homesickness. Suddenly she realised that Rusty and Tina were arguing again.

'Looks like we're coming up to a cross-roads,' Tina said, peering into the distance. 'Which way do we go?'

'I don't know.' Rusty was vague. 'Northwards, I suppose.'

Tina snorted. 'Yes. I *suppose*. But north-east or north-west, you booby? We do want to *see* this perishing wall, don't we? It would be a shame to come all this way and miss it.'

'We won't do that,' Rusty assured her. 'They built it right across, you know. It goes on for miles.'

'It used to, dear. But it's not all there now, is it? Like someone else I know!'

'Oh, ha, ha! *Very* funny, I don't think.'

Sara grinned. 'Hand me the map and I'll navigate if you like. We should be heading towards Haltwhistle or Haydon Bridge, I think, but we've got a long way to go yet.'

Gratefully Tina passed her the road atlas. 'Thank heavens somebody seems to know what we're doing.'

Sara studied the open page, tracing the coloured lines with her finger. 'Straight on at the cross-roads,' she directed. 'And then there's another ten miles or so before we need to turn off.'

After a few minutes Rusty put her head back and started to sing at the top of her voice. '"We'll be coming round the mountain when we come,"' she bawled. She had her window wound right down and was banging out the rhythm on the outside of the car door with the flat of her hand. '"We'll be coming round the mountain when we come" thump, thump. "We'll be coming round the mountain" thump "coming round the mountain . . ."'

'For the Lord's *sake*!' exclaimed Tina. 'What *do* you sound like, girl? It's worse than a creaking old hinge.' But after a while she began to join in. '"We'll be wearing red pyjamas when we come . . ."'

'"When we come,"' echoed Rusty, with operatic gusto.

'Mercy!' Sara laughed, and put her hands over her ears. Her eyes wandered idly across the map, following the lines of roads, river and railway, and the trail of black dots that marked out the Wall itself. She looked at the eastern coastline where it curved in a bit and saw the blue corkscrew of the Tyne twisting inland to Newcastle. Then below it, Sunderland sitting in its own little niche on the river Wear. Suddenly she gave a great shout. 'There's Redbrae!' she called. 'I had no idea we were so close. It's Redbrae.'

The singing came to an abrupt halt. Tina jammed down both feet and brought the car jolting to an emergency stop at the edge of the road. 'What is it, dearie? Red Bay, d'you say?'

'I'm sorry,' Sara stammered. 'I didn't mean you to do that. I was surprised, that's all. I just saw Redbrae, over on the edge of the page here. I had no idea.'

'Do you want to go there? Is it some place you know about?'

'Yes. No.' Sara felt confused. 'It's just . . . there's a woman I know . . . well, not me exactly. My gran. You know, the one who died last month, I told you . . .'

Tina nodded her head sympathetically. 'Yes, we remember, dearie. Of course we do.'

Sara took a deep breath. 'It's all a bit complicated.'

'Take it slowly,' Rusty told her. She rummaged in the glove compartment and pulled out a packet of fruit pastilles. 'Have a good suck on one of these, my beauty, and begin at the beginning. Fish out a purple one – they're the best.'

Sara smiled, the sweet rough and sugary in her mouth. 'During the war, my father's plane was shot down, you see,' she told them, selecting her details with care. 'And he was sent to a hospital in Redbrae. When my grandmother went up there to see him, she stayed with a woman called Mrs Edith Batey. She'd been a reader for Dad when his eyes were bandaged. He couldn't see for weeks.' Tina and Rusty bobbed their heads encouragingly and made gentle little clucking noises. 'Well, when Gran died, Dad wrote to let Mrs Batey know, and then *she* wrote to *me* and sent me a picture of her. Of *Gran*, that is.'

'An old photograph, you mean?' Tina wanted to know.

'No. A portrait she'd painted of the way she looked then. During the war, I mean. It was good. Just like her.' She gave a little laugh. 'When she was in a determined sort of mood her eyelids used to droop a bit and her mouth set in a long, straight line, and then we all knew we had to watch ourselves. Mrs Batey had got that, exactly. Anyway, she sent me the picture, and in her letter she said that if ever I was anywhere near Redbrae she would be very happy to meet me, and talk about what Gran was like, in the old days before I was born. That's all, really. I just suddenly saw Redbrae on the map. On the same page as the Roman Wall. I had no idea it was so near.' Her voice tailed lamely away.

A few hours later they dropped Sara off at the end of Cherry Villas, just where the road forked, one prong leading up to Redbrae Hospital, the other towards the street where Edie lived. Tina and Rusty had wanted just to leave her there for a while, then come back and collect her for the next leg of their journey north.

'We could go down to the coast for a few hours,' Tina suggested. 'All those lovely beaches looked fantastic. We could pick you up this evening and get to Corbridge before dark, ready for an early start tomorrow.'

But something told Sara that they'd come to the parting of their ways. 'You see, I have no idea how long I'll want to stay here,' she explained gently.

'You *might* decide just to get on the train and go home,' Tina suggested.

Rusty looked at her anxiously. 'You do have enough money for your ticket, don't you?' Sara nodded. 'And you *did* post that card to your parents this morning?'

'Yes! Don't worry. They'll get it tomorrow or the next day. Everything's going to be all right. Promise.'

'Well, I don't know,' grumped Tina. 'It just won't seem the same seeing the Wall without you to keep us right. And if Rusty's navigating, I don't suppose we'll even *get* there.'

Sara smiled. 'I'm sure you and old Hadrian will get it together one of these days.' And she gave them a kiss, quickly, one after the other, bundled them into the car, and turned resolutely away before she changed her mind.

She watched the old Beetle disappear down the hill, heard the last honk of its horn, raised her arm in one final wave. Then she straightened her shoulders and tried to think positively. She ran her fingers through her hair, attempted to smoothe out the car creases in her skirt and hoisted up her heavy bag. She must take a few deep breaths, she told herself, and that would help her to stop trembling. Then she must walk, calmly and slowly, along the neat little street. Count the numbers on the gates until she got to 11. Walk up the path, knock on the front door, and wait until Edith Batey opened it. And then she'd say . . . Her heart began to hammer against her ribs. What exactly *would* she say to the woman her father loved?

When the telephone rang Maureen was in the garden. She had no idea how long she'd been there, or what she'd been doing. She just seemed to be standing quite still, staring at the gate that led into the orchards. She was wondering, vaguely, not even caring very much, what Lewis was doing. How he was feeling. The sun beat down upon her head, the bees were frantic among the last of the lavender heads, but she felt cold. And very lonely.

She hadn't felt as lonely as this since she'd decided she had to send Jonny away, when she'd first heard the news about Lewis. That his sight had practically gone. That he couldn't manage without her. What would have happened to them all, she thought, if Lewis had never had his eyes burned? If Helen had not set her heart on having *her* and no other for her daughter-in-law? What if she had been strong-minded and insisted on marrying Jonny Crozier instead? All these years doubt had nagged at her mind and at last, when she'd met Jonny again and finally, completely, resolved it . . . then they'd lost

Sara. It was almost as if it were a judgement, a punishment. She always seemed to lose the people, she most loved. Jonny . . . Lewis . . . and now Sara. It wasn't fair. It really wasn't fair.

She stood quite still in the garden, consciously closing her eyes tight, trying to conjure up Sara's face, and felt panic overwhelm her when she found that, already, it was difficult to get a clear picture. Her eyes, hair, nose, chin – she could imagine each separate feature. But somehow they didn't fit together in exactly the right way. Sara was vanishing away from her. Maureen swallowed, determined not to cry again. She couldn't expect Lewis to bear her despair on top of his own. But, oh dear God, where *was* Sara? Was she even still alive? Was she ill, unhappy, suffering? Would she ever come home? And if she did come home, would she be the same Sara as the one who went away? Questions. Questions. The same questions over and over again. What had she and Lewis done to make her leave them? Did she hate them now? Was it all their fault?

At last, at the back of her mind, she was aware of a bell ringing. A long way off, it seemed, in another place. The telephone! She went rigid. She dared not answer it. It might be the police, wanting to see her, bringing her bad news, terrible news, that she could not bear to hear. Why didn't Lewis go and answer it for her? She wanted it to stop but it just went *on*.

And then she thought – oh! dared she hope? – it might be Sara, quite close to them, safe and happy, and on her way home. Maureen's feet flew over the lawn as she rushed to the phone. 'Hello! Hello! Maureen Harrison . . .' She fought for breath.

'Maureen! There you are! Whatever have you been doing? I've rung and rung.'

Maureen's thin, tired body sagged as she heard Jane's querulous voice. 'Sorry, Jane. I was in the garden.'

'Gardening! With all this hanging over us?'

'I don't seem to be able to sit down.'

'No.' Jane's tone softened slightly. 'There's no news, then?'

'None.'

'So what are the police doing exactly?'

'As much as they can. Sergeant Trespin—'

'You'll have to bully them, Maureen. Robert says nothing gets done these days unless you keep on at people. They should be making proper enquiries, ringing round the hospitals . . .' Her voice began to trail away. 'Maureen, are you listening to me? Maureen! Are you still there, Maureen?'

In the quiet shade of the hallway, Maureen laid down the telephone receiver on the polished table that smelled of lavender and roses, and then turned her back on it. When Lewis came in half an hour later he found her, still as a standing stone, in the corner, her forehead pressed against the wall, her face cold and glistening.

14

Edie was on her knees weeding the big flower bed in the back garden when she heard the click of the gate. She threw down her trowel and dabbed at the soil on her hands with her handkerchief. As she stood up and straightened her back, she felt a surge of irritation. She didn't want to be disturbed this afternoon. She'd promised herself an hour or two in the garden, and she wanted to get on with it. Reluctantly she hurried along the path round the side of the house and saw a thin, dark-haired girl standing on the front step, gazing steadfastly at the door. Edie looked at her carefully, trying to work out who she was, what she wanted. She seemed too young to be a Jehovah's Witness. She was simply dressed in a creased cotton skirt and blue aertex shirt, and she had a big canvas bag slung over one shoulder. Perhaps she was trying to sell something. There was a little worried furrow on her forehead, and she was chewing anxiously at her bottom lip. For all that, Edie could see that her face was beautiful, as delicate as a cameo with its determined little chin, high cheekbones and fine brows arching above huge brown eyes. Suddenly the girl turned her head slightly, realising that Edie was watching her, and the pale oval of her face flooded with colour.

'Oh, hello,' she said, taken off her guard. 'Mrs Batey? I . . . you don't know me, but I'm—'

'You're Helen's granddaughter.' Edie smiled. 'And the very image!' And, without thinking what she was doing, she stepped forward and wrapped her arms around Sara in a warm, enveloping hug.

Next morning, Edie served Sara breakfast in the little glass 'sun house' that Joe had built for her as an extension to the dining room, and then she picked up her drawing pad and sat beside her, sketching intently while Sara devoured two large boiled eggs.

'I think you should take it easy today,' she told her. 'You look a bit washed out, after all your travels.'

'I'm not tired, really,' Sara said dreamily, her eyes fixed on two yellow butterflies in the rose bush that grew close to the window. 'I'm just being lazy.' She crunched luxuriously on buttery toast. 'It's very kind of you to look after me like this.'

Edie laughed. 'I can't help it. I look after everybody – even if they don't want looking after. And Will's away for a couple of nights at a teaching conference, so I haven't got *him* to fuss over.'

'He's a teacher? I didn't know that.'

'A *head* teacher.' Edie laughed at herself, at the pride she still couldn't manage to keep out of her voice, and saw a glimmer of amusement dancing in Sara's eyes too. We're going to get on together, she decided. I just know it. 'Now,' she asked the girl, 'what do you want to do while you're in Redbrae? Anything special?'

'There is something.' Sara was embarrassed. 'I've been thinking, I'd really like to see some of the places my father knew, when he was here. Like the hospital. And the village.'

Edie nodded. 'You're your father all over. That's just what *he* wanted when he came up in June. "I want to *see* everything, Edie. Where we walked and everything."' She smiled happily. 'We used to walk all over the place, you know, and he made me describe every single step of the way.' She laid down her pad and looked thoughtfully at Sara. 'I really think that's what made me take up painting in the end. I didn't know how to look at things until Lewis made me do it properly. For him. He forced me to see things clearly, so that he could see them too.'

Sara caught her breath. There was such a closeness, such a warm intimacy in Edie's voice when she talked about Lewis, that she could hardly bear it. 'What was it like?' she blurted out suddenly. 'When Dad came back out of the blue like that. What did it feel like?'

Edie bent her head over her drawing for a while, then raised it and met Sara's eyes. 'It was . . . wonderful,' she said simply.

'A bit frightening at first – it had been all of twenty years since the last time. We'd been very good friends. And we'd never even managed to say goodbye properly during the war, so there were a lot of loose ends. But we had one perfect day together.' Then her eyes clouded. 'Sad, too, in a way. We both knew, at the end . . . that time had moved on. We remembered everything, every single detail. Like watching an old film. But we were watching – other people, you see.'

Sara was moved by the sorrow in her face. 'Did you mind my asking?'

'Not at all. I'll answer your questions whenever I can, but . . .'

The girl gazed at her anxiously. She didn't want any buts. Buts always seemed to complicate life. She just wanted to stay here in this funny little house, and watch Edie drawing, and listen to her gentle, musical voice, and not have to think or worry about anything at all for a long, long time. Edie must be a witch, she thought. A good white witch. And somehow she had fallen under her spell. Just the way her father had. 'But?' she echoed reluctantly.

'But . . . I'd like you to do one thing for me.'

'What's that?'

'Just ring your dad and mam, will you? And tell them where you are. Please.'

Sara flinched. Whatever had happened, Edie wondered, to give her this . . . stretched look? Like a wire that had been pulled too taut and might snap at any moment. It frightened her.

'I don't want to go home,' Sara said. 'I *told* you.'

'I know. And nobody's going to make you. They won't want you to. Not until you're ready.'

'But what if I'm *never* ready? You see, it doesn't really feel like home any more. So I might as well be anywhere, mightn't I? If I haven't got a proper home.'

Edie shrugged. 'All I'm saying is, as long as they know *how* you are and *where* you are they'll be happy, and then we can all stop worrying and enjoy ourselves.'

'Oh, they won't be worrying,' Sara insisted. 'They'll know—'

'Won't be worrying! They'll be out of their minds.'

She shook her head. 'I haven't been away long, you know. Just three weeks. And I did send them a postcard.'

'When?'

'Mmm . . . yesterday.'

'Sara! Why are you punishing them like this? What have they done?'

'You don't know them. They're such *hypocrites!* They say one thing and do another. Their whole life is a lie.'

'Don't you think you're being a bit unfair?'

'No! I don't, as it happens. I mean, they go on as if they're really happy together. They never shout at each other, like some parents do. Davey – David Walters, he's a friend of mine – he says his mum actually throws things at his dad. *Heavy* things. Books and pans. And a fruit bowl once, with the fruit still in it.'

'Poor Mr Walters,' murmured Edie, biting her lip. 'I wonder what he'd done to deserve it.'

'But my dad and mum are never like that. They both work in the orchards, of course, so they spend all their time together, and they never seem to have a cross word. Mum's not the shouty type anyway. She's always very calm. Sort of . . . in control of herself, you know?'

'She sounds nice.'

'She *is*. Well, usually she is. But now everything's different. I really think they might be going to split up.'

'Why ever do you say that?' Edie's pencil hovered over her drawing pad. She looked at the girl carefully. 'Surely they haven't said—'

'Oh, no!' Sara interrupted her. 'Of course not. They never say anything. Not to me anyway. But I know that's what Gran thought.'

'Helen did?' Edie frowned. 'I hope you're wrong, Sara. I really do. Because it would have broken Helen's heart if anything had gone wrong between them.'

Suddenly Sara's face was ashen with grief. 'That's the worst part of it. What they did to Gran. I used to think Dad really loved her . . .'

'He did!'

'. . . but he shouted at her, you know. When she was so ill. The day she died. I was downstairs in the cottage and I could hear him. She was lying in bed, and he suddenly started shouting at her, on and on at the top of his voice. Banging on the wall and shouting. That's what killed her. She was getting better. Dr Redwood said she could get up soon, but after the row she had a sort of stroke, and . . .'

'No. Sara—'

'I am not making this up, you know. I was with her. One minute she seemed OK. She was talking to me, telling me things. The next . . . it was horrible. She was making a terrible sort of snoring noise. And then she died. It was all Dad's fault.' She was crying now, with painful, gasping sobs, rubbing her knuckles into her eyes as if she were still a child.

Edie threw down her work and went to her, knelt by her side and rocked her in her arms, smoothing back the hair from her troubled forehead until she was calm again. 'You didn't say this to your father, did you?'

'No. Afterwards I couldn't *speak* to him. Neither him nor Mum.'

'Well, that's a pity, pet. Because he would have been able to put your mind at rest.'

'He might have tried. But I know what happened because I was *there*.'

'Listen to me, Sara. It was *not* his fault. You must believe it. Helen had a tumour on the brain. Lewis told me when he wrote to say that she had died. But it wasn't diagnosed in time.'

'A tumour! Yes, I know that's what they say now.'

'It's true. Apparently the doctor had his suspicions all along. Those terrible headaches she'd been having. He was keeping her under observation.'

'But before that they'd all made up their minds she had senile dementia. Just because she was a bit forgetful at times. And that was wrong too. When she passed out that day the doctor told Mum her blood pressure was up a bit, that was all. High blood pressure. You don't die of that, do you? Lots of people have it. It certainly doesn't kill them all. You just take pills or something.'

'You're going to have to accept this, pet. Whatever anybody thought, or said, Helen had a malignant tumour on the brain. And that is a fact. The post-morten proved it.'

Sara wouldn't look at her. Her eyes wandered round the room, resting on the red tablecloth that shone like rubies in the sunlight, the fly that buzzed helplessly in the top corner of the window. 'It was still Dad shouting at her that triggered it off,' she muttered defiantly. 'Brought it to a head, or whatever happens. With tumours, I mean. I'd been to see her every day. She was all right. She was getting better.'

'No!' The tone of Edie's voice showed that she would brook no further argument. 'Helen was terminally ill. She was going to die anyway. You must *not* go on blaming your father. It isn't fair. And he's suffering too, you know.' She stood up and patted Sara's hand. 'Now,' she said briskly, 'I'm going to go into the kitchen and get us both a cup of hot, strong coffee. And then I really think you should make that phone call. At least the police will be able to take you off their books.'

'The police!' Sara choked. 'They wouldn't have gone to the police!'

'Of course they would. It's the very first thing I'd have done if it had been one of mine. And I'd have been walking the floor hour after hour convinced that they were lying dead in a ditch with their throats cut.'

Sara clapped her hand to her mouth. 'Ah – what a horrible thought!'

'That's the way parents are,' Edie told her gently. 'We worry. It comes with the job.'

'I'd better go and do it now, then, shall I?' said Sara. 'Get it over with.'

Edie nodded, relief flooding through her. 'Use the phone up in our bedroom. You can be private there.'

When Sara came downstairs, almost half an hour later, her face was luminous with delight. 'I spoke to both of them,' she told her. 'Dad had just come in for his break.'

'And was it all right, then?'

'Yes.' Sara laughed shakily. 'We all cried. Even Dad. I don't know why. And they both tried to talk at the same time so I could hardly make out what they were saying, except that Dad kept shouting, "It's Sara! It's Sara!" over and over again as if he couldn't believe it, and poor Mum could just manage, "Thank God! Thank God! Thank God!" all the time.'

'So they were really quite pleased, then?' grinned Edie.

'I hadn't realised that I mattered so much.'

'Sara! You're their only child. You matter more to them than the whole world.'

'No.' Sadly Sara shook her head. 'I'm just a part of it. It's the orchards that come first. I suppose they have to. They're our livelihood. But that's why . . . I mean, I never minded, really, when Gran was around, but after she died . . .'

Edie watched, silent and helpless, as Sara struggled with the grief that threatened to engulf her again, but then the girl took a deep breath and straightened her shoulders. 'Anyway,' she told Edie, 'they really did sound very pleased. They wanted to drive up straight away to fetch me.'

'I should think so!'

'But I said . . . Is it really all right if I go on staying here? With you? I said that's what I'd like to do for a bit, if you'd have me.'

'Of course, pet. That would be great.' Edie's blue eyes gleamed. 'And Will's looking forward to meeting you too. I told him all about you when he rang last night. He'll be home tomorrow.'

Sara wandered over to the window and stood gazing out at the garden, her back towards the other woman, her voice so low that Edie had to struggle to hear what she was saying. 'The trouble is – I still don't understand anything. Nobody's explained anything. I mean, Gran told me the bare facts. When she talked to me just before she died. She told me about you loving Dad, when you had Will already. And all about Mum having an affair with that horrible Jonny Crozier, and—'

'You know about that?' Edie could hardly believe that Helen would do such a thing, burden the girl with stories of old passions and betrayals that were too powerful for her to comprehend. Too overwhelming for her to bear, or to forgive, being still such a child. She was torn between fury with Lewis's mother and pity for his daughter. 'But why?' she demanded sharply. 'Why should Helen tell you all that?'

'I don't know. I think it was because, when they had that terrible row, Dad blamed her for everything. She thought he might try to turn me against her. He kept saying that everything was her fault. All the things that had gone wrong. He said she'd forced him and Mum to get married to each other when they

were both madly in love with other people. That all she'd wanted
was to get her hands on Mum's family orchards so we could add
them to ours. And he said that she'd ruined their lives and he
hated her and he'd never forgive her, not ever.'

Edie stared at the girl's forlorn back, noticing with a pang how
slender the drooped neck was, how narrow the shoulders, how
the little winged shoulder blades projected slightly, making her
look immensely vulnerable. She longed to be able to ease away
the hurt. She tried to keep her voice level and controlled, though
her whole body was shaking with rage against Helen.

'Do you really believe your father would say all those things
to his own mother?' she asked her quietly. 'That doesn't sound
like Lewis to me. He was never a cruel man.'

'No . . .' Sara began to tremble. 'I didn't use to think so either.
But now I don't know. I can't think why Gran should lie about
it.' Suddenly she swung round and looked at Edie, her face grey
with despair. 'The thing is, you see, what I keep thinking – if Dad
really did say that, he was sort of saying that I should never have
been born. Wasn't he? That he and Mum should never have
had me.'

'Oh, pet!' Edie lifted her arms helplessly and then let them drop
again by her sides. So that was the notion that was haunting the
poor child, she thought. That her very existence was a cheat. 'Of
course he wasn't saying that,' she told her. 'Or thinking that.
Of *course* he wasn't.' She reached out and touched her cheek.
'Lewis talked about you a lot when he was here, and whenever
he mentioned your name, his face shone. He just loves you.'

'Does he?' Sara shook her head, but looked slightly reassured.
'I thought so, but when Gran told me all those things . . .'

'I *know* so,' Edie said.

Sara was still troubled. 'But even – even if you're right, what
about him and Mum, then? Has he just been pretending to love
Mum all these years?'

'I don't think so.'

'But Gran didn't make *you* up, did she? So he must have
been pretending. How could he love you and Mum at the
same time? And how could you love both Will and Dad?
It's not supposed to be like that. It doesn't make sense, does
it?'

'No. I don't suppose it does. If it's sense you're after, it's no good. It doesn't make sense at all.'

Suddenly Edie felt deadly tired, as if she could drop to the floor where she stood and never rise up again. She gathered together their breakfast things and carried them into the kitchen. Mechanically she turned on the taps, squeezed detergent into hot water and trailed her fingers in the bubbles. Why? How? What if? She was too old for all this, she thought. It was all too long ago. She'd come through – she and Will together. She didn't want to be dragged back again. First Lewis. And now his daughter. Both trying to drag her back.

Sara reminded her of Josie when she'd been that age, always demanding answers, never satisfied with what Edie told her. Expecting everything to be black and white, neat and tidy. But life just wasn't *like* that, Edie insisted. Why didn't they understand? Sometimes there weren't any answers. You might as well ask why the wind blows.

She swirled a cup under the tap, and heard Sara creep quietly into the room, behind her. Without looking round, she laid it on the draining board and reached for the next one. She could feel the girl hesitating, nervous.

Then, 'I'm sorry,' Sara muttered. 'I didn't mean to be rude.'

'No. I know.' Edie's voice was more abrupt than she had intended.

'What did I *say*? I wasn't . . .'

Edie poured away the water from the washing-up bowl, wiped it round with the dishcloth, tipped it on its side in the sink, then turned to face her.

'You tell me it doesn't make sense, Sara, your father and Will and me. But we're talking about hearts, you see, not balance sheets. And sometimes they just don't add up.'

Sara took the tea towel Edie handed her and began to dry up. 'I seem to be a bit mixed up, don't I?'

At once Edie relented. 'You have every right to be,' she said. 'You're just sixteen. And you've lost someone you loved very much. You remind me of Marigold.'

'Who's Marigold? Your daughter?'

'No. She was like a daughter, but she was really Will's little sister. Her mam died when she was born so she used to live with us. Ten years ago there was a terrible accident at the pit here. You might have heard about it? The Redbrae colliery disaster?'

Sara shook her head, her face shadowed.

'No. Of course not. You were just a bairn then. Marigold was sixteen, bright and bonny, just like you. Eighty-two men were killed down the pit. One of them was her boyfriend.' She smiled sadly. 'A real canny lad. Like your Davey, no doubt. "Little John", they used to call him, though he was about six feet two. His dad was killed as well.'

Sara gasped.

'It really knocked her back, poor mite. Everything changed for her after that. It was as if she couldn't settle back into her old life, the way things had been, before it happened.'

'Was she all right? In the end?'

Edie could see that it was terribly important for Sara to know that Marigold's story had a happy ending. 'Why, yes.' She beamed. She walked over to the shelf where she kept her cookery books and lifted down a photograph to show her. 'Look. *This* is Marigold. She's married now, as happy as a bird.' And she felt a surge of relief as she saw Sara's eyes light up as she gazed at the pretty face that smiled back at her from the picture frame.

In the heat of the afternoon they walked together up the long, straight hill that led from Cherry Villas towards Redbrae Hospital. Edie felt the years peel away as if they had never been. She looked sideways at Sara's face, and Lewis's presence moved steadily beside her. The road was peopled with ghosts, both of the living and the dead. A man passed them, hurrying down the path on the other side of the road. And as he went by a voice seemed to float towards her.

'Busy getting the old tonsils tuned up, Edie.'

She bit her lip as the memory of Bombardier Taffy Evans reared up to meet her. What was it he'd said to Marigold? 'Well, if it isn't little Miss Shirley Temple herself!' And hadn't poor Marigold been cross. 'I'm not Shirley Temple!' she'd rebuked him. 'I'm Marigold Batey, and I'm seven.'

The Redbrae doctors had done Taffy proud. His wounds had healed better than anyone could have hoped. His courage and cheerfulness had been held up as an example to all the other wounded men. Once Christmas was over he'd gone back to active service. Three months later his fiancée arrived – a bright, brave girl with green eyes and hair like the prize-winning bronze chrysanthemums that Joe grew in his back garden. She came to tell Edie that Taffy was dead.

'It's funny,' she'd told her, 'but he was really happy here, you know. His letters were always full of Edie and her Suppers and the bonny little girl with the golden voice.' She'd laughed. 'He always said that after the war he was going to be Marigold's manager, and we'd all be rich and famous.' Then she had broken down and cried in Edie's arms. And Edie had cried with her.

She walked on with Sara past the rowans that still grew by the edge of the path, and stopped to point out the high view across the fields and down towards the sea, lying blue in the distance.

'It's pretty here.' Sara sounded surprised. 'Almost like real country.'

Edie laughed. 'Almost! If you turn a blind eye to the pit heap over there you can imagine what it used to be like. Before they started digging it all up for coal.'

When they reached the hospital forecourt, explosively colourful now with carefully drilled borders of scarlet geraniums, orange marigolds and big white daisies, Edie stopped and put her hand on Sara's arm. 'We could go in and see Matron. I'm sure she'd organise a conducted tour for us, especially if I told her your father had been one of our wounded men.' Sara nodded enthusiastically, but Edie had other ideas. 'I think it would be more fun to take the place unawares, don't you? See it as it really is.'

She led Sara away from the red brick of the main building, towards a path made of concrete slabs, staring white in the bright light. It took them round to the back where they could see, marching away down the field behind, a regimented row of twelve large single-storey wooden huts, all painted with dark creosote, and joined together by a long corridor that ran through the middle of each.

'Just look at them!' Edie said. 'They were thrown up as emergency accommodation right at the beginning of the war, and they're still here.'

'They've been in use for twenty years?'

Edie nodded. 'And I bet they'll still be here twenty years from now!'

Quietly and steadily they walked down the path outside the huts, glancing in from time to time, seeing neat rows of beds, the bending shapes of nurses and slow-moving figures in dressing gowns. A brisk smell of antiseptic and carbolic escaped through the open windows, and mingled outside with the summer's day fragrance of cut grass and sun-warm earth.

'I'm very good at trespassing!' grinned Edie. 'The trick is never to look furtive. Now – follow me!'

She stepped towards a door that opened on to the corridor and once inside, made a sharp turn to the right. 'The ward Lewis was in is the third one down from here. Lilac Ward. They're all called after flowers. We'll just stroll past very slowly so you can have a really good look inside. Lewis used to have the first bed, by the door – a nice big corner space all to himself.'

They paused on the threshold, glancing at the dark-haired woman who sat up in the narrow bed, clutching a mauve, knitted shawl around her shoulders with one hand while, with the other, she fretfully turned over the pages of a magazine.

'Dad was exactly here?' hissed Sara, her eyes wide. 'In this very bed?'

And at that moment the Sister emerged from behind a screen at the far end of the ward and began to walk quickly towards them, her shoes tapping on the bare floor.

'Good morning,' Edie said brightly. 'Beautiful day, isn't it?'

The nurse nodded and smiled. 'Do you need any help?' she asked them politely.

Edie shook her head. 'No. We're fine, thank you.' And then she led Sara down to the bottom of the corridor and out through a swing door at the end.

Once outside again, her eyes briefly dazzled by the sunshine, Sara said, 'I thought we were going to be in trouble. Hauled off to Matron to explain ourselves.'

Edie grinned. 'When I was young I daren't say boo to a goose. But my father-in-law hated that. "Always behave as if you own the place," he used to tell me. "And people will treat you as if you do."'

Sara stood staring around her at the hospital and its grounds. 'Has it changed much? Since Dad was here?'

'It's uncanny.' Edie shook her head. 'It all looks exactly the same. I almost expected to see him in Lilac Ward, waiting for us.' She smiled. 'Even the weather! The day he arrived it was just like this. Hot and sunny and perfect. Very still. As if even our east wind had decided to do the decent thing and take a holiday, like the rest of us.'

'Shall we go and look at the village now?' Sara began to turn back towards the main building.

Edie hesitated. Standing a little apart, she gazed across the fields, to where the land fell steeply away. Sara, following her eyes, could see just the topmost leaves of a belt of trees.

'I'll take you to our very special place, I think,' Edie murmured. She nodded quickly, her mind made up. 'Yes. I'm sure Lewis would like me to do that.'

At once she began to hurry on ahead, her face serious, brooding. They walked away from the hospital huts, at first following a well-worn, level footpath. After about five minutes the walkway came to an abrupt end, and in front of them the land dropped towards a deep, green valley, so far below them that Sara couldn't see to the bottom through the crowding branches.

'We've lost the path!' Sara exclaimed. 'It doesn't go any-where.'

'No. The nurses and patients walk just as far as this and no further for exercise, and the groundsmen try to keep it cut back for them. That's the hospital dene you can see down there, but it's out of bounds to patients. The staff are afraid they'll lose too many of them, no doubt.' She laughed at Sara's apprehensive face. 'I've been doing this walk for more then twenty years,' she told her. 'I know every step of the way. So, keep close and watch your feet. The first bit is tough going, riddled with rabbit holes.'

Edie plunged away from the grassy level and began to clamber down a tiny, twisting track that was barely wide enough for Sara, stumbling along behind her, to put one foot down at a time. The soil beneath was bone dry and little eddies of dust spurted up around her ankles. Occasionally she slithered and lost her balance, grabbing dizzily at tussocks of coarse grass to steady herself, afraid that she might tumble headlong into the ravine. Her knees and calf muscles began to throb but Edie walked confidently ahead of her, upright and sure-footed. At last they reached the bottom and she found herself on a flat path again.

'Hang on a minute,' groaned Sara. 'Let me get my breath back.'

Edie beamed. 'Now aren't you proud of your dad? He used to do that blindfold.'

'He couldn't!'

'He did. He was like a mountain goat.'

'But why? Why didn't you stay at the top of the hill? It's quite nice up there.'

'Ah. But it's beautiful down here.'

'Dad couldn't see it, though, could he?'

'Oh, yes,' Edie assured her. 'I told you. I painted it for him. In words. That way he saw it even better. Come on, now. I can't wait to show you.'

At first the footpath led along the edge of a little stream, densely overgrown and choked with weeds. Trees arched above their heads almost shutting out the sun, which glimmered through the branches in tiny, shining prickles of light. It was cool and shady, almost gloomy, and Sara longed to go back to the warm brightness they had just left. As she was looking over her shoulder, wondering whether she dared suggest that they'd come far enough, Edie turned round and called, 'Close your eyes. I want it to be a surprise.'

Obediently she stood still until she felt her hand tucked through the crook of Edie's arm, its gentle pressure urging her forward. At first she felt nervous, afraid to move in case she stumbled. Then the gentle voice whispered, 'Trust me,' and she walked on with mounting confidence, not afraid of the dark, even though she felt the surface of the ground change beneath her feet, as the soft sponginess of the path gave way to something much more solid and unyielding.

'We're here,' Edie said at last. 'You can look now.'

Sara opened her eyes, dazzled as the sunny light flooded in, and stood speechless. Entranced. Edie had led her out on to the top of an old dam, grown over through time and neglect with bracken and brambles. Beyond it the stream spread away, not a strangled little rivulet now but a broad stretch of glittering water, deeply fringed by lush beds of mint and forget-me-not. From its banks the land shelved gently upwards so that the whole area formed a shallow basin, a natural amphitheatre. It was completely silent, and still except for the dozens of butterflies that skimmed among the seeding grasses and flowers. It looked like a painted landscape in a child's picture book. An ancient Eden.

'You see why Lewis and I loved it,' Edie said. 'We always thought it belonged to us alone.'

'Doesn't anyone come here?'

'No, because it's hospital property. People are very frightened about trespassing.'

'And about the climb down!' muttered Sara. 'Is that really the only way in?'

'There is a path down from the top fields, right along at the far end there. But that's across ploughed land and the farmer doesn't exactly welcome visitors. He once threatened Marigold and me with a shotgun!'

'What did you *do*?' Sara was horrified.

Edie laughed. 'Marigold called his bluff and blew him a kiss. Let's walk along by the stream, shall we? There's a little bridge further on.'

In two or three minutes they reached it, and Sara laid her hands on its wooden rail, feeling its warmth, rough and splintery, beneath her fingers. She leaned over and stared down into the water which bubbled around a clump of marsh marigolds spreading out into the stream. 'I hadn't expected so many flowers,' she said.

'Once I found orchids growing here,' Edie told her. 'I didn't even know what they were until I described them to Lewis.'

Suddenly, her eyes fixed on a pair of vivid blue dragonflies that skimmed the water, Sara asked, almost in a whisper, 'Can we talk a bit more about what we started yesterday, Edie?'

'Yes. If you think it will help.'

'And will you swear, cross your heart, to tell me the whole truth?'

Edie took a deep breath. 'Not "swear". But I'll try.'

'Did you really, truly love my father?'

'Oh, yes. Really, truly.'

'And . . . and . . . this probably sounds very cheeky and you don't *have* to tell me, but did you . . . sleep with him?'

'Sara, I really don't think that is the sort of question you should be asking me. Do you?'

Sara turned to look at her and saw that her face was glowing, and that the blue of her eyes seemed to have darkened to deepest violet. The answer was written there clearly. 'But did you ever think about Mum?' she reproached her. 'Waiting at home for him?'

'I didn't even know about Maureen,' Edie insisted. 'I promise you. Lewis never even mentioned her name to me. Not once in all those months.'

'But Gran said—'

'I think,' Edie told her, her voice sharp, 'I *do* think, you should take some of the things your gran said with a pinch of salt. Don't you?'

'What about Will, then? You have to admit you weren't fair to Will.'

'No, I wasn't.' Abruptly Edie turned her head, trying to blink away the tears as she remembered Will coming back to her after the war, his body scarred and emaciated, his face haggard, and his eyes . . . It had been his eyes that had really broken her heart, the wild, haunted look in them. At length she steadied herself and continued, 'I was eaten up by guilt for a long time about Will. When I heard he'd been taken prisoner by the Japs I didn't know how I could live with myself. But by then, you see, Lewis had gone. We'd become separate people again.'

Sara's face was a blank. 'I just don't get it. First you love one. Then the other. Then back to the first, just like that. As if it was . . . I don't know . . . just . . . whoever was with you at the time.'

'Sara!' Edie's hand shot up. For a moment she felt as if she might slap the girl's face. Not just once, but again and again. Desperately she fought to regain her self-control. 'You don't understand,' she said coldly. 'It wasn't like that.'

'Well, tell me, then. Please.'

Edie struggled to be calm and sympathetic, to find the right words, but her heart was beating so fast that she felt almost breathless. 'There was a war on, you see. It wasn't ordinary life as we knew it before. Everything was somehow . . . dislocated. I don't know how I can explain it to you . . .'

'"The times are out of joint"?' The quotation leapt into Sara's mind, something she'd heard quite recently but had not completely understood until now.

'Out of joint! Yes!' Edie's voice rose in excited recognition. 'Exactly. That's *exactly* what it was like.' She wrapped her arms tightly around her body, holding on to herself, as if that would help her to concentrate, to re-create those months. 'You see,' she explained, 'when Lewis and I met we were both suffering. Both of us lonely and frightened. He was *terrified*, Sara. The chances were, he'd have to spend the rest of his life in darkness. He couldn't bear it. And remember, he'd lost all his friends. All the men he'd lived and worked with every minute of the day. They'd become like brothers. He'd never had any, had he? He was the only one who survived the crash. And somehow, that made him feel guilty too. Because he was still alive and they were all dead.'

'Poor Dad!' The words were so quiet they sounded like a sigh.

'We needed each other, you see. And, I think, we healed each other.'

'So you don't really believe there's anything wrong then, in committing adultery?'

'For heaven's sake!' Edie glared at her furiously. 'Don't be such a prig. Putting stupid names like that on things! Judging. Labelling. You're sixteen, Sara. Too young to understand *anything* yet. You've hardly begun.'

'I – I'm sorry.' She was taken aback by the sudden lashing of Edie's tongue.

'When you're older you'll learn that life is never so simple. I just know – the way Lewis and I loved each other – I absolutely *know* there was nothing wrong in that.'

Sara studied her face, scared, but determined to stand her ground. 'So why was Gran so set against you? She must have seen the way you loved each other, mustn't she? Why did you hate you so much?'

'She didn't hate me.' Edie gave a wry laugh. 'I think, in her own funny way, Helen liked me. Recognised me as another bonny fighter like herself. We had a lot in common, you know. She didn't waste a lot of time worrying about what was right or wrong either. She'd stop at nothing to get her own way. And her own way did *not* include me.'

'Because of Will, you mean? You having to get a divorce and everything.'

'I don't think that was it. At first I couldn't understand why she was prepared to cause so much grief. When she took Lewis away I wanted to die. And he felt the same, I know he did. Worse, even, because he thought . . . you see, he thought then that I'd never really loved him.'

Suddenly Edie broke away from Sara and, crossing over to the other side of the bridge, she dropped down and stretched herself out on the grass, her hands behind her head. She lay quite still, staring up at the sky where tiny wisps of cloud seemed to hang suspended in the clear air. She wished she were up there, floating free and unfeeling, instead of being pounded by this girl's endless questions, thrust back, again and again, into the unbearable pain of the past.

Hesitantly, after a few moments, Sara came and sat down at her side. She picked a head of sweet clover, and began tearing off its petals one by one, sucking out the honey sweetness. 'But why would Gran hurt Dad? She loved him too,' she persisted. 'Didn't she?'

Edie nodded wearily. 'More than life itself.'

'So . . .'

'But you see the other person she loved was *you*.'

Sara's eyes widened. 'Don't be silly. It was ages before I was born. I wasn't even thought of then.'

'Oh, yes, you were. Helen thought of you. It took me ages to work it out, but I really believe that, even then, Helen was fighting for *you*. She wanted the child of Lewis and *Maureen* to pour her heart and soul into. Mould in her own image, perhaps. She was fighting for *you*, pet. So we must forgive her.'

Sara stood up. She scuffled around with her foot, picked up a little pebble and hurled it into the water. It landed with a round, satisfying plop. She watched the circles it made as they grew and widened and finally disappeared. Then she shook her head, puzzled. 'I didn't really know her, did I? To me, she always seemed wonderful. Funny and kind and clever. I had no idea, the things she got up to, organising everybody's lives to suit her own grand plan.'

Edie smiled up at her, shading her eyes from the sun. 'But she was right, after all, wasn't she? To send Jonny Crozier and me packing. And to marry off Lewis and Maureen.'

Sara looked at her anxiously. 'Do you think they'll stay together, then? You don't think she'll leave Dad and go off with Jonny now?'

'No. I really don't. I can't tell what's going on in their heads, Sara, but I really don't think that'll happen. What's Jonny like, by the way? Have you met him?'

'He's *horrible*!' Sara's face contorted. 'A horrible, smarmy *slug*! But he thinks he's absolutely "it", of course.'

'How do you know that?'

'One of my friends at school – Alex Bowman – he's sort of related to her and he went to stay at their house in May. She said he was a real creep. She actually saw him doing body-building exercises. She said he'd left the bedroom door open on purpose, so that she could admire his wonderful muscles! And, she said, every time he walked past a mirror he gazed at himself and sort of *smirked*! And he's old, you know. Older than Dad, anyway!'

Edie laughed out loud. 'There you are, then. Your mam couldn't have got stuck with him, could she? And my place – I had to be here really, waiting for Will to come home from the war. So, Lewis and me, it would have been the wrong thing. For everybody.'

'Do you really think that?'

'Of course I do. She was the most clear-sighted of us all, your gran.' She sat up, stretched, then scrambled to her feet. 'You see, that's what love does for you, Sara. Never mind the rights and wrongs. When you really love someone, the way Helen loved Lewis, then you seem to know instinctively what's best for them. That's why Helen wanted me to give him up for Maureen.' She gave a quick, decisive nod, as if she were talking to herself. 'Yes. And that's why I let her have her own way, even though I thought I would die of it.' She turned and gave Sara a hug. 'Your mam really was the right one for Lewis. You're *their* child, pet. The child Helen wanted. And that's just the way it should be. Never doubt it.'

Summer was slipping serenely by. Will broke up for the long holiday and the Batey household settled into a peaceful languor, untrammelled by the ringing of the school bell, lesson timetables or set meals. Occasionally Edie and Will took Sara off for 'days out'. They wandered along the steep old streets of Durham city, and picnicked in green shade by the river Wear before toiling breathlessly to the top of the cathedral tower. They paddled gingerly in the chilly waves at Seaburn and Edie bought Sara a kiss-me-quick hat and her first ever candy floss, then took her photograph so that she could send it to Lewis and Maureen. They clambered among the smoke-grey ruins of Finchale Abbey and Will enthralled her with stirring tales of the ancient bishop princes to distract her from the fact that Edie was sketching her.

'But you don't have to entertain me all the time, you know,' she told them one day as they sat dawdling over breakfast, making plans for a visit to Newcastle.

'Nonsense, pet,' Edie said. 'I need you to help me to choose my new daffs. The green market will have them in by now, and Will's useless at that sort of thing. He can't tell the difference between a King Alfred and a shallot.'

'True.' Will sighed. 'But what Edie's really saying is it's a treat to have you with us. Like having Marigold back. Or Josie. All that seems a long time ago.'

His face clouded and Edie rapidly changed the subject. If they were going to catch the ten o'clock train from Sunderland, she told them, they'd have to get their skates on.

Though Josie lived next door, Edie and Will didn't see a lot of her. She and her husband, George, were so busy running the shop, Edie explained. And she had the children to look after too. Josie was a good organiser. Her home, her business, her family – they all seemed to run like clockwork. But it did mean that the poor girl never stopped. She was on the go from morning till night.

One day, soon after she'd arrived, Sara had been sitting quietly on the bench under the cherry tree in the back garden. She'd been deeply engrossed in a letter that had just come from Davey, who'd got her address from Maureen and was writing to tell her about what had been going on in Donchurch since she'd taken herself off. Including the fact that he and a few of the others in their class had been interviewed by their head teacher *and* the police, which was a bit of a liberty, he thought, but at least it gave them all something to talk about when they were feeling at a loose end. Everybody, but everybody, he wrote, wanted to know what she was up to and when she was going to deign to waft herself back in their direction.

Suddenly, rousing herself from the pages in her hand, Sara got the prickly feeling that she was being watched. She raised her head, unnerved, and saw a young woman observing her intently from behind the hedge. She was quite pretty, slim and smartly dressed, with heavy fair hair like Edie's that she wore tied back tightly. Her face was pale, her eyes serious.

'Hello,' Sara said. 'You must be Josie.'

At that moment Edie came into the garden, a basket of washing balanced on her hip. 'Ah!' She smiled. 'There you are, Josie. Have you two introduced yourselves?'

Josie shook her head.

'This is Sara,' Edie explained. 'She's going to stay with us for a while. Sara Harrison.'

'Oh, yes?' Josie nodded with polite interest. 'Hello.'

'Her father, Lewis, was up at the hospital during the war. He came here quite often. I don't know if you remember him.'

'Really?' Josie's eyes swivelled. Suddenly the interest was genuine. 'Lewis Harrison? Oh, yes, I remember Lewis well. Bandages and all. The poor airman who had to be read to.' She stared at Sara curiously as if she were trying to conjure up the spirit of Lewis in his daughter's features. 'Lewis Harrison,' she repeated. 'Well!' Then she gave a dismissive shake of her head. 'Nice to meet you . . . Sara, did you say? But I'm afraid I've got work to do. So, if you'll excuse me . . .' And she turned abruptly on her heel and hurried towards her house.

Sara looked first at her retreating back and then at Edie's flushed face.

'Don't worry about it,' Edie said. 'We just took her by surprise, that's all.' She dropped the washing basket on to the lawn and went back inside, just as Josie had done.

Thoughtfully Sara rummaged for the peg-bag and began to hang up the clothes. Will's new blue shirt, upside down, pegged securely by its tail. Edie's cotton skirt, well spread out to catch the breeze, fastened at the hem so the peg-marks wouldn't show. Two snowy white pillow slips, neatly squared up, side by side as if they were on a double bed . . . Her mind was working overtime. Of course Josie remembered Lewis. How old had she been when he was here? About eight, Sara supposed, not much more. A little girl. Frightened of the black-out and the sirens and the air-raids, lying awake at night afraid that the bombs might be going to fall on her. And on her mum. Terrified, perhaps, that her mummy might get killed. Missing her daddy, too, because he's away fighting the Germans and she doesn't know when he'll come home. And then – a strange man arrives in her house. A scary man, a bit of a monster, because he can't see, and worse still, she can't see *him* properly since most of his face is hidden under terrible thick white bandages. Her little, ordered life is disturbed by the bandaged man who seems to take up so much of her mother's time. But the worst thing is, it sometimes seems to her that her mum has begun to think more about this – this Lewis than about *her*. She doesn't always hear the things Josie tries to tell her. She doesn't wait for her to catch up like she used to. She doesn't seem the same any more. The way she smiles at Lewis – even though he can't see her smile – the way she looks at him and listens to his voice . . . Josie doesn't like it. She doesn't like *him* either. She just wishes he would go away and leave them alone. And that her own daddy would come back home.

Sara looked at the red-checked tablecloth she was holding, then put it back into the basket and went indoors. Edie was standing with her hands in a sink of cold water, peeling potatoes. 'Is it because of my father that Josie was upset?' she asked her bluntly. 'I could tell from the look on her face. She knew, didn't she, about you and him?'

'She certainly did *not*.' Vigorously Edie rooted out the eye of the potato she was cleaning. 'Neither she nor Marigold had an inkling. They were far too young.'

'Too young to understand, maybe. But not too young to sense that something was going on.'

'That's rubbish.' Edie was angry. 'I was very careful. We both were. I made absolutely sure that it didn't affect their lives at all. Not at *all*!'

'But you can't know that, can you?'

'I *do* know that, Sara.' She dropped the potatoes into a pan of water and stood it on the stove. 'And that's quite enough about it! All right? I'm busy this morning. I have all the clothes to hang up now.'

Sara quailed before her fury. 'I have started them,' she said humbly. 'We'll do it together, shall we?'

As they hauled up the candy-striped double sheet and Edie showed her how to peg the corners to make it billow out like a sail, Sara gave a worried shake of her head. 'I suppose I'm a bit naïve,' she said, 'but I didn't realise that parents had problems too. I thought they'd got it all sorted out, but really they're just like us, aren't they? Like their own children, I mean. They haven't got the answers either. They just have to muddle through and try to find the best way.'

'You're absolutely right.' Edie smiled, beginning to relax again. 'The other big sheet now. You have got tight hold of the corners, haven't you? I don't want to have to wash it again.'

Sara's words flowed on, unchecked by the peg she was holding ready between her teeth. 'You see, most people seem to be OK from the outside, don't they? Mum and Dad always looked fine to me. And Gran. And you. Rusty – one of my Australians, you know?'

'I know,' Edie reassured her. 'Just pop the peg in now, will you?'

Obediently Sara took it out of her mouth. 'Am I talking too much?' she asked anxiously as she fastened the sheet.

'I'm still listening, pet.'

'You can tell me to shut up if you want to. Mum does sometimes.'

Edie laughed, shaking her head. 'Tell me about Rusty first.'

'Oh, yes. Well, to look at her you'd think she hadn't a care in the world. But she's had an awful time because her husband had an affair with their daughter's *best friend*. Would you believe it?

Not much older than me, Rusty said. And when she told him to leave, her son decided that he would go too, so they both cleared off. Then the next year her daughter got married and moved to Melbourne, hundreds of miles away, so Rusty would have been left entirely on her own if it hadn't been for Tina. She regrets it now, sending him away like that. Now she wishes she'd forgiven him, her husband, I mean, and kept the family together.'

'Poor woman,' Edie murmured. 'What a business.'

'But she's never sorry for herself. Rusty says that people are like onions. You peel them and you peel them, and often they make you cry, and there's layer after layer of packaging until you reach the heart. And that's the bit that really matters, you see, because that's where the growth comes from.'

Edie nodded and fitted the clothes prop under the line of washing to lift it high into the wind. 'And I think Rusty's right!' she declared solemnly. 'That will be my motto for the day, Sara. We are all . . . onions!'

'Sara! It's for you!'

Sara came bounding down the stairs from the little sea-facing bedroom that she had made her own. She'd been so busy searching through her drawer for a clean blouse that she hadn't even heard the telephone. 'Who is it?'

'Who would it be?' Will grinned, handing her the receiver. 'Your devoted dad, of course.'

Lewis had got into the habit of ringing practically every evening. Sometimes he passed the phone over to Maureen. Sometimes he had a long chat with Edie or, quite often these days, with Will. But usually it was a 'just-keeping-in-touch-darling' conversation in which he told Sara the latest news of the family, their friends and life at Greenways. It was quite strange, really. She sometimes thought that she'd spoken to her father more in the two brief weeks she'd been with the Bateys than she had in the whole of the rest of her life. And every time, just before he rang off, he reminded her that they missed her and were looking forward to having her home again just as soon as she was ready, but not a moment before.

Today it was a particularly long phone call. Sara couldn't wait to pass on the news to Edie. 'It's Auntie Jane!' she announced, hovering in the doorway of the sitting room. 'She's actually got herself a job!'

Sitting side by side on the pink sofa, Edie and Will lifted their heads at exactly the same time, as if they were fastened together by invisible elastic, and turned their surprised gaze upon her. In a way, Sara thought, they were very alike, the two of them. Gentle, tranquil souls who gave the impression that they had found their niche in the world and were well content with it.

'Jane?' Edie echoed. 'Did she need to?'

'Not for the money! Uncle Robert's a bank manager. Rolling in it. But it's good news all the same. Did you ever meet her?'

Edie shook her head. 'She never came here. But Helen showed me her photograph. And of the two little boys. Her youngest was the same age as David, I remember. Oh dear!' A look of horror crossed her face.

'What's the matter?' At once Will was anxious.

'Nothing.' She laughed. 'I've just worked it out, that's all. The bairn I'm imagining in the picture is about eighteen months old, but he must be getting on for twenty-two now. Old enough to be a dad himself.'

Sara nodded. 'That's all part of it, I suppose. When the boys left home Auntie Jane got very lonely, and now she's missing Gran terribly, Dad says.'

'Is it a good job, then?' Will asked.

'That's what's so wonderful! The one thing Aunt Jane is just marvellous at is cooking. She's brilliant. She was always trying to feed us all up, especially poor Gran who ate like a sparrow. And now she's gone into partnership with a man who's opening a posh little restaurant near Tillerton. One of Uncle Robert's clients, actually. So she can't lose, can she?'

Edie looked at her shining eyes. 'Are you very fond of Jane?'

'I am, really. And in a funny kind of way, I feel a bit responsible for her. She wasn't the sort of daughter Gran wanted, you see. It wasn't her fault, but she was too solid and practical. If she'd been different, or even if she'd had daughters instead of Mike and Peter . . . Well, Gran might not have needed me so much if she'd loved Jane more. And you do need your mother to love you properly, don't you, if you're going to be really happy?'

'You're right.' Will nodded. 'You've got a wise head for such young shoulders, Sara. But the fact is, love comes unbidden. We can't decide who we love. Or the way we love. It just happens. And some of us are luckier than others.'

And he turned a smile of such sweet radiance upon Edie that Sara felt her own heart contract.

Next morning Sara woke early to the sound of the blackbird clamorous in the cherry tree. When Edie padded downstairs to make some tea she found her in the kitchen, putting the finishing touches to a huge pile of ironing.

'What are you doing?' she asked. 'It's not eight o'clock!'

Sara grinned. 'I like ironing. I often do it for Mum.'

'I *hate* it.'

'I know. And you worked round the house all day yesterday. You need a break and I'd quite like to go into Sunderland this morning. Get an early start.'

'Do you want me to come with you?'

'No. Thanks.' Sara folded up the last tea towel. 'I thought if I did this you could have the whole day painting, couldn't you? And Will's been saying for ages that there's school work he must get on with.'

Edie laughed. 'He's been more than happy to postpone *that*. Will you be back for your dinner?'

'I don't know. But don't bother about it. I'll just have an egg or something.'

Edie stretched, stood up stiffly and rubbed the back of her aching neck. She looked at her watch in amazement. The afternoon was half gone already. She'd been sitting in the sun house at her easel for four hours without a break. And Will, bless his heart, had just left her alone to get on with it. She took a step back and scrutinised the portrait of Sara she was doing from the sketch she'd begun at Finchale Abbey. Had she really captured her, she wondered. Those large eyes under their delicate winged eyebrows – they had to be the focal point, the essence, dominating the other features. She frowned. Why was it that the image in her mind was always so elusive when she tried to capture it on paper?

She heard the door click behind her and Will came and stood

quietly by her side. He stared at the portrait, then shook his head slowly. He looked so serious that Edie felt ridiculously nervous, waiting for his verdict.

'It's the best thing you've done,' he said at last. 'No doubt about it.' He smiled. 'What a look she's giving us!'

Edie felt a swift surge of pleasure, then she turned and put her hand on his sleeve. 'Do you think she's all right, Will?'

'Of course she is. She said she might be late back, didn't she?'

'I don't mean that. I mean in herself. Has she got over it all? Helen dying, and – and everything?'

'Oh, all *that* old stuff!' Will gave a rueful grin. 'Yes. I think she has.'

'Are you sure?'

'You just need to listen to her. She's turned into a regular little chatterbox.'

'Mm. Sometimes I think she'll *never* stop talking.' Edie laughed.

'When she first came here, can you remember, her face had a wary look? As if there were things going on in her head that she didn't like. That's gone now. I don't know how you've done it but you've worked wonders with her.'

'It's not my doing.'

'I think it is.'

'I don't know. I just love her, that's all. Like my own.'

Will was silent, his face grave. 'Lewis's child. Your own . . . ghost child?'

'Will!' She stared at him. 'Oh, love, I didn't mean . . . It doesn't upset you, does it?'

He shook his head, smiling down at her. 'It might have done. At one time. But not any longer. I sing the song of "a man who has come through", remember.'

'Ah!' She pursed her lips. 'But who are "the three strange angels"?'

When Sara got back it was clear that she had had a very good day. Her eyes were bright, her face glowed and her arms were full of gifts. 'I brought you some freesia,' she told Edie. 'I had a feeling that they were your favourite.' And she gave a delighted grin as Edie thrust her nose among the delicate flowers, breathing in their sweetness. 'And this for you,' she said, handing a bottle of malt whisky to Will. 'I hope you like it.'

'You have been extravagant!' he exclaimed, reading the label with approval.

'My dad always says it's the nectar of the gods! *And* I found this book. D H Lawrence's poems. Edie told me you were a fan.' Then she fished around in the pocket of her jacket and pulled out a small package wrapped in thick red and gold-striped paper and tied with gold string. 'And this one's just for you.' She pressed it into Edie's hand.

Edie turned the parcel over and over, examining it from every angle, then she looked from it to Sara. 'But why? What is it? It's not my birthday for ages.'

'Open it,' Sara urged her.

Once the paper was stripped off a small black leather box was revealed, shabby and worn as if it had been well used.

'Open it,' repeated Sara as Edie held the box on her out-stretched palm, studying it.

Slowly, obediently, she lifted the tiny hinged lid, and then her eyes widened. Inside, on a pad of inky velvet, lay a round silver brooch. In its centre, picked out in tiny seed pearls, was the initial 'E' mounted on a background of lapis lazuli as blue as a summer sky. She stared at it intently, her mouth a little open, but she didn't say a word.

'You do like it?' Sara asked her.

'Like it? I've never seen anything as beautiful. But it must have cost you a fortune. It's exquisite.'

'It's Victorian,' Sara told her proudly. 'I drew the money out of my savings book. I found it in that funny little antique shop near the Bridge.'

'May I see?' Will took the silver circle from Edie and laid it carefully in his big, cupped hand, carrying it to the window, noticing that when the light shone on it the pearls seemed to glow and the lapis lazuli blue intensified. 'It's the same colour as your eyes, Edie,' he said. Then he turned it over and looked at the back. 'What's this? There are some numbers here.'

'Where? Let me see.' Edie took the brooch from him. '9 3 3.' She studied Sara's face, saw that her eyes were dancing.

'I had it engraved for you,' Sara explained.

'But what does it mean? 9 3 3? It's not from ... from a poem, is it?'

Sara laughed out loud. 'It's my telephone number! Donchurch 933. Remember?' And then her face grew serious. 'To remind you to ring me up sometimes. When I've gone. I'm going to miss having you to talk to.'

'But that won't be for ages,' Edie protested.

'No. Soon, I think.'

'But do you really want to? Are you ready?'

She nodded. 'The brooch is a little thank-you.' A slow flush rose to her cheeks. 'I can't say exactly what I feel, Edie. I'd probably start crying all over you. You've just made me understand what matters, somehow. And you too, Will. You're part of it all. The two of you together.'

He shook his head. 'It's a long time before the new term begins. You could have another week or so . . .'

'No.' Her voice was firm. 'I've loved being here.' She grinned. 'I think it's really beautiful, pit heaps and all. But it's not *my* place. We're into August already. We'll be picking the early apples soon. That's where I should be – out in the orchards. I've helped bring in the harvest since I was five years old, you know. So I've made up my mind. Tonight I'm going to ring Mum and Dad and ask them to come and take me home.'

15

Lewis stared gloomily through the windscreen. The wipers clattered rhythmically against the glass, sending large raindrops splattering sideways. The cars ahead threw up a dense silvery spray which made visibility even worse, and the pewter-coloured sky offered no glimmer of hope that the rain would clear. It looked as if it was set in for the day. He stretched out his legs, pressed his back firmly against the upholstery of his seat and switched on the radio. At once the Mini brimmed over with music. He closed his eyes in delight. Vivaldi's *Four Seasons*. His absolute all-time favourite. He tried to surrender completely to the glorious sound of brisk strings . . . and failed. He could not relax. He opened his eyes again and looked across at Maureen's face, wondering what was going on in her mind. She hadn't spoken to him for miles. Perhaps she was thinking about Sara and what it would be like seeing her again after all this time. Or perhaps she was anxious, embarrassed even, about coming face to face with Edie. He was feeling a bit nervous about meeting Will at last. It was, after all, a rather curious situation for them all.

They'd got off to an early start, leaving Greenways at seven o'clock. The route from Kent to Redbrae was not an easy one, especially since Lewis's sight made it impossible for him either to take a turn at the wheel or navigate. When they'd discussed things on the phone Edie had offered to put them up overnight but he'd thanked her and refused. Both he and Maureen had the feeling that once they'd been reunited with Sara they would want to get her back to Greenways as soon as they possibly could.

Lewis felt a thrill of excitement at the thought of having Sara at home again. Even when she had telephoned them and broken the news that she was with Edie, even then, when they knew she was safe and well looked-after, her absence had been a bleakness at the heart of their lives. Neither he nor Maureen, he thought, had completely understood how much they depended on Sara to give them a steady focus.

He shifted uneasily in his seat. Since the middle of May – because it all went back to the Blossom Procession, really – since then, he felt, he'd been living in chaos. It was as if a tornado had blown across the farm, lifted them in its power, whirled them about and blown them this way and that. Just like *The Wizard of Oz*. It seemed to him, considering it cautiously, that somehow he had managed to land safely with both feet on the ground, knowing at last what he hoped for, what his life was about. And Sara too – on the phone she'd said very positively that she wanted to come home, that she knew now it was the right place for her.

But Maureen . . . Lewis had no idea what Maureen wanted. She hadn't even told him whether she was still toying with the idea of trying to get a place at college in the autumn. Since he'd got home from Redbrae they'd talked about many people. About Helen, and Jane, and especially about Sara. On and on about Sara, sometimes, when she was still missing, sitting up in bed all night long, drinking tea, worrying about her, trying to imagine where she was, what she was doing. Praying that she had not been hurt in any way.

The one person they had not talked about was Jonny Crozier. The man was rarely out of Lewis's mind, but he dared not ask Maureen about him. And Maureen chose not to mention his name. She seemed to have closed herself away, wrapped herself around in a protective layer. It was possible, of course, that she and Jonny were keeping in touch with each other in secret. Biding their time until Sara was home before they told him their plans. Perhaps Jonny telephoned her sometimes, and wrote to her. Even managed to get down from Suffolk to meet her. Maureen and Lewis had always respected each other's independence. Had made a point of not interfering. They'd never been in the habit of checking up on each other, keeping tabs, and he didn't intend to start now. But suddenly, he felt he couldn't bear her . . . separation any longer. He *must* persuade Maureen to talk to him.

Abruptly he switched off the radio and cleared his throat. 'How long will it take us to get there, do you think?' he asked.

'Hours! At least another four or five, I imagine. Depends on the traffic. And this weather doesn't help.'

'Perhaps we should talk, then. Could we? Since we have time on our hands.'

She didn't answer. He looked at her intently. Her pale face was grave and expressionless. The upturned collar of her coral-coloured shirt made her skin glow. Her dark hair gleamed. He took a deep breath. Sometimes he forgot what a beautiful woman she was.

'Since . . . everything happened,' he began, 'Mother . . . and Sara, I mean, we don't seem to have had a chance to talk about ourselves.'

She smiled faintly. 'The story of our lives.'

'What do you mean?'

She shrugged. 'Other people. Other things. We've never had much time to think about *us*. As a family, I'm talking about. To think about family things.'

'I wouldn't say that.' Lewis was genuinely surprised.

'For instance,' Maureen tried to explain, 'we didn't even know that Sara had a boyfriend.'

'What? David Walters, you mean? Oh, I don't think he's a boyfriend exactly.'

'He seemed mightily worried when she went missing.'

'Mm. And he was at Helen's funeral, wasn't he? I must say, that surprised me.'

'I'm sure Helen knew all about him. You see, Lewis, we told Sergeant Trespin that we were protective parents and Sara loved her home and all that, but really, because we're always so preoccupied with the orchards, it was your mother who was Sara's anchor. That's why she's taken her death so badly.'

'But we do have the farm to run. And there's only you and me and Luke – and the casuals when we need them.'

'I know. I've been thinking about that. Perhaps it's time you took on another pair of hands. To help on the management side.'

'Why?' He looked at her sharply. 'What do you mean?'

She glanced in her wing mirror as a big black car overtook them. 'It's just – we're doing pretty well, aren't we? Financially? It seems to me the business might be able to afford another wage. Work isn't the whole of life, is it?'

'No. No, it isn't.' Again, he was taken by surprise. He didn't know what she was saying, whether he should be downcast or elated. Did she want him to take on another worker, on the management side she said, so that she could ease herself out of Greenways without leaving him in the lurch? Or was she trying to tell him that she wanted them to make a new start, a new sort of life in which the orchards took second place? He felt absurdly frightened. He dared not allow himself to be too hopeful. He'd been tossed around so much that he couldn't bear the thought of being hurt again. He peered ahead into the rain. 'Maureen,' he said, 'we haven't talked about it at all, but when I was on the train, on the way to Newcastle, I . . . I wrote . . .'

'. . . you wrote me a letter.'

'Yes. And I said . . . and I meant . . . that if you wanted to . . . go to Jonny . . . I wouldn't stand in your way.'

He saw her hands tighten on the steering wheel, the knuckles stretched, shiny.

'You also said—' she reminded him, 'I probably know the letter off by heart – that you had to find Edith Batey. To "lay the ghost".'

He grimaced. 'An unfortunate choice of words. I'm sorry.' And felt a glimmer of relief as Maureen spluttered into sudden laughter.

'But you have never told me what happened,' she said. 'When you saw her again.'

'When I saw her for the first time,' he corrected her. He moved restlessly, uncomfortable. 'I'm sorry. This is hard for me.'

'It has to be done, Lewis.'

'Yes.' He waited while she changed gear, overtook a huge lorry that was sending up fountains of water from beneath its heavy wheels, and then slid smoothly back into the inside lane. 'You too. I need to know what *you've* been thinking.'

'But you first.'

'Right. Me first.' He gazed out at the road, then took a deep breath. 'The truth is . . . I did love Edie. Part of me still does. And I think it will always be the same, because, you see, when I first met her I wanted to die. In fact, at the very moment she found me, I was standing at the edge of a railway line thinking about throwing myself down on to it. The only thing that held me back was that I couldn't hear a train coming and my brave suicide bid would have just looked like a pathetic little tumble.'

'I can't bear to think of you like that.'

'It didn't last long. She pulled me back from the brink and made me want to live. The silver answer – from one of those sonnets she used to read to me. "Not death, but love".'

'I see.' Her face was like granite now, no trace left of her brief laughter.

'No. You don't. Oh, you *don't*, darling. I've come to understand – I've been doing a lot of thinking these last few weeks as well. I realise now that loving *her* didn't mean I couldn't love *you*. In a way it made me love you more. Value you more. The bad thing was not knowing why she seemed to have rejected me. Once she had shown me that it wasn't a rejection, more a . . . setting me free . . . for you, and Greenways, and Sara and our whole good way of life together, then it all settled into place.' He shook his head, smiling, trying to find a way of explaining. 'It was like doing the crossword, Maureen. You know, sometimes we get just one of the clues wrong and then none of the other answers fits, so it all gets horribly complicated and won't work out properly. It was just like that. Do you understand?'

'I don't think so. Not really.'

He realised that Maureen's voice was shaking. 'No. I didn't at first. The truth is, Helen told Edie all about you. Showed her photographs. Convinced her that *you* were going to be my wife. Our time together in Redbrae – Edie said that was "dreamtime". But you and me, love, what we have had all these years is *real*.' He looked beseechingly at Maureen's face, but her profile was still fixed and rigid. 'I know what you must be thinking,' he pressed on desperately. 'What a nerve! These two women sorting out *your* life, *your* future, and neither of them bothering to fit Jonny into the equation. But Edie didn't even know about Jonny. Helen just behaved as if he didn't exist.' Maureen made a little choking noise and Lewis looked at her in alarm. 'I'm sorry. This is upsetting you. It's upsetting me too. But it would help if you would tell me what's happening now, about Jonny, I mean.'

'I can't, Lewis.'

'I know it made you ill with misery when you met him again. I suppose it's still—'

'I mean I can't talk about it while I'm driving,' Maureen interrupted. 'You've forgotten what it's like. There's so much water being thrown up I can hardly see, and there's an idiot in a green Jaguar trying to overtake, and we've just passed a notice saying Road Works Ahead.' She leaned forward and switched on the radio again. 'There!' she said. 'Sit back and shut up and let's listen to Vivaldi. The autumn allegro must be coming up soon, the one that I love. When we stop for lunch, we'll talk then. Promise.'

Two hours later they found a table in a rather grimy roadside café, ate their way in ravenous silence through mounds of bacon, eggs and chips, accompanied by thick slices of white bread and butter, and finished off their meal with large cups of very strong tea. Then they sat for a while, wordless.

At last Lewis said reluctantly, 'I suppose we'd better be getting on the road again.'

'Let me rest just a little longer,' Maureen murmured. 'There's plenty of time.'

Anxiously, he rubbed his hands over his eyes. 'What will it be like, do you think? Seeing Sara again?'

Maureen laughed, nervous herself. 'I don't know. I've been trying to imagine. We'll all talk too much, I suppose. And not listen properly.'

'Mmm. Or not be able to think of a thing to say.'

'We must try not to go on about the weather,' she warned him. 'She can't stand that.'

He nodded. 'Or tell her she's grown. That's her pet hate.'

'All this time. I hope she hasn't changed too much, Lewis.'

'She's bound to be different. All the new people she's met. New places.'

'Yes. And just . . . looking after herself. Managing to do it. Without us.'

Lewis sighed. 'It'll never be quite the same again, will it? She'll come home for a little while. A year or two. But she's beginning to break away. Leave the nest.'

She looked at him curiously. 'But you wouldn't want it any other way, would you?'

'Of course not. But everything's changing. I still don't know . . .' His voice trailed off. His eyes pleaded with her.

'All right, you've been very patient,' she conceded at last, wiping her fingers with a paper napkin. 'My turn now. I promised.'

Lewis sat quietly, feeling like a prisoner in the dock while the judge gave his summing up.

'I did see Jonny again,' she told him, 'Just once, after the Bowmans' party. He rang up on the Monday morning and said he'd managed to fix things with his locum so that he could stay on in Donchurch for an extra week. He wanted me to have lunch with him at The Dancing Frog.'

'And you agreed?'

'I said I'd meet him the following Friday. I didn't want to meet him again too soon.'

'What was I doing? On the Friday?'

'You and Luke were cutting the grass in the bottom orchard. It was a perfect May day, very warm and still. I came down and brought you a jug of lemonade. Do you remember? I told you I had to go into town and that I'd left a ham and egg pie in the fridge for your lunch.'

'You didn't tell me you were going to meet Jonny?'

'No. I was going to invent a visit to the dentist. I had worked out a lie, you see. But you never even asked.'

'I always thought that was the way you liked it,' he explained. 'Would it have been better if I'd been the sort of husband who did ask questions?'

'I don't know. Anyway, I didn't tell you, I just went. He bought me an excellent lobster salad. And I drank one glass of very fine champagne, because he insisted.'

Lewis looked down grimly at the Formica table, at the bottle of tomato sauce and their empty plates, smeared with congealed egg yolk. 'Sounds a bit different from this.'

'Yes, it was. It was all delicious. And then, when I had enjoyed every mouthful, I told him I didn't want to see him, or hear from him, ever again.'

Lewis felt a slow flood of relief seep through his veins. 'I see,' he said, realising how lame it sounded. 'I see.'

She smiled, conjuring up in her mind's eye that uncomfortable lunch. She had felt compelled to go and see Jonny again. She had reached the restaurant at exactly the appointed time, but he was late.

'Table for two? Mr Crozier?' The head waiter nodded serenely and guided her to a secluded corner, deftly removing the Reserved card as he pulled out the chair for her.

Almost immediately Jonny appeared at the doorway, smiling radiantly, raising his hand in delight, striding across the room to her side.

What an entrance! she thought, and wondered vaguely whether he'd been hovering outside, giving her time to get settled. She noticed how people sitting at the other tables looked up at him as he passed and then automatically glanced across at her as if to see who was lucky enough to be lunching with this handsome man. He bent over her, dropped a light kiss on the top of her head and laid a flower in front of her. One perfect red rose in a Cellophane box.

'You look beautiful!' he breathed. He sat down, nodded to the head waiter that he was ready to see the menu, reached out and took her hand in a firm grip. 'Maureen, I've been longing to see you again.'

It was then that she knew without a shred of doubt that she'd been right about the *real* Jonny, when she'd seen him so clearly, looked directly into his eyes, at Phylly's party last Saturday night. It was all too practised. Too polished a performance. He was going through a routine so familiar that it came as second nature to him. He didn't even need to remember his lines.

She had a sudden vision of all the other women Jonny had wined and dined in exclusive little restaurants all over Suffolk. Women approaching middle age, she imagined, with time on their hands. Their children left home. A bit bored with their husbands, perhaps. Beginning to feel slightly disenchanted with the routine of their lives. He knew exactly how to charm them. The perfect single bloom he laid before them. The gentle pressure with which he held their hands. The wide-eyed, intimate smile. And then, no doubt, the discreet hotel where afterwards he made accomplished love to them, as only Jonny could.

She flushed, remembering as if it were yesterday the feeling of his warm, urgent body upon her own, and the scent of a thousand blossoming cherry trees. Poor Jonny! He was what Helen would describe as 'A rake, darling. A philanderer!' Helen, she thought, had probably seen right through him the first moment they'd met.

Maureen's smile, as she'd gazed into Jonny's eyes across the immaculate tablecloth, had the allure of the sphinx. 'How lovely all this is,' she'd said. 'Oh, yes, champagne! Why not!'

There was absolutely no point, she told herself, in ruining a superb lunch just because the man who was paying for it was such a second-rate *poseur*. It wasn't every day she had the chance to eat in a place as elegant, as ludicrously expensive, as The Dancing Frog.

Now, sitting by Lewis's side in Nell's Transport Café, Maureen realised that she was grinning. It really had been funny, the look on Jonny's face, when he'd realised that his plan had backfired, and that he'd run up a very large bill for nothing . . .

But Lewis was lost. 'No, I don't see,' he corrected himself. 'Not really. After the Bowmans' party, that night when I found you crying, you were devastated.'

'I was,' she agreed. 'I was in agony. Because of all that waste of emotion. All those years thinking he was someone special when he wasn't. Thinking that I was "in love" with that – that paper cut-out.'

'So Mother wasn't wrong, then?'

Maureen grimaced. 'Don't let her off the hook, Lewis. She wasn't wrong in what she saw. But she was very wrong in what she did. If she'd just left me alone I'd have got over that silly infatuation and seen through him myself. She dragooned me into sending him away, and so I made myself a martyr. Why did she have to interfere? I mean, just look at him now – all that bouffant hair and rippling pectorals. Anyone can see the man's a *joke*!'

She began to laugh, and as Lewis realised that the laughter had an edge of desperation in it, he put his arms round her and held her.

'What will the lorry drivers think?' she protested, pushing his face away.

He grinned. 'They'll be jealous. But if a man can't hug his own wife . . .' And then he kissed her. 'Now they can put *that* in their pipes and smoke it!'

'But I should have known, shouldn't I?' she wailed, emerging from his embrace. 'What sort of a man he was, I mean. Not just that he was a flirt. The other things as well. All the clues were there. I was just too – too stubborn to believe them. When the travellers came, you know, while you were away – the ones who used to camp in our back lane every April – he was awful to them. Accused them of *stealing*.'

'Good grief. It's a wonder he didn't get lynched.'

'They got their own back, don't you worry. Cans of petrol, free veterinary services.' She laughed. 'Even a bottle of whisky, I seem to remember, before they'd finished with him. But the sad thing was, they never came back. I did need them that year, but he'd hurt their pride.'

'To be fair, you can't really blame Jonny for that. He wasn't to know.'

'He was. He did. That's the whole point. I'd explained it all. Told him that their moral code was different from ours and that my father had always turned a blind eye. But he knew better. It needed "a man's authority", he said. Can you believe it? Pompous idiot!'

Lewis grinned. He couldn't help admitting to himself that he was beginning to quite enjoy this.

'And,' she went on, 'he told me that he'd fiddled his way out of the war so that he could "stay with my animals". His way of taking a stand against violence. "The animals are innocent," he said. And what's he doing now? Making a killing out of old ladies by pushing pills into their overfed poodles! Did you realise he was such a money-grubber, Lewis? Back in the old days, I mean?'

He studied her face thoughtfully. 'It never crossed my mind. Not then. But I must admit . . .' His voice trailed away.

'Tell me.'

He shook his head.

'Please.'

'Well, it really shook me when he made that crack – what did he say? – something about me marrying you for your fortune as well as your "lovely self"?'

She nodded. 'I thought . . . all these years I've been thinking he really loved me and that I'd broken his heart. Destroyed him, even. But when I heard him say that . . . It was the money, wasn't it? That was the real attraction. He came to the house often. He must have known that my father was a rich man, and dying.' She looked down at her plate and pushed a cold chip around with her fork. 'I'm so sorry, Lewis,' she mumbled, staring at a little pool of tomato sauce. 'All these wasted years lusting after a creep like Jonny Crozier and I didn't realise . . .'

'What didn't you realise?'

She swallowed. 'I didn't realise that I was thoroughly in love with my own husband.' She dropped the fork with a clatter, took hold of his hand and held on to it. 'That day I had lunch with him I couldn't wait to get back to you. I drove home like a maniac. I parked the car and came flying down the orchard to find you. I wanted to tell you everything. The whole stupid story from start to finish. I wanted us to make a wonderful new start. I felt like a teenager. It was ridiculous, how happy I was.'

'But you didn't say a word.'

'No.' She gave a rueful laugh. 'A matter of bad timing, I'm afraid. Luke was working on his own. He said Jane had been, and that you'd sat and talked for a while. I imagine she must have told you all about Jonny and me, down to the last detail. She always disapproved. Anyway, before I knew where I was you were beginning to pack, telling me you had to go away for a few days. I couldn't blame you. But I thought I'd lost you completely. Just when I'd found you.'

Lewis sat like a statue, staring ahead of him. The café windows were completely steamed up. Dampness rose like a mist from the shoulders of the lorry driver who sat at the next table, his newspaper propped against the vinegar bottle, his jaws champing methodically. The walls of the room were an indeterminate, shiny cream colour, the table tops glaring orange, the floor littered with crisp bags and empty cigarette packets and ground-in dirt. He felt that perhaps, just possibly, it was the most beautiful place in the world.

'Tell me,' he said, not daring to look at her, 'tell me that everything's going to be all right.'

He felt her grip tighten on his hand and stifled a wince as he felt his knuckles crunch. At last he turned his head and saw that her face was alight.

'This time I really believe it.' She smiled. 'Everything's going to be all right.'

September 1960

I love thee with the passion put to use
In my old griefs, and with my childhood's faith.
I love thee with a love I seemed to lose
With my lost saints.

16 ∫

September. A full, mellow sun shone over the deserted orchards. Wasps droned, darting greedily over the feast of fallen fruit that lay beneath the stripped trees, and a cidery smell hung heavy in the air. The slatted shelves in the big barn were covered with rows and rows of apples, the apple-pickers' baskets stood stacked high in the corner, the tall wooden ladders were back in their place against the walls, suspended from iron hooks.

Lewis and Maureen sat side by side on the shabby bench, lazy and contented in the late warmth.

'It's been a good crop,' Maureen said.

'Mmm. The best ever, I think.'

She nodded, sleepily. For weeks now the big green lorries had been rumbling away, laden with prime fruit for their wholesalers and the London market. But this morning, the last one had left. The harvest was gathered in.

'I think we've earned a little rest,' she said.

'We certainly have. And Sara too. She's been a tower of strength.'

'Where is Sara? She was here not half an hour ago.' Maureen shaded her eyes and gazed along the green ways between the trees.

Lewis said, 'She went off to meet Davey. He rang and asked if she'd like to go swimming.'

'That's good.' Maureen smiled. 'What a strange summer it's been. Lewis . . .'

'Yes. Action-packed, you might say. Just one thing that saddens me . . .'

'Lewis, I've got something to tell you.'

'Hang on a minute. Me first. You never did anything about enrolling at the college, did you? Is it too late now?'

'I imagine so,' she said, her voice vague.

'You could give them a ring, darling. There might be some vacancies now, kids dropping out because of their exam results.'

'I don't think I'll bother. I wanted to tell you—'

'Are you sure? What about having a go next year, then?'

'No. I'll be too busy next year.'

'We can get help.'

She nodded. 'We're going to need that too.'

'What do you mean?'

'I'm trying to talk to you. Seriously.'

'It's too hot to talk *seriously*.' Lewis yawned, resting his head back against the old bricks of the barn wall and turning his face up to the sun.

Maureen slid her hand into his and felt him squeeze it gently as he held it on his lap. 'I don't think I can wait much longer,' she told him.

He gave her a sideways glance. 'Important, is it?'

She nodded. 'I don't quite know how to tell you . . .'

'It *must* be important. Better get it out.'

'Do you remember that night, months ago, when I couldn't sleep . . . and I went into the spare bedroom . . . and you thought . . . ?'

'Yes.' Suddenly Lewis looked overwhelmed with sadness. 'I remember all too well. I thought you were pregnant. Why I should think *that*, after all those years of trying, I can't imagine. Stupid!'

'Now, try to stay calm, darling, and don't get into a flap. I told you that night that you wouldn't hold a baby in your arms until Sara made you a grandfather.'

Watching him carefully while she spoke, Maureen was alarmed to see the expression on his face change.

'What! Oh, no!' he groaned. 'I don't believe it.'

She quailed under the desperate look in his eyes. 'What do you mean? I thought you . . .' she began. 'I never imagined . . .'

'But this is terrible. What are we going to *do*, Maureen?'

'Whatever are you talking about? We don't have to do anything. You don't, anyway. Not unless you want to.'

'Of course we do. We'll have to work it out together. We can't let it happen. Not now.'

'Lewis! Please! Don't say that.' She was shaking, panic rising within her.

'We *can't*. For heaven's sake, she's much too young. It would ruin her life. Her education. Davey's too. I suppose he is—'

'*Lewis!*' She heard herself shouting at him, desperately trying to stop his flow of words, to force him to listen. And then she felt laughter beginning to bubble up from deep inside her as she looked at his baffled face. 'Oh, darling!' she gasped. 'It's not Sara I'm talking about! It's me. It's us. Next April, to be precise. *We*'re having a baby, you idiot.'

And then the laughter erupted and engulfed her whole body, leaving her feeling as helpless as a child, as Lewis gathered her into his arms, his face glowing with joy, and held her there, for a very long time, as if he would never, ever, let her go.